A HEART'S Journey

The Three Sisters - Book Two

BETH E. WESTCOTT

Published by Scrivenings Press LLC
15 Lucky Lane
Morrilton, Arkansas 72110
https://ScriveningsPress.com

Printed in the United States of America

Paperback ISBN 978-1-64917-220-4
eBook ISBN 978-1-64917-221-1

Editors: Shannon Taylor Vannatter and Susan Page Davis

Cover by Linda Fulkerson, www.bookmarketinggraphics.com

All characters are fictional, and any resemblance to real people, either factual or historical, is purely coincidental.

Scripture taken from the New King James Version®. Copyright © 1982 by Thomas Nelson. Used by permission. All rights reserved.

Published in association with Jim Hart of Hartline Literary Agency, Pittsburgh, PA.

*To my granddaughters, Caylin, Katiann, Isabelle, Emily, and Aryanna,
so dear to my heart. Your hearts' journeys have only begun.*

*May the desires of your hearts agree with God's plan for each of you,
"being confident of this very thing, that He who has begun a good work in
you will complete it until the day of Jesus Christ." Philippians 1:6 NKJV*

ACKNOWLEDGMENTS

I'm grateful to God and to Scrivenings Press for the privilege of being a published author. Many friends and family members have prayed for, encouraged, and supported me in my writing endeavors. I love being part of the writing community from which I have learned so much and derive inspiration to continue.

I also want to thank my niece Beth Bronson Troop, a former EMT, for her assistance with the accident scene in *A Heart's Journey*.

1

*M*idnight!

Haleigh Abbott snuggled under her comforter and closed her eyes. The drive across New York to Greenlawn tomorrow would take five hours. She had to get some sleep!

Hanging her arm over the side of the bed, she met empty space where her fingers should have found warm furriness. Tears sprang into her eyes, and she cuddled her hand against her chest. Sunshine, her loving companion for over seven years, no longer lay on the rug beside her bed.

With the edge of the sheet, she wiped the tears from her face and tried to ease away the pain of missing her pet. Was her dog's death God's punishment for her past mistakes?

She closed her eyes and drifted off.

Sunshine? Barking came from the woods behind the house. Sunshine wouldn't wander away like that. Haleigh ran toward the sound, not caring that branches grabbed her, tore her clothes. She had to find Sunshine!

The woods disappeared and the barking stopped. From the twisted wreck of a car, Leanna Nelson stretched out her hands to Haleigh. "Help me," she screamed.

The face morphed into Aubrey White, her friend's mouth open in a silent scream.

"Nooo!" Haleigh sat up, soaked in sweat, twisted in her sheet. As her breathing slowed and her heartbeat returned to normal, she retrieved her pillow from the floor and lay back. She hadn't had this nightmare for a long time.

She changed into dry pajamas, then curled up on her side and fell back to sleep.

MONDAY MORNING HALEIGH awoke with the sweet scent of lilacs floating in through her open window. A nearly cloudless sky promised good traveling weather. The aftereffects of the nightmare wore away gradually as she dressed. She set her suitcase and backpack in the entryway at the foot of the stairs before joining her parents in the kitchen for breakfast.

"Remember to pick up the key for the Sousas' house at the real estate office. We'll be in Greenlawn late next week for the wedding."

"Yes, Mom." How could she forget when Mom constantly reminded her?

Dad pushed out his chair and stood. "Your pancakes were delicious as usual, dear." He leaned over and kissed Mom.

"You go ahead, Haleigh." Mom lifted the plates from the table and set them next to the sink. "I'll clean up here."

Stepping up behind her mother, Haleigh put her arms around her. Tears threatened to spill from her eyes. "Thanks, Mom."

If Mom turned around, they'd both be crying.

Dad waited for her at the foot of the stairs. "If you can bring down the rest of your things, I'll help you pack them in the car."

Haleigh's stomach tightened at the extra lines in her father's face and his slower than usual movements. With her move and Jeremy's wedding, he had a lot on his mind. She didn't want to consider another possibility.

"I didn't pack anything too heavy since I'm going to unload the car by myself." Although stronger than she looked, she didn't want to spend the next few days with an aching back.

"Wise thinking."

Excited and nervous, Haleigh didn't talk much. Dad didn't say much either. His mind seemed to be elsewhere.

It took half an hour to pack the car with suitcases, boxes, and bedding, everything Haleigh planned to take with her.

As she looked around her room one more time, her eyes fell on Sunshine's dog bed under the window. She couldn't bear the finality of putting it in the attic yet.

When Haleigh agreed to return to Greenlawn for the summer, to house-sit the Sousas' log home, she'd looked forward to exploring all her favorite places with her dog. Would Sunshine have had memories of their hometown? She'd never know.

Pressing her lips together to hold back tears, she descended the stairs for the last time and stepped outside.

Dad grasped her shoulders. "Please call to let us know where you are. Our mechanic checked your car, and you should be fine. But if you have trouble —"

"I know." Tears welled in her eyes as she gave Dad a farewell hug. "I'll let you know."

"Be careful, Haleigh." Her mother hugged her especially tight.

Haleigh swallowed around the lump in her throat. "I will." Her stomach clenched as she pulled the key ring from her pocket.

When Dad opened the car door, she slid in behind the wheel and fastened her seatbelt. Resisting the urge to get out of the car and give Mom and Dad one more hug, she rolled down the window.

"I'll check in with you along the way. I love you."

Was the sadness in their smiles because she was leaving home, or was it something they weren't telling her?

She backed out of the driveway, gave another wave, and headed for Greenlawn.

Haleigh took three deep cleansing breaths. As the youngest Abbott and the only girl, she had to prove she could make it on her own. And, somehow, she had to figure out how to make up for her mistakes. The Sousas' offer opened the way for her to finally put the past behind her so she could move ahead with her life.

Glad for light traffic on the highway, she loosened the tightness in her shoulders and her grip on the steering wheel. She stopped once for a rest stop, once for lunch, and once for gas, checking in with her parents by phone each time.

In midafternoon, she turned off the highway onto Main Street in Greenlawn. She rolled down the car window and drew in a breath of fresh spring air.

"Welcome home," she whispered to herself. Had she really been away six years?

Somewhere along Main Street should be a florist shop and greenhouse. Yes, there, Floral Creations, something new since she'd lived here. After parking in front of the shop, Haleigh remained in her car as she read the rest of the sign, 'Flowers and Landscaping by Will White.' She wanted a geranium for her grandmother's grave but wasn't sure she could face Willie yet.

She stepped out of her car and pulled the lower edge of her T-shirt over her hips. Taking a deep breath, she headed for the shop door.

A bell over the door jingled when she opened it. The scent of damp earth and flowers greeted her. Haleigh glanced around and slowly let out her breath, relieved and disappointed at the same time. No Willie.

A young woman about her age, with short, dark hair, waited on a customer at the cash register. Haleigh spotted the greenhouse and browsed through the potted plants. She found two perfect, bright pink geraniums, her grandmother's favorite, among the many beautiful flowers.

Haleigh set the plants on the counter and pulled her wallet from her purse.

"Is this everything?" The clerk tapped the register keys.

"Yes, thank you. You have so many beautiful flowers, it was hard to choose."

Nodding as Haleigh gave her money, the clerk made change and handed it back. "A lot of people say that."

"Well, thank you." Haleigh lifted the pots and looked around once more before heading out the door. The floor on the front passenger side of her car was the only place she could find to set the flowers.

She turned into the driveway of Rose Hill Cemetery. Following the bumpy drive, she pulled to the side near Gram's gravestone and parked, then removed her sunglasses and laid them on the passenger seat. Other than a few more gravestones and the fresh flowers left at loved ones' graves, Rose Hill Cemetery looked the same.

With her water bottle tucked under her arm, she grabbed the potted geraniums and Gram's old trowel from the corner of the car trunk.

As she approached her grandmother's grave, a cardinal greeted her with a cheery hello, and the spring-scented air filled her with peace. She wasn't sure why a cemetery would make her feel this way, except maybe it brought her closer to Gram.

Kneeling before the gravestone, she brushed away some specks of dirt and rested her hand on top of the stone as she read the inscription

Amanda Abbott ... Always in our hearts

After digging a hole on either side of the gravestone, she placed the geraniums gently in them and replaced the soil, patting it firmly around the plants. She poured the water from her bottle on the ground around the flowers and rubbed her hands together to get rid of the grime.

"Yuk! I have dirt under my nails now. I should have remembered gloves," she muttered.

Sitting on the grass, Haleigh focused on the gravestone. "I still miss you, Gram. You were the best."

She wrapped her arms around her bent knees and rested her chin on top. Haleigh and Gram had a special relationship from the time Haleigh was small. She'd learned so much from Gram, and Gram had encouraged her to get Sunshine.

After her stroke, Gram had insisted on moving into the Senior Home instead of living with Haleigh's family. Haleigh visited her there often. Because Gram knew the names of most of the residents in the home, so did Haleigh.

They talked about everything, from flowers and gardens to Haleigh's friends, school, and dogs. Gram helped Haleigh train Sunshine and had died shortly before the Abbott family left Greenlawn six years ago. Her death left a big, empty space inside Haleigh, alongside the hole left by the breakup of her friendship with Aubrey and Katie.

Gram had often reminded Haleigh that God had a special purpose and plan for her.

"Yeah, right, Gram. What does God want me to do?"

"Haleigh Abbott, is that you?" A masculine voice behind her startled her.

Haleigh cringed. Had he heard her talking to herself?

A glance over her shoulder confirmed his identity. Auburn hair, brown eyes, that grin – Willie White. He was taller, with broader shoulders than she remembered. Her heart fluttered.

"Hey, Willie." She pushed herself up and self-consciously brushed off her jeans. She caught herself before she hugged him and held out her hand instead. Too late she remembered the dirt.

"Hmm, your hand is dirty." He examined the hand he held between his own.

The contact sent a current up her arm. "I brought some

flowers for Gram." She pointed with her free hand while tugging to extract her other from Willie's.

He looked at the flowers but didn't release her hand. "Ah, pink geraniums, her favorite. If you'd bought them at my greenhouse, I'd have given you a discount." He turned his gaze to her face.

Her face warmed. "I did buy them at your place, but you weren't in. Your flowers are beautiful."

During middle school and high school, Willie could have played several sports, like his older brother, Mike. He played on the basketball team during the winter, but his passion became gardening. "Good for the environment," he said. He experimented with organically grown vegetables, as well as growing all kinds of flowers and his butterfly garden.

He nodded. "Thank you. Next time I'll make sure you get a discount."

She waited for him to tease her about blushing, but he didn't.

"I opened the greenhouse a year ago. I have a degree in horticulture and business management, and I worked for a nursery for a couple years to get the experience. Now, here I am, a successful entrepreneur." Willie tipped his head up, looked down his nose at her. Finally, he released her hand and pretended to grasp lapels on a suit jacket that wasn't there.

Laughing at his pose, she clutched her hand, which felt strangely cold. "Good for you." He always knew what he wanted and found a way to get it.

Lowering her eyes, she dug the ground with the toe of her shoe, not knowing what else to say.

He stuffed his hands in his pockets. "What took you so long to come back, Halo? I missed you."

Her eyes met Willie's, then she looked away.

Why hadn't she returned sooner? Fear. Guilt. After his sister's accident, the Abbott family left Greenlawn, and Haleigh refused to talk to Willie. She never communicated with anyone in Greenlawn, and she always managed to find excuses not to visit when her family did: a school activity, her dog, the therapy program. Her parents never forced her to come.

Haleigh turned and ambled toward her car. Willie fell into step beside her.

"You know I just graduated from college." She put her hands in her pockets. "Before that, it was high school and I was busy with Sunshine."

Willie nodded at her weak excuses, his gaze burning through her.

She could have visited with her parents, or at least written. She sighed. "Sometimes coming back is a long journey." Six years. Haleigh pushed back the urge to explain. "I'm glad Aubrey and Jeremy chose May for their wedding. It's my favorite month. Mom and Dad sent me here to get the house ready for the family. I'll be house-sitting the Sousas' log home for the summer, and we'll all stay there for the wedding." She was babbling.

"How is Sunshine? Is she with you?" Willie looked toward her car.

Haleigh's throat tightened and she stopped. "Sunshine had an inoperable tumor. I had her put down last week." Her voice broke, and Willie squeezed her shoulder, sending a zing down her spine. She wiped the tears from her face with the back of her hand. "It was the hardest thing I've ever had to do."

"I'm so sorry. I know what that dog meant to you." Willie chuckled. "Whoever heard of naming a black dog Sunshine?"

Haleigh sniffled, and her chin went up. "I think it was a good name. She was like sunshine, always cheering people up. You know how the people in the Senior Home responded to her."

Willie grinned and nodded.

"Oh, you!" She swatted the air between them and smiled. "You did that on purpose."

His grin broadened. "I'm glad I still know how to make you smile."

"Remember when you said you thought I should get a pot-bellied pig?"

"Yeah, I tried to convince my mom to let me have one, but she emphatically said, 'No!' Then you reminded me that my flowers might be in danger from a pig rooting around."

They laughed. How good to laugh with Willie again.

"And I got Sunshine, and Gram helped me train her." She gestured back toward Gram's gravestone. "I miss her."

"She was a special lady. Everyone's grandma. And a real inspiration for me to become a florist."

"Even after her stroke, when she lived at the Senior Home, she loved life." Haleigh watched a gray squirrel scamper up a tree. "Seeing her so frail and in a wheelchair, I didn't understand how she could be so happy."

"I know," he said.

Next to Aubrey and Katie, Willie had been her best friend in Greenlawn. She ran out of things to say, at least about the subjects she cared to discuss.

"So, Halo, you're here." He kicked at a stone in the path. "What are your plans?"

Haleigh shrugged. "For now, I need a job. I have school loans to pay, and I owe my dad for the car."

"Aubrey's glad you're in the wedding."

"Is she really?" She had talked briefly to Aubrey on the phone and had agreed to be a bridesmaid for Jeremy's sake.

"Why not? You're her friend, as well as being the sister of her future husband."

"Friend in the past tense."

"I don't think she sees it that way." He shook his head. "Even though Aubrey and Katie both had other friends and followed other interests, I don't think either one of them wanted to lose you as their friend."

Haleigh shrugged and continued walking. Long ago, she'd suspected the truth of what Willie said, even before she decided to return to Greenlawn.

"Well, here's my car, such as it is." She held out her hand toward the dark red, older model Toyota. "What do you think?"

He strolled around the car. "Nice." He opened the door for her. Haleigh smiled and slid in behind the steering wheel. She laid the trowel on the floor and her empty water bottle on the seat.

"Thanks. Dad and I decided it would do for now. The engine is clean, and the upholstery still looks nice. It will get me safely where I need to go." She reached into the glove compartment for a couple of hand towelette packets and offered him one. "Can I give you a ride anywhere?"

Willie cleaned his hands, then he leaned toward Haleigh and wiped the end of her nose. "You had a streak of dirt."

Heat rose in her face. She tucked both used towelettes into the trash bag.

"You're looking for a job?" He shut the car door and leaned against it.

She slipped on her sunglasses before looking at him. "That's one of my goals for the summer."

"You need work, and I need reliable help. I have a few landscaping jobs lined up, and I need someone to take over in the shop for me when I'm not there. And I've signed on for a missions trip in the fall and will be gone for about a month."

Fear tightened her chest. "I don't know, Willie. I'm not sure I can do that."

Willie folded his arms. "Why not? You're a responsible person, and you know a lot about flowers, thanks to your grandmother."

"But you know how hard it is for me to meet strangers." Sunshine couldn't help her now. "What if I don't say the right thing, or I give them the wrong change?" And what if someone comes in who remembers the teenage Haleigh?

"Tia will run the cash register, so she'll handle the money most of the time. Just supervise the shop and help the customers, maybe answer a few phone calls. Piece of cake." Willie grinned at her. "If I didn't already have a commitment, we could discuss this over dinner tonight."

She couldn't think of any more excuses, and she really needed a job. She liked flowers, and working for Willie wouldn't be so bad, would it?

"Well ..."

"That's great, Halo!" Willie slapped his hand against the car door. "Come to the shop in the morning to fill out your application. Mother's Day is Sunday. You can begin right away."

"Willie, you're impossible!" Once again, he'd gotten his way.

He grinned. "I know." He looked so proud, she had to laugh.

"I'm not sure I'll be staying in Greenlawn."

"Well, let's call it a summer job, until the end of August. Then we'll see from there."

"All right." Haleigh started her car. "Do you need a ride?" She held her breath, wishing she hadn't asked again.

"No, thanks. I'm walking today. Rain check?"

When Haleigh nodded, he pushed himself away from the car and walked toward the cemetery entrance. He skipped a step or two.

He'd been a good friend when she lived in Greenlawn. After the Three Sisters broke up and Gram died, Willie tried to help her get past her anger, sadness, and lostness, but she'd shut him out.

How interesting she met Willie first on her return to Greenlawn. Had he come to the cemetery because he knew she was coming and suspected she would come here first?

She rubbed her hand, feeling the warmth of his grasp. Dinner out with him would have been nice. On second thought, maybe not. She shifted her car into drive.

An old friend, this grownup, more mature Willie caused the stirring of unfamiliar feelings within her.

LIGHTHEARTED AND LIGHT-FOOTED, Willie skipped a few times on the way out of the cemetery. He couldn't help it. Haleigh had come back!

Perhaps he was crazy. When she left Greenlawn and refused to write, talk on the phone, or visit, he thought he'd lost her forever. Her rejection hurt, after all they'd shared. They were young, teenagers back then, but he could've helped her if she'd let him.

His mother had mentioned that Haleigh planned to arrive today. He knew she'd want to visit her grandmother's grave and hoped she'd be at the cemetery when he took his afternoon break. He had to find her.

Seeing her sitting by her grandmother's headstone had nearly stolen his breath away. She welcomed him with her dark brown eyes framed by thick lashes and her smile. Her brown hair, cut shorter than she used to wear it, framed her oval face and slightly pointed chin. She talked to him, almost hugged him.

He couldn't resist teasing her about the dirt on her hands. Gardeners had a thing for dirt.

Even before she moved away six years ago, his feelings for Haleigh reached deeper than friendship. She'd remained in his heart, in a spot reserved just for her. Would she ever see him as more than a friend?

What had kept her away? He saw through her excuses. Would the truth make her run again?

Why did she come back now? Jeremy had told him that she kept something from the past boxed away so she didn't have to deal with it. Aubrey and Jeremy's wedding and house-sitting for the Sousas this summer gave her a perfect opportunity to let go of the past.

With his education behind him and his business established, perhaps God was giving him another chance to win her heart.

Or not. She promised to remain in Greenlawn only for the summer.

He needed God's wisdom. The walk back to Floral Creations gave him time to think and pray.

2

Haleigh drove slowly out of the cemetery and headed across town. Flowering shrubs and trees bloomed in yards and along the street. With her window open, she breathed in the scent of lilacs, apple blossoms, and freshly mowed lawns. Vegetable gardens and flower beds displayed careful grooming.

The grade school, middle school, and high school hadn't changed much. As she passed the Senior Home, she wondered if Mr. Evans still cared for the grounds. Several new shops had opened beside old, familiar ones, along with Willie's place, Floral Creations.

Reaching the outskirts of town, she turned left on a dirt road. The Sousas' log home was the only house on the right. Two other houses stood on the left side, and a yellow bungalow claimed the lot at the edge of the woods.

Haleigh unlocked the door and stepped inside. The house smelled fresh and lemony-clean, and the woodwork gleamed. She couldn't find even a cobweb. It didn't take long to bring her belongings in from the car.

She called her parents to let them know she arrived safely and had a job.

A little later, she shopped for groceries at the store near the mall. She watched for familiar faces but saw only strangers.

After putting away the groceries and eating, Haleigh walked to the end of the road, where it stopped at the edge of the woods. A young boy rolled on the lawn of the bungalow, playing with a black dog, still a puppy. The dog pranced on gangly legs. The boy laughed and the dog barked. Haleigh paused to watch them. Tears filled her eyes.

The boy stood up and brushed off his jeans. "Hi." His fingers curled around the collar of the dog, whose tail wagged furiously. He managed to keep the dog beside him.

"Hello," Haleigh said. "You have a nice dog. He looks like my dog."

"Do you have a black dog? What's its name?"

Grief spearing her chest, Haleigh shook her head. "I did, but not anymore." With a quick wave, she turned and hurried back to the log home. Closing the door behind her, she leaned against it, sobs shaking her body, her heart broken again.

Her tears spent, she took a deep breath and found some tissues. She had work to do.

The small bedroom with the lacy white curtains at the window and handmade throw rugs on the hardwood floor had a warm, homey feeling. Perfect! She unpacked her belongings, put away her clothes, and made the bed, covering it with her own green and white comforter.

From her purse, Haleigh pulled the *to do* and *to get* lists her mother had given her and laid them on the dresser. She had plenty of time to get ready for her family's arrival for the wedding next week.

After showering, she sat on the bed, wrapped in a fluffy, multi-colored robe. Surrounded by quietness, she heard the floor creak, and something tapped on the roof. Living alone felt ... spooky.

Picking up her journal from the bedside table and leaning back against the pillows, Haleigh began to write about her return to Greenlawn. She often journaled about her experiences with Sunshine and the people she met and their response to her dog. Her journal included her heartbreak when the vet informed her of Sunshine's tumor, and she saw her beloved dog's obvious pain.

Three framed photos sat propped on the dresser where she had placed them. In the first one, Gram wore her favorite dress, the black one with bright pink flowers, and smiled at her from a wheelchair. The second, taken at Jason's wedding, included Mom, Dad, Jason with his arm around Carmella, Jeremy, and Haleigh. The next family photo would include Aubrey as Jeremy's wife. In the third photo, she crouched next to Sunshine, her arm around the dog, smiles on both their faces.

"You always wanted to make people happy, didn't you, girl? It didn't matter if they were senior citizens or kids, you had a smile for everyone. Their faces glowed when they saw you. And without you ..." Tears filled her eyes. "You gave my life purpose when I had nearly given up. How I miss you, dear friend."

She tried to swallow the lump in her throat. The decision to put Sunshine to sleep, even though necessary, made a deep wound that had not yet healed. She might get another dog one day, but not until the pain of Sunshine's death lessened. To lose someone else she cared about was too much to think about right now. She wiped tears from her cheeks with her fingers.

"Nothing remains the same," she muttered. "Circumstances change, people change. We can never go back." However, some things about her past she'd redo if she could.

Setting her journal on the bedside stand, Haleigh rose. She padded to the dresser and pulled a small jewelry box from the top drawer. She opened the box and lifted a necklace, a gold chain with a pendant, and laid it gently over her palm. She ran her fingers across the words 'Best Friends Forever' inscribed on the gold pendant.

Best Friends Forever. Shopping at the mall outside Greenlawn had been one of the favorite pastimes of the Three Sisters. Their last trip to the mall together sometimes seemed like only yesterday, not ten years ago. She still had the jeans and T-shirt she bought that day, although they were ragged and too small. Did Aubrey and Katie still have theirs?

Back then, she'd thought their friendship would never end. Her brothers had nicknamed them Goldie, Red, and Beanie. Her nickname, Beanie, faded away rapidly when she expressed adamant disapproval.

'Best Friends Forever' had been their motto. But when Aubrey and Katie found new friends and new interests, Haleigh had felt left out in the cold. Had she been wrong to give up on them?

That night, her dreams became a jumble of people and memories, jolting her awake several times.

Awaking before sunrise, Haleigh contemplated the unfamiliar ceiling in the dim light. A gentle breeze moved the shade and curtain at the window. Her own green comforter lay over her. She sat up. Oh, yes, she'd returned to Greenlawn yesterday.

Her fuzzy brain needed more sleep. Lying back down, she dozed on and off until her eyes refused to remain closed. She chose to wear jeans and a forest green blouse. Her breakfast included a cup of green tea with honey that cleared away the brain fuzz.

The beautiful day invited her to walk, but she decided to drive in case she needed her car later. She parked in one of the spaces in front of Floral Creations. After she checked her hair in the rearview mirror and examined her nails for dirt, she took a deep breath. She'd procrastinated long enough. She got out of her car.

"Hey, Willie," she called out as she pushed open the door of Floral Creations. The bell attached to the door jingled. Haleigh breathed in the floral scents. "Hmmm. It smells good in here."

Willie turned from the counter, where he stood talking to the young woman at the cash register. "Good morning, Halo … uh, Haleigh." Willie grinned. His eyes welcomed her.

Glancing at his hands, Haleigh raised her eyebrows. "I see your hands are clean."

"Well, I wash them for special occasions, like seeing you." He winked at her.

Her cheeks grew warm. She cleared her throat and turned toward the young woman watching them. "Hi, I'm Haleigh." She held out her hand.

The young woman didn't smile. Her black hair was cut short with bangs, and her brown eyes looked large in her thin face. "I remember you."

Did she remember Haleigh from yesterday or from before?

Willie took over introductions. "Haleigh Abbott, this is Tia Merino. Tia is running the cash register for the summer. She just finished her first year at the community college." He reached across the counter to answer the telephone.

"I guess we'll be working together." Haleigh tried to think of a way to ease the tension emanating from Tia. She didn't know what she'd done to offend her.

"Looks that way." Tia fiddled with the cash drawer and checked her nails.

Taken aback by Tia's cold reception, Haleigh didn't know what else to say to her. She gazed around as she waited for Willie to finish the phone call.

He hung up the receiver and turned to her with a grin.

Tia observed them curiously then shifted her gaze when Haleigh smiled at her.

"Well, Willie, I'm here to fill out the application."

With a bow, he gestured toward his office. "This way."

The small, neat room impressed Haleigh. Large windows allowed Willie to see into the shop and watch the cash register from his desk. The knotty pine paneling, the file cabinet, and the desk that held a laptop computer, were stained with a light finish. A photograph of Willie's family, probably taken several years ago, stood on one corner of the desk. Haleigh identified Jim and Annette White, Mike, Aubrey, Willie, and Jesse.

"After you finish the application, I'll show you around the greenhouse and the rest of the shop, and I'll teach you how to fill out orders."

He indicated for her to sit in one of the two chairs in front of his desk and pulled a paper from his file.

"If I'm not here, you or Tia will open in the morning and lock up at night. Tia will take care of the cash register and the money. She's worked for me before and knows how to do that. You can assist customers, make arrangements, and take orders. Now, fill out this application." He handed the paper and a pen to her. "Please."

Haleigh hesitated. "Do you really think I can do this?"

"Sure, you can." His grin reassured her.

After a glance back at Tia, who straightened displays and brushed dirt from display areas, she leaned toward Willie. "Who is Tia?"

He looked at Tia, then back at Haleigh. He couldn't have missed the tense interplay between the two of them. "Tia's best friend is Cheryl Nelson."

"Nelson. Cheryl. Hmmm. Leanna had a sister named Cheryl."

Willie nodded. "One and the same."

"Oh, no wonder Tia doesn't like me." Leanna hadn't liked her and had probably told Cheryl, who told Tia. Haleigh laid the application on the desk and began to fill it out.

"I don't think you'll have any problems with Tia. She's a good worker." Willie opened a file drawer. "Don't you think it's time you put the past away?"

His question caught her unprepared. "What?" Haleigh looked up, pen poised to write.

"You didn't cause the accident, Haleigh. Don't you think it's time you forgave yourself for whatever it is you think you did? Everyone makes mistakes."

"I'm not here for a therapy session, Willie, just a job." Haleigh shifted uneasily. He came too close to the truth, and she didn't want to discuss it with him. At least not yet.

He persisted. "Aubrey's my sister. I know how much your friendship meant to her, but after the accident you hardly ever saw her or talked to her."

The pressure of tears built up behind her eyes, and she bit her lip. She bent over the application to hide her face from Willie.

"Don't you think God had something to say about the accident? Wasn't the drunk driver at fault?" The sharpness of his tone made her wince, but she knew he was sincere, trying to help. "And why do you think you were the only one who could talk to Leanna? Aubrey did, although we don't believe Leanna became a Christian."

Haleigh continued to write, hoping he would drop the counseling session. In her peripheral vision, she saw him shake his head as he sat at his desk.

"Did you ask for God's forgiveness?"

Haleigh nodded and pushed a lock of hair behind her ear. "Of course." She didn't look up.

"Don't be so hard on yourself. Let go of your guilt. And talk to Aubrey."

Haleigh finished the application. She took a deep breath and handed it to her new employer. "Here's my application, Mr. White. I hope it's satisfactory."

"I'm sure it will be, because I know you." His intense gaze gave her butterflies. He took the paper from her without looking it over.

She broke eye contact. "How can you be so sure? It's been six years." She gestured toward the application. "I've included references."

"I'll check the references, if it will make you feel better, but

I'm sure everything will be fine. Our families did keep in touch, although you tried to be invisible. You've grown up, but you haven't changed. You're ..."

Stubborn? Aggravating? She held her breath, but he didn't finish.

He cleared his throat and looked away. "Today I'll show you what you'll be doing. You shadow me. Tomorrow, I'll let you start doing things on your own. My first landscaping project starts later this week."

Ashamed of her attitude, Haleigh rested her hand on his arm. "Did anyone ever tell you what a good friend you are?" Willie had always been perceptive where she was concerned.

"Not for about six years." He laid his hand over hers.

Warmth spread through her. Tia watched them from the cash register. Haleigh pulled her hand free.

The bell jingled. Willie rubbed his arm and stepped back.

"I heard the door open, so there must be a customer. Shall we get started?"

Haleigh nodded. When Willie turned away, she blew out a breath and rubbed her fingers together before following him out.

Obviously, he'd chosen the right career and enjoyed his work. Her confidence increased under his patient teaching about running the business, caring for the plants and flowers, and assisting customers. She could do this.

He showed her how to use the cash register. "This is Tia's job, but it will be good for you to know how, just in case."

The frown on Tia's face disappeared at his words.

During a pause in business, Willie walked into the greenhouse, where Haleigh deadheaded a basket of petunias. He leaned against a post with his arms folded.

"Jesse sometimes comes in to help me. He's going to work on landscaping with me this summer."

"What's he up to?" The fun-loving youngest White had often made a pest of himself when they were kids.

"He'll want to tell you himself. I don't want to spoil his fun."

Willie pushed himself away from the post and stepped nearer. "By the way, Mom wants me to bring you home for dinner tonight. Do you have other plans?" He pulled off a few dead petunia blossoms.

"I only intended to look over the lists my mother gave me and relax. I probably won't do much to get ready for the family until next week. I'd love to have dinner with your family. I appreciate the invitation."

"Good. Why don't you drive home after work, and I'll pick you up on my way."

"I can drive myself. I know where you live. You don't have to go out of the way for me."

"It's not out of my way. I'll be glad to do it."

A customer came in. Willie walked out of the greenhouse into the shop and greeted her.

Haleigh wiped her hands on her jeans. She didn't know why she was being so stubborn, except to prove her independence. Tia's stare shot daggers at her. She turned her attention back to her job.

Near closing time, Haleigh walked through the greenhouse, once again admiring the flowers. "Maybe working here won't be so bad," she murmured to herself. If she could get along with Tia.

"What's that? Have you taken up talking to yourself?" Willie called out from the front counter, where he'd been talking to Tia.

All the way from there, he heard her? She wished she had water to splash on her hot cheeks. Willie used to tease her about blushing.

She stepped back into the shop. "Just admiring your flowers."

"Thanks." He grinned at her then turned toward Tia. "Tia, why don't you show Haleigh how you take care of the money before you leave. That way, she'll know what to do if you're not here."

"That won't be necessary. I never miss a day."

Willie's body tensed slightly, and he frowned. "True, you

haven't yet. Your work record is perfect." The frown smoothed out. "But you never know. Do it just in case."

Willie returned to his office and sat at his desk. Haleigh watched him for a moment. Tia's defiant tone had ruffled his usually even temper. She turned back to Tia, who was also watching him.

"Have you been working long for Willie?" Haleigh asked the younger woman, who obviously had a crush on her boss.

"Huh? Oh, I worked last summer and then during school vacations." She examined her nails again. "Sometimes I came in during school, especially near holidays when there was extra business. Will is one of the nicest guys I know. Good-looking too." Tia blushed. She opened the cash register drawer.

Haleigh said nothing, but her heart agreed with Tia's assessment of their employer.

"I don't know why I have to show you this," Tia muttered.

Silently, Haleigh watched as Tia counted the money, recorded the tally, and removed the cash register tape. She placed everything in a green zippered bag with the words "Greenlawn National Bank" printed on it in large white letters. Haleigh followed her to Willie's office, where she placed it in the safe. She felt Willie's eyes on her as she watched Tia from the doorway.

"If Will's not here, I lock the safe," Tia nodded at Willie and left the office.

Haleigh glanced at Willie. He smiled at her and winked. Her stomach turned a somersault.

Not quite understanding her own reaction to Willie, she followed Tia back to the employee break room, where they retrieved their purses from small lockers and returned to the front of the shop.

She had to make things right with her co-worker before they left for the day. Haleigh touched Tia's arm. "Tia, since we'll be working together, I'd like to be friends. I have the feeling you're not comfortable with me, and I thought it might have something to do with Leanna."

"Leanna Nelson?" Tia shouldered her purse strap. "Cheryl said Leanna didn't like you much." Tia shook her head. "But that has nothing to do with you and me."

"Then what?"

"I should oversee the shop, not you." Her eyes narrowed. "I've been here longer. And things were going fine between Will and me."

Haleigh's mouth dropped open. She hadn't noticed anything special in his treatment of Tia. "You mean you and Will ...?"

"Yeah, that's the way it is." Tia whirled and flounced out the door.

Willie came out of his office. "What was that all about?"

"It was just—" Haleigh shook her head. Nothing seemed to escape his notice. "—girl talk. I'd better get going if you're mom's expecting me for dinner."

He stared at the door for a moment, as if he wanted to say more about Tia's exit. "Okay, Halo, I'll see you in a few minutes. Dress is casual, as usual."

"Make that thirty minutes," Haleigh said over her shoulder as she closed the shop door behind her.

THROUGH THE FRONT WINDOW, Willie watched Haleigh get into her car and drive away. What had gone on between Haleigh and Tia that caused the latter's dramatic exit from the shop?

The tension evident between his two employees puzzled him. Tia, a good worker, had never given him a problem until today, when she challenged him about taking care of the money. Why she'd left in a huff, he didn't know.

Most of the day had gone well. He'd made the right decision to hire Haleigh. She knew flowers, she handled herself well with customers, and she tried to be friendly to Tia. The problem was, how would he keep everything on a friendship basis when he had to work with her every day?

As he cleared his desk, he found Haleigh's application. He'd check out her references ... tomorrow. He read over the application to be sure she filled in all the necessary information before locking it in the file.

He'd drop the money in the night deposit box at the bank before picking Haleigh up.

Why did he insist on giving Haleigh a ride? Because he wanted to. He liked having her close by.

If only she'd tell him what still haunted her from the past. She'd resented Leanna, but the feeling had been mutual. To help her, he had to break through her protective wall first. Should he try?

He shook his head. Perhaps it would be better to let it go and enjoy her friendship while she remained in Greenlawn.

3

*H*aleigh couldn't count the number of times she'd eaten at the Whites' house during her growing up years. Besides her own friendship with Aubrey, the White and Abbott families had been close.

After taking a quick shower, she dressed in khaki jeans and her favorite mint green, knit top.

She looked in the mirror as she picked up her hairbrush. Maybe she should have her hair in curls for the wedding. She'd always been envious of her friend Katie's curls. But the bob style she'd chosen was easy to care for, and she loved its sleek shine. Besides, it made her look older, and she could use help in that department.

Katie Mann: where was Katie now? Haleigh had lost track of Katie after leaving Greenlawn. Had she let too much time pass to make things right?

The sound of a motor outside the cabin alerted her to Willie's arrival. She grabbed her purse and light jacket, then with one more glance in the mirror, she opened the door just as Willie put up his hand to knock.

For a moment their eyes connected. "Hi," they said simultaneously. Then they laughed.

Haleigh closed the door behind her, twisting the knob to be sure it was locked.

The height of the step into the van presented a challenge to her short legs, and she appreciated the pressure of Willie's hand against her back, giving her a boost. The warmth of his touch spread through her. She settled in and fastened her seat belt as he walked to the other side and got in.

Would Aubrey be home? She'd find out soon enough.

Willie spoke after he turned onto Main Street. "What do you think? Will you be able to work for me?"

Haleigh nodded. "I don't see why not. Thanks for taking the chance on me."

"You're welcome."

He didn't look at her, and she missed his grin. Was he mad at her for something she did at work, or for her confrontation with Tia?

"Would you prefer that I call you Will? Your sign says 'Will White,' and I noticed that some people call you Will."

"I'm afraid people might not take someone called Willie seriously, so I use Will or William professionally. My family and friends usually still call me Willie."

"Which do you prefer?"

A smile tugged at the corners of his mouth. He shrugged. "Well, Halo, I don't mind if you call me 'Willie' as long as you take me seriously."

Was he teasing, or did his words have a double meaning? He pressed his lips together and averted his gaze as though he'd said something he regretted.

"I'll have to see how Will sounds. You've always been Willie."

All conversation died away after that. Her stomach clenched with worry. She shouldn't have come, or she should have driven herself.

When Willie pulled into the Whites' driveway, she started to get out.

"Wait." He came around to open the door for her and took

her hand to help her step down. Letting go, he closed the door behind her and walked silently beside her to the house.

While she greeted his family, he went to shower and change.

"Haleigh, it's so good to see you." Mrs. White, Willie's mother, gave Haleigh a big hug.

Willie's father took his turn. "It's good to have my other daughter back."

Then Jesse, Willie's younger brother, gave her a hug and whirled her around. "I see you haven't grown up too much." He looked down at her petite form from his lofty height, a little taller than Willie.

When she wrinkled her nose at him, he ruffled her hair. She stepped back and smoothed it out before they all gathered around the dining table.

"Aubrey is finishing her on-campus job this week and will be home on Friday." Mrs. White offered Haleigh the dish of green beans. "Mike will be here sometime next week for the wedding. He has someone special for you to meet. I think you'll like her."

"His wife? Mom and Dad said the wedding was beautiful." Haleigh took the bowl and spooned green beans on her plate. She should have been there, but she'd found 'reasons' not to go. A summer job and therapy dog work had given her an excuse to be invisible. She'd seen a few photos of the wedding but hadn't examined them closely.

Mrs. White nodded. "They've been married almost a year now. Maddison's not from Greenlawn. Mike met her at work." Mrs. White reached for a framed wedding picture of Mike and his wife that stood on a stand near the table and handed it to her. The smiling bride stirred Haleigh's memory.

Haleigh had known a Maddison in the therapy dog training program eight years ago, but she couldn't be the same person, could she? She handed the picture back. "And we always thought Katie ..." Haleigh stopped, afraid she'd let out a long-time secret of the Three Sisters, that Katie Mann had a teen-age crush on Mike White.

This time Willie commented when she blushed. "You know, Mom, Haleigh blushes as easily as ever. I think pink cheeks become her, don't you?"

Haleigh nudged him with her elbow, happy for his teasing and more relaxed attitude.

"Yeah, cute," Jesse commented.

Mr. and Mrs. White just smiled.

The teasing and laughter that continued during the remainder of the meal filled her with a comfortable, at-home feeing.

When they got up from the table, Mrs. White announced, "It's time for girl talk, so shoo!" She flapped her hands. "You men go to the living room. We want to talk in private."

"You mean I can't help with the dishes?" Jesse threw his arm across Haleigh's shoulders.

She laughed and stepped away.

"Aw, can't I stay?" Willie grasped his mother's arm.

"No. Go!" His mother pushed his hand away and pointed.

Chuckling as they went, the brothers followed their father out of the dining room.

"Thank you for inviting me for dinner. It's like coming home." Haleigh removed the plates from the table and carried them into the kitchen. "The food was delicious."

"Willie nearly begged to have you over. But it seems natural to have you here. Aubrey will be glad to see you." Mrs. White put leftovers into storage dishes.

Having her over for dinner was Willie's idea? "Willie told me Aubrey would be glad. I wasn't sure."

Mrs. White set an empty bowl in the sink. "Haleigh, I won't pry, but if you need someone to talk to, woman to woman, I have good listening ears. I don't have as much opportunity to hand out advice since my children are adults now."

"My mom says the same thing." She placed the plates in the dishwasher. Even her own mother didn't know all that happened when the Three Sisters broke up.

"So, how did things go at Floral Creations today?"

"I think well. His flowers are beautiful, and he obviously loves his work. You must be proud of him." Haleigh found places for a couple of bowls.

Mrs. White opened the refrigerator and put away containers of leftovers. "You didn't know, but there was a time we thought we were losing Willie. During high school, he really questioned God and his faith."

Haleigh paused with a serving bowl in her hand. "Willie always seemed so stable, so sure. Always ... Willie."

"I'm glad you didn't have to see him then. It wasn't open rebellion, but a kind of apathy. He was like a lost soul looking for direction." She closed the refrigerator door. "We're not sure what triggered it, maybe his sister's accident, but he had a rough time for a while."

"What happened? He seems okay now."

"We had a revival one weekend at church. The messages on God's faithfulness and our commitment really struck a chord with him. He's been pretty focused ever since."

"Is he seeing anyone special?" She moved dishes around in the dishwasher, her back to the older woman.

Willie's mother hesitated. "I'm not sure."

"Oh." What was Mrs. White not saying? Tia? Were Willie and Tia more than just employer and employee? It really wasn't her business.

Haleigh checked the counters and table to make sure she hadn't missed any dishes and then closed the dishwasher door. "There, that's about it." She washed her hands and dried them.

"Thanks so much for your help. My guys help me in the kitchen, but it's nice to have another woman around the house for a change."

"You're welcome."

Mrs. White turned on the dishwasher then snapped off the light as they left the kitchen.

Willie and Jesse had set up the Monopoly board on the

coffee table. Jesse grinned. "Are you up for a challenge, Haleigh? Mom, Dad, how about it?"

Soon they were all intent on the game. Haleigh, ahead at one point, sat back to relax, keeping her eyes on the board. "So, Jesse, what are your plans?"

"Military. I've joined the Air Force. I go sometime in the fall." Jesse almost upset the Monopoly board when he spread out his arms like wings. "I attended college for two years and have an associate's degree in Criminal Justice, but I've always wanted to join the Air Force. Dad let me get a pilot's license. Want to come with me?" He grinned at her.

She shouldn't be surprised at his choice. Jesse's energy needed to be channeled in a beneficial way. But the thought of another big change made her stomach clench.

"Maybe to be in charge of a flying dog unit?"

Everyone laughed at her quip, and her stomach relaxed.

"Willie told us about your dog. We're so sorry." Mr. White pushed the Monopoly board back into position.

"When I went home for spring break, she was grumpy and touchy, not at all like herself. I took her to see the vet, and he said it was cancer." Her voice wobbled. "When I had her put down, it hurt almost as much as when Gram died."

Willie handed her the box of tissues.

"I'm surprised Aubrey didn't tell us." Jesse groaned as he landed on Park Place, owned by Haleigh.

"I haven't talked to Jeremy since graduation. I'm sure they've been busy." And talking about Sunshine hurt too much. Probably Mom or Dad had told Jason and Jeremy by now. "Pay up, Jess." She held out her hand. With another moan, Jesse counted out the rent payment and laid it in her hand.

First Mrs. White, then Mr. White, then Haleigh went bankrupt. The game ended with a fierce competition between the brothers.

"Hah, big brother, I beat you but good," Jesse gloated.

Willie took his ribbing with a grin. "Next time."

As Willie drove her home that evening, Haleigh laid her head back against the van seat, contented. Even though she'd isolated herself from them for six years, the Whites had welcomed her into their home and hearts.

Willie pulled up in front of the log home in a matter of minutes. He switched off the ignition and turned toward Haleigh, his left arm resting on the steering wheel.

"It was fun, Willie, uh, Will." Haleigh grimaced and Willie laughed. "Your family has always been special to me."

His eyes met hers. "How about Friday? Aubrey will be home, and we all want you to come over."

Haleigh dropped her gaze. "Are you sure Aubrey will really want to see me?"

Without answering, he got out of the van and came around to open Haleigh's door. She tried to think of something to say as they walked up to the front door, an uncomfortable silence between them. When she found the key in her purse, Willie took it from her and unlocked the door, then handed it back to her. He leaned against the door frame, only inches from her.

"I know I tease, Haleigh, but do you think I'm a liar?"

It took a lot to ruffle Willie's feelings. Her question had obviously done it. "I-I'm sorry, Willie. I didn't mean to imply you lied."

"Apology accepted. You will come on Friday?"

Haleigh nodded and fumbled to open the door.

"See you tomorrow, Halo." Willie walked back to the van and left.

How could she have ruined an otherwise perfect evening? She hadn't intended to hurt Willie's feelings.

Why did what happened six years ago still affect her so much? Willie had once said she should get on with her life. Did Mom and Dad encourage her to return to Greenlawn because they knew she had unfinished business here?

Sleep didn't come easily that night. She missed her dog. For an hour she tossed and turned in bed, then got up to get a drink of water and gaze through the kitchen window into the shadows of the back yard. Would she ever make up for her mistakes?

ON THURSDAY AND FRIDAY, Haleigh and Tia ran the shop while Willie and Jesse worked on their first landscaping project at a new home on the outskirts of Greenlawn. Nearly the entire population of Greenlawn must have stopped in on those two days, swamping Floral Creations with business. They barely had time to eat lunch. Because Sunday was Mother's Day, Willie had asked both her and Tia to plan on working all day Saturday.

Haleigh stood beside the counter, tempted to put her head down for a nap, when Mr. Evans, the groundskeeper at the Senior Home, came in on Friday afternoon. Haleigh had always liked the old man and his wife. She greeted him with a smile. "Hello, Mr. Evans."

"Well, well, if it isn't little Haleigh Abbott, all grown up." His smile made his eyes crinkle. "The wife and I were talking about you just the other day, wondering what you were doing. Are you still taking your dog around?"

Haleigh shook her head. "No, Mr. Evans, I don't have Sunshine anymore. She died."

"Oh, I'm sorry to hear that. You made quite a pair. It's like losing a family member when you lose a pet."

Nodding, she bit her lip to keep from crying.

He tapped his fingers on the counter. "Now, I'm needing some potted plants for the Home. Used to grow my own, you know, but these old bones protest at times now. I see you have some nice annuals for the flower beds too."

She and Gram had often admired Mr. Evans's flowers at the Senior Home. "We have some lovely fuchsias and petunias in hanging baskets that will be just right, Mr. Evans. Here, let me show you." She led him into the greenhouse.

"So, you're working for young Will now? As I remember, your

grandmother had a real green thumb, could grow just about anything."

"Yes, Gram missed working with her flowers after her stroke. She taught me a lot, so when Willie ... ah, Will found out I needed a job, he offered me this one."

Mr. Evans examined the baskets of flowers and chose eight, along with six flats of annuals. "These are quite nice. Your young man has established quite a reputation for himself. Has people coming from all over."

Why did Mr. Evans call Willie her young man? Haleigh pushed a lock of hair behind her ear. "Will has always loved growing flowers, so I'm not surprised. He's not my young man, though. We're just friends."

They each carried two hanging baskets to the counter. "Here you go. Tia, will you take care of Mr. Evans? I'll bring the rest of the baskets."

After he paid Tia, Haleigh helped him load his purchases into the back of his truck.

"These are going to look nice. Will you put them around the circular walk in back?" She listened as he explained his plans.

As he drove away, Tia snickered. "You know Mr. Evans?"

"Yes, my grandmother lived in the Senior Home for a while. Since she couldn't grow her own anymore, she always appreciated Mr. Evans's flowers. Mrs. Evans worked as activities director there, and she helped me get into the therapy program with my dog."

"He's a funny old man, but I enjoy his visits. He comes in often." Tia brushed her bangs away from her forehead. "I think the amount we've sold over the last couple of days will please Will." She paused, running her hand along the back counter where Haleigh busied herself with an arrangement ordered for late afternoon. "You've known Will for a long time."

"Will's sister Aubrey, another girl, and I were best friends in elementary school. Our families all attended Greenlawn

Community Church together, and we spent a lot of time together. Aubrey's brothers are like brothers to me."

It was true. She still thought of them that way. Willie and Jesse both welcomed her back, almost as though she'd imagined her six years of self-exile.

"Oh." Tia examined her nails. "I just wondered."

What if she could go back and live her life over? Would she make the same foolish mistakes? And would she be back in Greenlawn after college, wondering what she should do with the rest of her life?

4

aleigh took a breath and blew it out as she locked the shop door. She checked her watch. Six o'clock. She had just enough time to shower and change before going to the Whites' for a cookout.

When Haleigh pulled up in front of the Whites' house, the family van and a tan car were parked in the driveway, but Willie's van was absent. Aubrey sat on the front steps. Haleigh paused before opening her door, still uncertain of Aubrey's reception. She stood beside her car and straightened her jeans and brown and white striped blouse. The sound of voices and the smell of barbecued chicken greeted her.

Aubrey jumped up and ran toward her. "Haleigh, you're here!"

Haleigh hesitated only a moment. As they met in the middle of the front lawn, she held up her hand. They high-fived, then hugged.

"I'm sorry, Aubrey." Haleigh whispered the first words that came to mind, and a weight rolled off her. "I'm sorry I wasn't there for you."

"Oh, Haleigh, it's so good to be together again!"

"Really? I thought you'd never want to see me again."

35

Aubrey stepped back, her hands still on Haleigh's shoulders. "Let's go for a walk. The boys aren't home yet, and Mom said there'd be time."

Haleigh nodded.

"Have you been by your old place yet?" Aubrey asked. "We could walk that way."

"No, I haven't dared. A part of me is afraid to go. But we can go together."

"Like old times." Aubrey looped her arm through Haleigh's, and they strolled along the sidewalk.

"I'm so sorry about Sunshine. It must have been awful for you."

"It was." Haleigh sighed. "Even now, I think I hear her barking at night."

"Will you get another dog?"

Haleigh shook her head. "Not right away, if ever. It's hard losing someone you love, even a dog."

"The two of you were so close."

Only Haleigh knew how many times Sunshine's love and companionship had pulled her through periods of sadness and loneliness, especially after the Abbotts left Greenlawn.

Haleigh breathed in a floral fragrance she couldn't identify as they passed a house. "One thing I noticed, even after six years. The flowers here are just as beautiful as they always were. Isn't May a wonderful month?"

"You always did notice flowers and butterflies and stars." Aubrey smiled at her.

"Gram taught me. She loved life and all creation. I wish I could embrace life the way she did."

"I think you're a lot like her."

She shook her head. "Why do you say that? Gram was so kind, and talented, and generous."

"Well, you are. You shared many interests and traits. You look a lot like her too."

"Me?" Even after her stroke, Gram was a beautiful woman, inside and out.

"Certainly."

"But, Aubrey, I'm shy around people. Gram loved people, and she lived a fulfilled life. I don't even know what my next step will be."

"Maybe you needed to come back to Greenlawn to find out." Aubrey looked at her from the corner of her eye. "What about Willie?"

"What about him?" Haleigh pretended not to know what she meant.

"You know what I mean." Aubrey stopped walking and turned Haleigh to face her. "Willie has been crazy about you for years."

Haleigh wanted to avoid thinking about a deeper relationship with Willie. She hurt or lost those she loved. She pushed her hair behind her ear. "We're just friends. Besides, he's younger than me."

"Huh, only by a couple of months. You know Willie loves you."

Haleigh shrugged. "I'm not so sure about that. And I don't know why he would." Aubrey had more important things to think about right now, with the wedding a week away. "Do you have things pretty much set for the wedding?"

Turning with a sigh, Aubrey continued to walk. "You're quite adept at changing the subject. Yes, almost everything is set. Your mom has been a great help. As best friends for years, our moms have had a great time planning this wedding."

They stopped in front of a white house with green trim, the large yard enclosed by a white picket fence.

"It hasn't changed much. Look!" Haleigh pointed. "The apple tree swing is still there. And the new owners have kept up my grandmother's flower garden."

"We made a lot of memories here."

As they stood by the fence, Haleigh's mind filled with happy memories: Gram's kind face and loving ways, fun with her brothers and their teasing, the love of her parents and family. The Three Sisters had spent a lot of time together in the house and yard.

Haleigh faced her friend. "Back then I believed in 'Best Friends Forever.' What do you think happened to us?"

"We grew up, and our interests became different. Even so, I still wanted your friendship."

Guilt and embarrassment washed through Haleigh. She had been so childish. "I was jealous. I thought you deserted me for Leanna. It scared me when you got hurt in the accident and she died. If I'd been a better friend, maybe you wouldn't have been in that car."

Aubrey checked her watch. "We'd better get back." They continued around the block. "I'm sorry, Haleigh. You didn't like Leanna, but I did. We had fun together, and she was a great friend. We both liked sports, and she encouraged me to be a better athlete."

With her limited athletic abilities, Haleigh had managed to pass PE in high school.

"I thought I could convince her that she needed Christ." Aubrey's voice caught. "I don't think she ever became a Christian, although she claimed to be considering it. When she died, I thought it should have been me."

Haleigh squeezed her arm. Aubrey had lost a dear friend when Leanna died.

Aubrey waved her hand. "I felt as though I failed her, and that God had too. I was so angry at Derek for drinking and driving. I should have known better than to get in that car, but Leanna insisted on going, and we were excited about winning the basketball championship."

"Do you remember the accident?"

Aubrey shook her head. "Not everything. I remember Derek drove too fast and zig-zagged all over the road. I remember being scared and asking God to protect us. Then I remember waking up in the hospital in so much pain I wanted to die, especially when I knew Leanna had been killed. I was so alone." Aubrey wiped the tears from her face.

"Why didn't you come back to be my friend?"

Aubrey stepped in front of Haleigh and turned to face her. "Haleigh, I never stopped being your friend. You didn't let me back. Sunshine took up much of your time, then you got sick with some kind of virus, and you moved after Gram died. I had a lot of physical therapy and tutoring to catch up on schoolwork. I never had another chance."

The sharpness of her friend's tone hurt. Haleigh had walked away, never allowing Aubrey an opportunity to renew their friendship.

"I'm so sorry." Haleigh forced herself to look directly into Aubrey's eyes. "Gram kept telling me I should be glad you and Katie were using your God-given talents, but I was angry at you both. Sunshine became my best friend, and the therapy program gave me something worthwhile to do." Her voice broke with a sob. "I'm sorry I shut you out."

Aubrey hugged her for a moment then turned, and Haleigh fell into step beside her. "Why didn't you find some new friends, like Katie and I did?"

"I did have a few friends, but never like you and Katie." Haleigh sniffled. "I didn't get close for fear of losing them. When Gram died, I felt totally abandoned, except for my family and Sunshine."

"I'm sorry."

"Gram told me God had a special place for me." She sighed and spread out her arms. "Here I am, still looking for it."

Aubrey pulled her long, blond ponytail over her shoulder. "Can we put the bad times behind us and begin again, Haleigh? We're going to be real sisters now, and it would mean the world to Jeremy and me."

"Friends forever!" Haleigh lifted her hand. They high-fived again, and both wiped a few tears from their eyes. Haleigh's burden of guilt and loss she carried for too long lightened. But she hadn't talked to Katie yet.

They turned up the driveway.

"When I left Greenlawn, Katie was pregnant," Haleigh said. "I know she gave the baby up for adoption. Do you know where she is and what she's doing?"

"I haven't seen her much recently, but she's planning to come to the wedding. She's still a vivacious redhead, she lives in Greenlawn, and she's a nurse, not an actress."

"Good. I'll get to see her then." Maybe in church on Sunday.

Jesse peered at them from behind the house.

Haleigh leaned close. "Remember how Katie hated being an only child, and when we complained about our brothers, she said she wanted six or seven?"

"She didn't know what she was asking for. Three are enough for me."

"About time you two came back. We're starving," Jesse called out as they entered the back yard. "We wanted to come and get you, but Mom said to leave you alone."

"We haven't been gone that long." Haleigh lifted her chin.

Aubrey pulled herself to her full height and stood on tiptoe to look her little brother in the eye. "You weren't home when we left."

"That's right." Haleigh linked her arm with Aubrey's.

"They're finally here, Mom." Jesse put his hand over his stomach and moaned. "Can we eat?"

"It seems like you were gone for days." Willie placed the platter of chicken on the picnic table. "Food's ready."

"Good, I'm hungry." Haleigh's stomach growled as she sat next to Aubrey, where her friend indicated. Willie slid in on her other side.

Mr. and Mrs. White laughed at them from across the table. After Mr. White asked the blessing, they passed the dishes of food around.

Willie leaned toward Haleigh. "At first I thought you didn't come."

"Didn't you see my car parked out front? I told you I'd be here." She passed the platter of chicken to him.

"I know. But you girls were gone a long time."

"It wasn't that long. Half an hour. We had some important things to discuss."

"Oh, like what?"

Haleigh shook her head. "That's for us to know."

"Secrets. Like in the old days. Well, I'll find out."

"Oh, do you think so?"

The smiles on the faces of Willie's family as they listened to their banter made Haleigh blush.

"Are you going to church on Sunday?" He laid his napkin on his lap.

"That's the plan." Haleigh took a forkful of potato salad.

"Want a ride?"

She shook her head and swallowed. "No thanks. I think I'll walk."

"But what if it rains?"

"Then I'll drive. It's no problem, Willie."

"Oh, okay."

A question from his mother diverted Willie's attention, to Haleigh's relief.

Aubrey smirked at her, and Haleigh shook her head.

"Are you busy tomorrow morning?" Aubrey asked.

"Yes. Why do you ask?"

"I have the final fitting for my wedding gown, and I thought it would be fun to have you go with me."

"Oh, that would be so much fun!" Haleigh's face fell. "But I won't be able to go. I have to work tomorrow. This is a busy time for Willie. I'm sorry."

"I forgot it's Mother's Day weekend." Aubrey made a face.

Haleigh tapped her finger on the table. "Unless Willie will let me take break time and lunch together. I can grab something at the café and meet you at the dressmaker's shop for the fitting. Let me ask Willie."

"Ask me what?" Willie leaned toward her.

She explained the situation to him, Aubrey looking over her shoulder at Willie.

He nodded. "I think we can work something out." They agreed on a time.

"Now, let me check with Mrs. Hayes. I have to be sure it's a good time for her." Aubrey pulled her cell phone from her pocket and punched in a number. She walked a little distance from the picnic table. When she returned, she smiled. "Mrs. Hayes said that one o'clock would be fine for the fitting. So you'll go with me?"

"Certainly. I'd love to."

THE NEXT DAY, after a very busy morning, Haleigh sighed with relief when she walked out the door of the shop at twelve fifteen. She met Aubrey for lunch at the café, where they sat across from each other at an outdoor table shaded by an awning.

"Thank you for coming with me." Aubrey sipped her iced tea. "I'm not sure I'm going to make it to next Saturday. It's hard to believe the waiting is almost over, but there are a lot of little details to see to."

In one week, Aubrey would become her sister-in-law. The oldest and tallest of their threesome, Aubrey had been the big sister, always looking out for the other two friends.

I'm so sorry, Father God. If I had forgiven her, I could have helped her when she needed me. Instead, I selfishly rejected her. And Katie too.

"Yoo-hoo! Haleigh! Are you still with me?"

Aubrey's words and hand waving in front of her face startled her. "I'm sorry, Aubrey. I was thinking about all the time I lost with you because of my immaturity and lack of forgiveness. And now, here I am with you, going to your bridal gown fitting, and soon you'll be marrying my brother."

"Don't give it another thought." Aubrey reached for her hand. "I think we'd better get going. I don't want to keep Mrs. Hayes waiting, especially since she willingly changed the time for the fitting."

It took less than five minutes to arrive at the dressmaker's shop, located down the street from the café.

Haleigh had been in the shop only a couple of times when she lived in Greenlawn, but she knew Mrs. Hayes from church. As she waited in a chair, she gazed around at fabric samples, sewing notions, and several of Mrs. Hayes's own creations. A large metal file held patterns.

Mrs. Hayes pushed back a curtain, and Aubrey glided out in her bridal gown. Haleigh gasped.

"Oh, Aubrey, you're gorgeous! Jeremy won't be able to take his eyes off you, except maybe he'll faint when he sees you." The thought of Jeremy fainting at his wedding made them both giggle. "Mrs. Hayes, you did a beautiful job."

"Thank you, dear." The dressmaker motioned with her hand. "Now, turn around, Aubrey. I have to be sure the hem is straight and everything fits right."

Aubrey spun in a slow circle, the gown swirling gently above the carpeted floor.

Mrs. Hayes nodded. "You may take the gown home with you, Aubrey. And I wish you so much happiness, dear. I remember when you were just a little girl, and now you're getting married." She smiled warmly. "Sometimes it makes me feel old."

"You'll never be old, Mrs. Hayes, because you're young at heart." The dressmaker had been one of Haleigh's favorite Sunday school teachers.

"Thank you, Haleigh. You're kind. Perhaps I'll be able to make your wedding dress in the near future."

Haleigh blushed, and Aubrey smirked.

After Aubrey changed back into her street clothes, she paid

the last installment for the gown, then Mrs. Hayes enclosed it in a zippered dress bag.

The two friends left the dress shop, Aubrey carrying her gown and Haleigh several smaller bags.

"That was almost like going to the mall, like old times, only better. Thank you for asking me to come with you today." Haleigh helped Aubrey load the bags into her car. She gave Aubrey a hug. "Thank you for forgiving me and taking me back."

"I'm so glad to finally get things settled between us." Aubrey pulled her key out of her pocket. "You'll be in church tomorrow?"

"I plan to be. Do you think Katie will be there?"

"Maybe. I don't know Katie's schedule. She may have to work."

Haleigh waved to Aubrey as she drove away. How blessed to be forgiven and accepted by Aubrey! Would it be the same with Katie?

As she drove back to work, she worried about returning to Greenlawn Bible Church tomorrow. Haleigh and Leanna had clashed during youth activities, which Leanna sometimes attended with Aubrey. Leanna had always irritated Haleigh. She flirted with Jeremy and Jason, made comments about elderly people, and teased Haleigh about her lack of athletic ability.

One night, Haleigh had shocked herself and everyone else when she screamed at Aubrey's friend. She couldn't remember exactly what Leanna had said or done to make her lose her temper. It happened just before the accident. She hadn't apologized to Leanna then, and now she couldn't.

Although most of the teens in the group had grown up and probably moved away, Haleigh wondered how many people might remember. For a while after Gram died, she'd fought with her parents over church attendance. She'd been angry at God.

It mattered to her, but after all this time, would it really matter to anyone else?

5

It rained during the night, but patches of blue peeked through the gray cloud cover as Haleigh walked out the door Sunday morning. She waited until the last possible moment to leave the house, so she'd arrive just before the service started.

The sun burst out from behind the clouds, and raindrops sparkled like diamonds on the grass as she breathed in the fresh morning air and stepped carefully over puddles on the sidewalk.

As she entered the familiar front door of her first church home, her stomach tightened. The usher, a new face to her, greeted and welcomed her. Thanking him for the bulletin he handed her, she looked around the almost full auditorium.

Willie must have been watching for her, because he stood and motioned for her to join his family. Self-consciously, she made her way toward him, trying to ignore the thrill his smile stirred within her.

Haleigh greeted Mr. and Mrs. White and sat between Aubrey and Willie. She pretended to ignore Jesse, who, from Willie's other side, tried to make her laugh. When he folded his church bulletin into a paper airplane, his father leaned over and reproached him. He nodded at his father, sat up straight, and faced the front.

Watching from the corner of her eye, Haleigh covered her mouth with her hand.

Willie nudged her and murmured in her ear. "You know when you laugh at him, it only makes him worse."

Yes, she knew. She nodded and opened her bulletin. The service began, and she joined in worship.

Pastor Pete, now the senior pastor instead of the youth pastor he'd been when Haleigh lived in Greenlawn, caught her attention with his topic: forgiveness.

"God has forgiven us so much. He has buried our sins in the depths of the sea, so we should be willing to forgive those closest to us, our family members. This should be easy, but it is often the most difficult kind of forgiveness. I think this is because we expect so much more from our family and our closest friends, and when they disappoint us or hurt us, we hold on to that disappointment or hurt, and it keeps us from moving forward with our life and goals."

After the benediction, the White family left. Haleigh lowered herself to the pew and rested her arms on the back of the one ahead of her. She laid her forehead against her arms. The sanctuary became quiet around her, except for the voices of people leaving. Tears filled her eyes, and the lump in her throat made swallowing difficult. Whether or not Pastor Pete had intended the words for her, God had spoken to her.

Something rustled as someone slid into the pew beside her. She looked up. Amy, Pastor Pete's wife, smiled at her and handed her a tissue. Haleigh wiped her eyes.

"Haleigh, it's so good to see you! How are you?" Her hug was just what Haleigh needed. And Amy was just the person to talk to.

"I-I'm trying to clear some things up with God ... about forgiveness."

"Isn't God good? He knew the message you needed to hear today."

"Yes." She took a shaky breath. "Remember the time I lost my temper over something Leanna Nelson said?"

Amy had been there. "You had a hard time accepting Aubrey's friendship with Leanna."

"I was so jealous that Leanna had taken my friend away from me. And Katie had Nathan. Leanna said something, I think it may have been about the elderly, but I'm not sure now. Gram was dying at the time, so I let my jealousy and anger stand in the way of doing right. I said some horrible things to Leanna, and I never asked her forgiveness. Now it's too late. I ... " Haleigh swallowed. "What do I do?"

Amy sat back. "Have you confessed your sin to God?" Haleigh nodded and Amy continued. "God says that when He forgives us, our sins are as though buried in the sea, and as far away as the East is from the West. The enemy wants us to believe we must wallow in guilt, but that's not true if you've confessed and repented. Although you can't ask Leanna to forgive you personally, if you write a letter to Leanna, telling her how you feel, perhaps it will help you."

"Maybe." She rubbed her palms against her legs. "I wish I could go back and do that part of my life over." Haleigh saw Aubrey watching from the sanctuary doorway. "Oh, I have to go now. Thank you so much for taking the time to talk with me. And it's good to see you again."

They stood. "Haleigh." Amy placed comforting hands on her shoulders. "If you need to talk, please come to see me. Or make an appointment with Pastor Pete. Will you be around long?"

"At least for the summer, maybe longer."

"Good. You can become involved with our young adults. We have a hike to the fire tower planned soon, and if I remember correctly, that's something you like to do."

Haleigh thanked Amy, who walked to the door with her, then

across the parking lot to her house, where two young children greeted their mother.

Aubrey was waiting for Haleigh and linked arms with her. "The boys have made a special Mother's Day dinner for Mom. Did Willie remember to invite you?"

"No." She planned to go back to the log home and heat a TV dinner in the microwave.

"I'm surprised. Will you come?"

She hesitated. Meals with the Whites were becoming a habit. She wanted to be independent, to do for herself. Living at the log home gave her that opportunity. However, she enjoyed being with them, and she was curious about the meal Willie and Jesse had prepared. "I'd love to, but only if I won't be in the way."

"You should know by now, Haleigh, that my family never considers you 'in the way.' Besides, I'm the clean-up committee, and you can help me."

"Now I know why you want me to come over." How good to laugh with Aubrey again.

THE CHURCH HAD SCHEDULED a family concert for the evening of Mother's Day. After the concert, Haleigh stayed to speak with Pastor Pete for a few minutes. She said goodbye when Aubrey approached her.

"A group of the young adults are going out to eat. Do you want to go with us? Willie has the van with the seats in, so there's plenty of room."

Haleigh nodded. "Sounds like fun."

"This might be my final chance at freedom." Aubrey sighed, but she didn't look at all troubled by the thought. "I wish Jeremy could be here, but he can't get away until Thursday."

Discussing the week ahead, they walked out together. Willie stood by his van with a young man who looked familiar to Haleigh. Aubrey slowed her pace with a quiet, "Oh!"

Willie turned toward them. "Derek Hall, you remember Haleigh Abbott and, of course, my sister."

Aubrey nodded and said nothing, but Haleigh felt her friend's body tremble.

With a mocking smile, Derek nodded at her. "Well, well, if it isn't little Haleigh Abbott all grown up." His voice held the same tone it had in high school, his attitude the same swagger.

Haleigh cringed inside, but she reluctantly acknowledged the backhanded greeting from the blond former football hero of Greenlawn High. She did her best to steady her voice. "Hello, Derek. Do you come to church here now?" To her knowledge, he had never been a churchgoer.

"Just visiting with my mom. She got religion and asked me to come with her. What are you doing back in Greenlawn?"

"Haleigh is working for me this summer." Willie stepped closer to Aubrey and her.

"Should have known. Little Haleigh working for the garden jock. And Aubrey, I hear you're marrying Jeremy Abbott. Keeping it all in the family, I see."

Willie's fist clenched. "I think it's time to go, girls. Jesse's waiting. We'll have to catch up with the others. See you around, Derek."

"Sure." Derek shrugged and turned away.

"The gall of that guy," Aubrey hissed through clenched teeth, watching as he swaggered away. "The time he spent in prison for the accident didn't sweeten his personality any!"

"Are you okay, Haleigh?" Willie put his arm around his sister. "I planned to ask Derek to join us, but I decided it wasn't such a good idea."

"I'm okay. Just a little shaken. I never was a recipient of his schoolboy charm. I guess some people don't ever change." Haleigh turned toward Aubrey. "Are you all right, Aubrey?"

"I am. I thought I'd forgiven him a long time ago, but the bad feelings resurfaced just then." Aubrey, visibly trembling, gave her friend a hug. "Why don't you sit in front with Willie while I calm down back here? Move over, Jess."

WILLIE PRONOUNCED a silent blessing on his sister as he opened the van door for Haleigh. "I'm sorry about Derek. I thought maybe he'd grown up by now. I'm surprised he came to church."

"I'm not sure he'll ever change." Haleigh climbed into the front seat.

Willie didn't regret reaching out to Derek. He knew people changed, and God could change Derek. He prayed God would use him to help Derek.

As he started the van, he caught his sister's eyes in the rearview mirror. She winked at him. Aubrey knew how much he cared for Haleigh.

From childhood, Willie and Haleigh had developed a trusting friendship, until the split up of the Three Sisters had broken her heart. Aubrey's accident, Gram's death, and Katie's pregnancy had torn away Haleigh's trust, and she closed herself off from her friends. She wouldn't talk to him, wouldn't let him help her, then left Greenlawn with her family. For a while Willie struggled with his own faith, not sure where the God he thought he knew was in the turmoil.

He'd wanted to be the one Haleigh confided in that morning after church. Amy signaled him away, and Aubrey pulled him out the door. He'd been relieved when Haleigh joined them for dinner, composed and happy.

Aubrey and Jesse talked softly in back, but Haleigh watched the passing scenery without speaking. Willie respected her silence. Haleigh still struggled with the past, and Derek had probably awakened some bad memories. Maybe one day soon she'd let go so she could move forward with her life. And maybe she'd allow him to be an important part of it.

6

*T*ia arrived as Haleigh unlocked the door at Floral Creations on Monday morning.

"Good morning, Tia.'

"'Mornin'." Tia put away her purse and took up her position at the cash register.

Oh, well. This was Tia's usual greeting in the morning.

Haleigh walked through the shop and greenhouse. The greenhouse plants would need watering. The rumble of a truck alerted her that the fresh flower order had arrived. Willie hadn't.

Although Willie had explained the procedure to her and she'd watched him do it, the responsibility for a flower order was out of her comfort zone. It involved a big expense for Willie's business.

She helped the delivery person bring in the flowers, checked the invoice, and signed for the delivery, hoping she did everything right. She didn't want to betray Willie's trust in her.

As the truck pulled away, Willie rushed in the door. "Good morning. Sorry to be late and miss the truck. I had to stop by the bank."

"Hi, Will." Tia smiled at him and touched her hair. She hadn't offered to help with the flowers.

"I hope I did it right." Haleigh handed him the invoice and held her breath.

He checked the invoice and the flowers. "Everything looks good."

She breathed again.

"Starting this morning and later this week, Jesse and I have a landscaping jobs. I'll be in and out. If you have a problem, you can call me."

She and Tia both nodded.

"On Friday I have a big order for a wedding. I promised the bride I would provide the flowers as my wedding gift."

"That's a generous gift, Willie, but are you going to have enough time?" Willie would be sure to make the flowers extra-special for his sister.

"I'll make it, Haleigh, but will you check the inventory to make sure I have supplies? Here's a list of what I'll need."

"Sure." She read the list he handed her. "I'll get to it first thing."

Stepping into his office, Willie placed the invoice in his file, then turned on his computer for a few minutes.

After he left, the phone rang, and Tia answered at the front counter. Haleigh checked the inventory and laid the list of needed supplies on his desk.

On Tuesday, Haleigh took advantage of the beautiful May weather and walked the mile to work. She inhaled a long breath of the mild air, made sweet with the scent of apple blossoms.

"Haleigh!"

She turned around to see who called her name.

"Haleigh Abbott, wait for me!"

Haleigh spotted a jogging figure with bouncing red curls coming toward her. "Katie?" Haleigh's feet propelled her forward. She stopped in front of Katie, watching her face for signs of resentment, but a big smile lit her face.

Without reserve, Katie threw her arms around Haleigh. "It's good to see you, old friend. It's been too long!"

"I know. I'm sorry." Joy flowed through her as she returned the hug. "I wasn't sure what happened to you. I didn't see you in church on Sunday."

Katie grasped both Haleigh's hands and looked into her eyes. "How are you? What are you doing now? Are you here just for the wedding?"

Haleigh couldn't suppress a grin. Some things never changed, like bubbly Katie. She had always kept their trio lively, and her exuberance spilled over to Haleigh.

"I'm staying at the Sousas' log home. They didn't want to leave it empty for the whole year, and they knew from my parents that I was graduating from college and wanted some time to decide what to do next. So, here I am."

"You're staying?"

"For the summer anyway, and maybe for the whole year. What are you doing now?"

"Oh, I just got back from a church drama conference, and I stopped to see my grandmother on the way home. I'm a nurse, an RN, and that pays my way. But I'm also the drama director at church, which satisfies my love for drama. I write plays too."

"So that's why you weren't in church." Haleigh glanced at her watch. "Oh, I have to get to work!" She turned and quickened her pace.

Katie fell into step beside her. "I'll walk with you. I'm on second shift, so I have plenty of time. Where do you work?"

"At Floral Creations."

"You're working for Willie White? That's great, Haleigh! With all Gram taught you about flowers, it's the perfect job for you."

"I enjoy it, and Willie's a good boss. Gram taught me so much. I still miss her."

Katie touched her arm. "She was sooo special, like everyone's grandmother. Aubrey and I always thought you were like her."

Haleigh raised her eyebrows. "Like a grandmother?"

"No, silly." Katie laughed. "You always encouraged us to keep trying. Like a cheerleader for the Three Sisters. And you look like her."

Haleigh shrugged. Gram had always encouraged her, and the Three Sisters had encouraged each other.

She wanted to ask Katie about her baby but didn't feel comfortable opening a subject so deeply personal. Maybe one day Katie would tell her.

"How are your parents, Katie?"

"They're doing okay. Thanks for asking. Dad is still a lawyer, and Mom's a nurse, but they seem closer to each other since I moved into my own apartment. You'll have to come see me. How about dinner at my place on Thursday night? I'm off Thursday."

"You have an apartment here in Greenlawn?"

Katie nodded as they stopped outside Floral Creations.

"I think Thursday will work. I'll call you." Haleigh started to pull out her key, but she saw Tia standing by the cash register examining her nails. She checked her watch. "See you later, Katie."

Katie handed her a card. "My cell phone number."

"Thanks." Haleigh slid the card into her pocket and walked into the shop, the bell jingling overhead. "Good morning, Tia." Katie's cheerfulness had rubbed off on her. "You're here early this morning."

"Mornin'," her co-worker muttered, opening the cash register drawer.

"Haleigh." Willie called to her from his office.

"Yes?"

"Will you come here for a minute?"

What had she done now? Haleigh cringed inwardly at the impatience in his voice.

Tia gave her a smug smile. What did Tia know that she didn't?

The file drawer grated as he opened it to place a folder inside. He turned when she entered the office. "Did you make out that list of what I need to order?"

"Yes, I did it yesterday, and I left it right here on your desk for you. Didn't you find it?"

"No, I didn't. Are you sure? I really have to get going. Jesse and I are meeting at the Gallaghers' in half an hour for a big landscaping project. See if you can find that list. I need to make the order right away."

"I'll do my best."

Tia watched them closely. Did she know what happened to the list?

Haleigh sighed. She didn't mind working with her. However, Tia found little ways to get under her skin—nothing Haleigh could really complain about. Now Willie had spoken sharply to her.

After he left, she looked everywhere for it. "Have you seen the list, Tia? I'm sure I can't miss a piece of paper that's hot pink. I don't know where it can be."

"Maybe you just thought you made one."

Haleigh shook her head. She'd been thorough and could almost remember the complete list. She had a lot to do today, but she drew another paper from the stack under the counter and made another list.

So many little things had gone wrong at the shop, and they all seemed to be her fault: misplaced orders, confused delivery and pick-up times, supplies not where they should be. Maybe this wasn't the right job for her.

In the early afternoon the doorbell jingled. Haleigh looked up from a flower arrangement she was working on. The young man who stood inside the door looked around. When they made eye contact, he smiled, but she groaned inwardly. Oh no, not

Stuart Webber. She wanted to duck behind the counter. Tia stared at him.

"Haleigh Abbott, I found you!"

If only he hadn't been looking for her. Well built and good-looking, with blond hair and blue eyes, he'd always turned female heads at college, including Haleigh's, until the female attached to the head realized what a conceited jerk he was.

Haleigh chided herself for her unkind thoughts, glad Tia didn't hear them.

"Hello, Stuart." She forced enthusiasm into her voice. "I'm surprised to see you in Greenlawn."

"You're a hard person to find. I called your home, but your parents only agreed they'd let you know I called. I found your summer address on the college website and thought I'd drop by. I live only a half hour from here."

"That's ... that's nice of you, Stuart, but I'm really busy right now."

"What time do you get off? How about dinner tonight?"

"We close at six," Tia said.

Haleigh glared at Tia and shook her head. Tia wasn't being helpful. She'd fallen under Stuart's spell once. After that she'd tried to avoid him, glad when he graduated the year before she did.

Before speaking, Haleigh took a deep breath. "Tia Merino, this is Stuart Webber. We attended the same college."

Tia put out her hand and fluttered her eyelashes.

"I'm delighted to meet you, Tia." Stuart took her hand and gazed into her eyes. "This town must be filled with beautiful women."

Gag!

"I see you're busy, so I won't bother you now." Stuart headed for the door. "See you at six."

The door shut behind him before Haleigh could open her mouth to tell him, 'no.' She whirled around to Tia, trying to keep her voice calm. "Why did you answer him?"

Tia's eyes widened. "He obviously knows you, and he's hot. How could you not want to have dinner with him?"

"Tia, you don't know Stuart. He's opinionated, controlling, and conceited. His beauty goes only skin deep."

"But didn't you go to a Christian college?"

"Yes." She didn't have time to explain everything to Tia. "Be careful, Tia. Don't be fooled by guys like Stuart."

Their conversation ended when the jingle of the bell warned of the arrival of more customers.

As she waited on them, she tried to think of a way to avoid Stuart. She even suggested to Tia they leave a few minutes early by the back door. Tia only giggled. Maybe Haleigh could pretend to be sick and leave early, but subterfuge didn't sit well with her. Even if she couldn't avoid dinner with Stuart this time, maybe if she went out with him once, she could convince him she wasn't interested.

"Have fun." Tia hurried to her car as Haleigh locked the shop door.

Stuart's red classic Mustang convertible waited for Haleigh in front of the shop. She regretted her walk to work to celebrate the beautiful day. Reluctantly, she got into the Mustang.

Self-conscious in her jeans and T-shirt because Stuart wore neat khakis and a light blue, three-button shirt, she suggested the local pizza parlor, Pizza Land. Its informality allowed her to convince herself it wasn't a real date. Haleigh ordered a slice of cheese pizza and a diet cola, and Stuart had a personal pan pizza with mushrooms and a root beer.

She gladly let him do most of the talking about his favorite subject—himself.

"I'm doing well. My dad gave me a position in his company. He said I'll have to work my way up through the ranks, just like anyone else. But I figure it won't take more than a few years to reach management level. Then I'll try for an executive position. I'm already looking into buying a house. I have my eyes on one, if Dad will help me buy it."

"Why don't you just buy something you can afford?" She took a bite of pizza and caught a string of mozzarella on her finger.

"Oh, but this house is a real beauty, a real investment. I figure, in a few years, I'll be able to sell it for a huge profit and build the house I really want. What are your plans for the future? How did you end up in Greenlawn?"

Haleigh picked up her glass of cola. "I'm originally from Greenlawn, and I wanted to come back for a while."

"Do you own the florist shop?"

"No, I just work there." If he'd read the sign, he'd know she didn't own it.

There was a pause in their conversation while they finished their food. Stuart leaned toward her and smiled. "How about a date on Friday night? We'll find a nice restaurant and make it a dress occasion. Maybe we'll take in a movie. What time can you be ready?"

"Wait, Stuart, I'm busy Friday night." Stuart's mouth turned down. "My brother is getting married on Saturday. I'm busy all weekend." Although she didn't want to go out with him again, Haleigh didn't know why she felt guilty saying no.

"How about next week, then? I live near Waverly. It's not far. I can come over any time."

"Stuart." Haleigh kept her voice even, pushing back her empty paper plate. "I-I don't want to go out with you again."

His eyes widened. "Why not?"

"I'm not interested in a relationship with you, and I don't want you to think I am. I told you that after our other date. I appreciate that you came all the way over here to see me, but this is it, Stuart." Her firmness surprised even Haleigh.

"You don't really mean that." He tried to grab her hand across the tiny table.

Haleigh nodded as she laid both hands in her lap. "Yes, I do, Stuart."

A customer stood at the counter ordering pizza, and two other tables were occupied. She glanced out the window, trying to figure out how to get away. Willie stood just outside in his stained work clothes, frowning. When their eyes met, he waved and entered, greeting the proprietor at the counter. As Willie approached their table, Stuart scowled and sat up straighter.

With a smile at Stuart, Willie and held out his hand, one of the few clean parts of him. "Hi, I'm Will White. You must be new in Greenlawn."

Relieved, Haleigh pushed back her chair. Her knight in shining armor, albeit rather soiled armor at the moment, had come to her rescue. "Stuart Webber, this is my employer. Will White owns Floral Creations. Stuart and I attended college together, Will, and he stopped by to see me since he lives over near Waverly."

Stuart stood and shook hands with Willie. "Nice to meet you, Will." The two young men eyed each other. They were about the same height, but Stuart was less muscular than Willie.

"I hope you don't mind, but I need to speak to Haleigh for a minute." When Stuart shrugged and sat, Willie turned toward her. "Did you do the list?"

"Yes, Will." She stumbled a bit over the name, "It's on your desk. I'm sorry about the delay."

"I'm sorry about my impatience this morning. I'll go back and send in the order right away. Good to meet you, Stu. See you tomorrow, Haleigh."

Willie peered at them through the window from outside the restaurant. He probably wondered why Stuart 'stopped by to see her.'

She turned back to Stuart. His narrowed eyes and grim mouth indicated his anger as he tapped the tabletop with his fingertips.

"Are you interested in him?" Stuart demanded, nodding toward the door.

Haleigh pushed a lock of hair behind her ear. "He and I have been friends for a long time. Remember, I used to live in

Greenlawn. Now he's my employer and runs a successful floral and landscaping business."

"That's all?"

With pursed her lips, she looked him in the eye, and spoke quietly but firmly. "I don't think that's any of your business." Why didn't he get the message and leave?

Stuart glanced down at his empty plate. "Can I drop you off at your house?"

Tempted to offer to pay for her own food, she decided not to insult Stuart. "No, thanks. I like to walk, and it's not very far." She preferred he not know where she lived. "Thank you for the pizza. I wish you well with your life."

"You're sure you won't reconsider?"

Haleigh shook her head, stood, and headed for the door. Stuart stopped long enough to leave a tip, then followed Haleigh out.

The Mustang's tires spit gravel as he drove off.

A RED MUSTANG whizzed by as Willie inserted the key in the door of his shop. *What a car!* Was that the one he'd seen parked in front of Pizza Land? The guy driving had to be crazy to accelerate that fast on Main Street. Willie shook his head.

Blond hair. It was that Stuart guy, Haleigh's friend. No one had ever mentioned to him that Haleigh had a boyfriend. What was their relationship? She didn't look particularly happy to be there with him. In fact, she looked relieved when Willie came in and interrupted their conversation.

The Mustang turned the corner and disappeared.

When Willie entered his office, he found Haleigh's list where she said it would be. He made his order online, then sat back for a moment in his chair.

Willie regretted his snappish tone this morning. He'd been pressed for time and thought she'd forgotten to make the requested list. Things had been missing or misplaced in the shop since he hired Haleigh. Although he didn't want to believe her irresponsible, he didn't want to blame Tia, who had always been a reliable employee.

He removed the money bag from the safe and checked the receipts. The girls had done well today. Everything looked in order as he entered the information onto his computer spreadsheet. He would stop by the bank and put the money in the night deposit.

Giving one last look around his office before turning off the lights, the edge of a pink paper in the trash can caught his eye. Since he didn't usually use hot pink paper, he pulled the paper out and recognized the handwriting. Haleigh's original list? How did it get there, and why hadn't he noticed it before?

He laid the paper on his desk and ran his fingers through his hair. He shouldn't have doubted Haleigh.

7

Haleigh phoned Katie on Wednesday. "Katie, I can't make it to dinner tomorrow. I'm sorry. Willie has asked me to help him tomorrow night because the wedding flowers are due to come in, and my brothers are both coming."

"Oh, I was really looking forward to having a long talk." Katie's voice indicated her obvious disappointment.

"We'll find another time. How about next Thursday? The wedding will be over, and my family gone. I'll have more time."

"Sounds good. We'll make it next Thursday at six-thirty." Katie sounded like her cheerful self again.

"I'll see you at the wedding."

"I wouldn't miss it. Bye, Haleigh."

"Bye, Katie."

Haleigh held the phone in her lap for a couple of minutes. First Aubrey, now Katie: both valued her friendship. Had she been to blame when the Three Sisters broke up? What if....? She shook her head. The past couldn't be changed.

WILLIE AND JESSE worked on a landscaping project on Thursday morning. Haleigh returned from lunch to find Willie talking to Tia.

"Are you all done with the landscaping already?"

"Jesse is finishing up this afternoon. I have some things I need to do here," Willie gestured toward the stack of boxes behind the counter. "The supply order just came in. Oh, by the way, I found your first order list in the wastepaper basket. Must have blown off my desk."

Haleigh's eyes met Tia's as she glanced at them over her shoulder on her way out of the door for lunch.

Many customers came in to purchase garden plants that afternoon. Haleigh stopped counting the flats of pansies and petunias, along with many other varieties of flower and vegetable plants they sold. The time flew by.

She stayed an hour past closing to help Willie check in the supplies and prepare for making the wedding arrangements. He was still there when she left.

Haleigh yawned as she turned toward home that evening. She bought groceries first, expecting Jeremy, Jason, and Carmella that evening and her parents the next day. She'd told them where to find the spare key so they could let themselves in if they arrived before she got home.

When she pulled up in front of the log home, she squeezed her car in behind two cars parked in the driveway. Jeremy came first out the door, with Jason on his heels. The J brothers were probably the best brothers a girl could have.

"Hey, Haleigh!" Jeremy grabbed her around the waist and spun around.

Not to be outdone, Jason did the same in the other direction. "It's good to see you again!"

Laughter spilled from her. "Where's Carmella?"

"Aw, she's taking a nap. You know how it is with expectant mothers."

Haleigh squealed. "Oh, Jason, really? You're going to be a papa? Wow!" She gave Jason a bear hug.

"Oof! For a little squirt, you have a hefty hug."

Standing with feet apart, arms akimbo, Haleigh tilted her head and raised her eyebrows. "Watch it, Bro. How do you know I haven't been lifting weights?"

"You could always pack a wallop." Jason rubbed his arm where she'd hit him with her fist or a pancake turner when he teased her about her size.

She turned to Jeremy. "I thought you'd be with Aubrey. Why are you here?"

"Thanks for the warm greeting, Little Sister." Jeremy tweaked a lock of her hair. "Did you know you have a smudge of dirt on your nose?"

She'd been to the store looking a mess?

"There." He rubbed the tip of her nose with his finger. "It's gone. Aubrey had a few wedding details to see to, so I came here to be with my family."

Haleigh joined her brothers as they sat on the porch steps.

"Mom said to tell you we've all been invited over to the Whites' house for a cookout after the wedding rehearsal," Jeremy said.

"I can't believe they want to have so many people at their house tomorrow night." Jason shook his head. "I'm sure Annette has enough to do with the wedding on Saturday."

"Yeah." Jeremy nodded. "Well, our parents are having it catered, so there will be only a little preparation and clean-up. It's been a long time since the Whites and Abbotts have all been together."

"Before Gram died." The thought saddened her.

"Before we moved away from Greenlawn." Jason brushed a black ant off his pant leg. "Are you okay now, Haleigh? We've been worried about you."

A brother on either side of her waited for her reply. "I'm sorry. I guess I got caught up in my own problems and didn't consider other people." She looked at Jason, then Jeremy. "I'm sorry you worried about me. I should have come back long ago, but it was easier to move and stay away. Coming back hasn't been as hard as I thought it would be."

Willie's welcome on the first day, and Aubrey's and Katie's forgiveness, had convinced her she'd made the right choice for the summer.

"Do you have any good memories?"

Discovering dirt under her fingernails, Haleigh sat on her hands before she answered Jeremy. "Yes, but for a long time all I could think about was Gram dying and leaving me, and losing my best friends. Too many changes, too many goodbyes. I would never have made it without Sunshine."

"That dog of yours was something special. When are you getting another one?"

With a response ready, Haleigh opened her mouth.

"What's this?" A voice behind them spoke. "I take a nap and wake up to find my husband out here with a younger woman."

Haleigh jumped up, bumping into her brothers. "Carmella, it's so good to see you! Jason told me your good news. Congratulations! You look wonderful." She threw her arms around her sister-in-law.

Carmella's long, dark hair glistened, her eyes sparkled, and her skin glowed. She looked happy and healthy.

"How does it feel to be a college graduate, Haleigh? Have you made any plans yet?"

"Maybe I'll hire out to be your nanny. When is the baby due?"

"Around Thanksgiving."

"Somewhere near my birthday."

Carmella grinned and nodded.

"So, are you having a boy or a girl?"

Jason stepped up on the porch behind Carmella and put his arms around her, leaning his chin on her head. "We decided not to tell anyone beforehand. In fact, we told the doctor we don't want to know."

"We think it will be more fun to be surprised when the baby comes, like in the 'old days.'" Carmella curled her fingers around Jason's arms.

Haleigh sighed and looked away. Would she ever share such an intimate moment with someone? She quickly pushed thoughts of Willie away.

"I'd better get the groceries from the car."

Her brothers raced for her car.

"Hey, you guys, I don't have that much!"

Laughing, she and Carmella stood back as her brothers wrestled with each other for the bags, cleaned out the car, and raced to the door.

"I won," Jeremy shouted.

"No, I did," Jason shouted back. "Will somebody ..."

"... please open the door," Jeremy finished.

"They always did compete." Haleigh opened the door wide for them. "It must be their twin-ness."

"Hmmm, I wonder what else I should know. Maybe you and I should have a talk, Haleigh." Carmella said, loudly enough so the men could hear her. "Wait a minute, we'd better let Aubrey know too."

"Aubrey knows."

Carmella laughed and put her arm around Haleigh's shoulders, and they entered the cabin together. "We'd better check up on those two in there."

"Do you really think you can wait until the baby is born to find out if it's a girl or boy?" Haleigh closed the screen door behind her.

TO FREE HALEIGH TO help him with the flowers for the wedding, Willie asked Jesse to work in the shop on Friday. His brother made the most of Tia's attention. Jesse liked an audience, and he liked girls. Willie didn't mind their chatter and laughter so long as it didn't interfere with their work or shop business.

"This is our work for today." Willie set his laptop on the back counter and opened it. He clicked from frame to frame. "Aubrey told me what flowers she wanted, and this what I came up with."

"I love your designs. They're beautiful, Willie." Her hair brushed his cheek as she leaned forward to see the screen.

The fragrance of her hair rivaled the floral scents that permeated their work area. She didn't know what it did to him to have her so close.

"Okay, let's get started. Why don't you work on the centerpieces for the reception? There are twenty of them. I'll do the two church arrangements."

Leaving her to gather her flowers and supplies at the counter, he worked at a smaller table with his back to her. Safer for his heart this way, although he couldn't resist looking over his shoulder occasionally. His heart raced when she glanced up and smiled at him.

Absorbed in flower arranging, she appeared relaxed and happy, and she hummed while working. Maybe it had something to do with him.

The arrangements completed, he stepped up beside her at the counter. "Want some help?" They'd finish faster if they worked together.

"Are these all right, Willie? I've finished ten of them."

"Perfect. You've done a great job, just like you do every day."

As they worked side by side, he reached for some flowers, and his arm zinged when it brushed hers.

Remaining focused on her work, she bit her lip and her cheeks turned pink. Haleigh blushed easily, and he loved it.

She helped him set the arrangements and centerpieces in the cooler, then they cleared their workspace.

"The supplies for the corsages and boutonnieres are in the

blue plastic tote. I'll get the flowers." He'd organized everything last night.

This time they sat side by side on stools at the counter, his laptop in front of him.

"Okay, it's time for corsage and boutonniere 101."

She leaned closer as she watched him, then copied what he did.

"Like this, Willie?"

"This way." His fingers brushed hers as he helped her hold the flowers in place so she could tape them, and a current passed up his arm. He loved to feel the softness of her hands beneath his roughened ones. "There, that's good."

"Thank you."

Although he reserved the bridal bouquet to do himself, they still had the four bridesmaids' bouquets to make. If he didn't keep himself busy with the flowers, he might sweep her into his arms and kiss her.

No, he couldn't risk his heart yet. Haleigh promised to stay only to the end of the summer. And even though every minute he spent with her weakened his resolve not to give in to his true feelings for her, she still considered him a friend.

What am I to do, God?

Wait.

WILLIE'S SKILL with flowers and his patience as a teacher amazed Haleigh. She treasured their friendship. If she ever married, she'd want someone like Willie, someone dependable, caring, and capable. But she wasn't ready, and maybe never would be, to have such a relationship with anyone. Life held too many uncertainties, and she often failed those she loved.

After they closed the shop at four, Haleigh headed home at four-thirty. Tia and a friend of Willie's would open Floral

Creations from eight to noon the following day. The wedding was scheduled for one o'clock.

Jeremy drove his car to the rehearsal, and Haleigh rode with him. Jason and Carmella rode with Mom and Dad. When she got out of the car in the church parking lot, she saw Willie in a group with several other people.

With his heart-warming smile in place, he approached. "Hey, Ha ... Haleigh, there's someone here we want you to meet. It's Mike's wife ..."

At least he didn't call her Halo in front of everybody.

"Maddison, it's really you! You married Mike White?" Seeing her in person, Haleigh realized she was the Maddison she'd known from dog training classes.

The two young women embraced.

"Haleigh! When they said your name, I didn't think it could possibly be the same person. I didn't remember your last name. Besides, the Haleigh I knew lived in Greenlawn, and they said Jeremy's family lived in Wellsburg." She laughed. "Look at them, Haleigh. They can't figure out how we know each other."

Mike, Willie's older brother, looked astonished.

"Haleigh here was known as the best dog handler in the class," Maddison said. "Our dogs were in obedience class together, and we both trained for the therapy dog program."

Mike snapped his fingers. "I should have realized. You take Hammurabi to hospitals to cheer up kids, like Haleigh does with her dog."

"How is Sunshine, Haleigh? Is she with you?" Maddison asked.

"No." Haleigh shook her head. "She had an inoperable tumor. I had to have her put down." She wrapped her arms around her middle.

"Oh, I'm so sorry," Maddison put her arm across Haleigh's shoulders. "You must have been devastated. I know how I'd miss Hammurabi. A friend is caring for him this weekend."

Mike took her hand.

"Maddison." Willie looked serious for a moment. "What I'd like to know is: why did you name your dog Hammurabi?" Haleigh appreciated Willie's attempt to lighten the moment.

Maddison shrugged and smiled. "He looked like a Hammurabi. I had read about Hammurabi in history class. I liked the sound of the name, kingly and exotic. He likes his name too. I know because he wags his tail when I say it."

Laughing, the group made their way into the church and greeted the Abbott and White parents and Aubrey's college roommate and maid of honor, Christina. She introduced them to her fiancé Daniel. Jason, of course, was best man, with Aubrey's brothers as ushers. Haleigh, Carmella, and Maddison were bridesmaids.

"Well, is the wedding party all here?" Pastor Pete called out. "Here's what we'll do."

She listened to Pastor Pete's instructions for the ceremony. Everything had to be perfect for her brother and his bride. Only that could make up for her unwillingness last year to reconcile with Aubrey that had nearly kept them apart. Truly happy for them, she wondered what it would be like to feel the joy obvious on Aubrey's face when she looked at Jeremy. Or the tenderness between Jason and Carmella when they talked about their baby.

Her eyes met Willie's. Her cheeks became hot, and she looked away, giving her head a little shake. She couldn't trust anyone enough to be that close. She couldn't trust herself not to make a mistake or fail.

THE NEXT MORNING, Haleigh awoke with a start. Was that a dog howling? She recognized Jeremy's voice, bellowing from the shower, "Oh, what a beautiful morning..." She giggled.

Someone knocked on the bathroom door, and her father's sleepy voice called out. "Jeremy, son, try to remember there are people still sleeping out here."

"Sorry, Dad!"

Jason opened his bedroom door and looked out at the same time Haleigh opened hers. "That's okay, Dad, we're awake now."

"Me, too, Dad." Haleigh yawned.

"Well, okay, but let's not tell Jeremy," Dad said.

Jeremy turned off the shower. "Tell me what?"

"Nothing!" They replied in unison and disappeared from the hallway.

Haleigh closed her door and sighed. Although she was happy for Jeremy and Aubrey, sadness for the changes coming to her family enveloped her. And loneliness.

$\mathcal{M}$orning plans included the groomsmen taking Jeremy out for breakfast and miniature golf. They joked and laughed about kidnapping him until Mom gave them stern looks. The two fathers cleaned, washed, and waxed Jeremy's car. Haleigh and the other bridal attendants met Aubrey at the church at eleven to dress and pose for a pre-ceremony photo session. One of the larger classrooms had been rearranged for that purpose.

Standing to the side, the three bridesmaids waited their turn as the photographer gave Aubrey, her mother, and Christina instructions.

The camera flashed as Christina straightened Aubrey's train. It flashed again when Aubrey pinned her mother's corsage to her dress then leaned over and kissed her cheek.

Fingering the single strand of pearls around her neck, Haleigh drew a deep breath to calm her fluttering stomach.

Maddison leaned toward her and Carmella. "Aubrey looks so calm. My mother threatened to give me a tranquilizer, I was so nervous."

"Jeremy was pretty calm this morning as well." Carmella grimaced. "But I can't say much for that awful rendition of 'Oh,

What a Beautiful Mornin" he sang in the shower and woke us all up."

To keep from laughing out loud, Haleigh placed her hand over her mouth. Yeah, that had been bad.

Aubrey stood before the floor-length mirror donated for the occasion by Amy, and everyone held their breaths as Christina placed and arranged Aubrey's veil. The camera flashed multiple times.

Tears filled Haleigh's eyes. She'd been a bridesmaid at Jason and Carmella's wedding. That had been fun and meaningful, and she loved her sister-in-law. But if she hadn't been willing to face and accept her responsibility in her split with Aubrey, she would have missed out on this special time.

Thank you, God.

"Everything about this wedding is beautiful." Carmella raised her bouquet of blue forget-me-nots, white stephanotis, and pale pink lilies to her nose. "Willie has a gift with flowers."

Haleigh nodded. "He does." Only now had she seen the bride's cascading bouquet of white roses, stephanotis, forget-me-nots, and white lilies, with trailing ivy greens. "Isn't Aubrey's bouquet stunning?"

"Yes, and I love the color and style of our gowns and how the blue matches the color of the flowers in our bouquets." Maddison held her bouquet against her skirt. "My grandmother made my gown because my sewing skills are basic."

"In another month, I'd probably have to let out the seams." Carmella patted her stomach. "Jason said you made yours, Haleigh."

"I did. It took me the entire week of spring break, but it was worth it. I had to take out and redo a couple of seams, and the zipper didn't want to go in straight." The princess styling with a jewel neckline fit her to perfection. The skirt swirled around her ankles.

Soon after the photo session ended, the organist began to play a prelude of hymns chosen by Aubrey and Jeremy.

As the time for the ceremony approached, Haleigh's excitement mounted. Lined up behind Carmella and Maddison, she couldn't take her eyes off Willie, striking in his tuxedo. He held out his arm to her mother and escorted her to her seat, bending slightly to say something to her. Mom looked up at him and smiled.

As Mike escorted his own mother to her place, Carmella turned her head. "You know, I believe the White men are nearly as handsome as the Abbott men."

"Ahem. The White men may be a tad bit handsomer." Maddison twisted toward Haleigh. "What do you think, Haleigh?"

"What?" Oh, no, had they seen her staring at Willie? These two were trouble. "I, uh, I think they all look great." She buried her nose in her bouquet to hide her hot face.

The music changed from hymns to a processional piece. The men entered through a side door near the front of the church, including the three ushers.

Everyone quieted, and anticipation filled the air.

The pastor nodded, and Carmella proceeded up the aisle, followed by Maddison.

Haleigh trembled with excitement and took a deep breath. When her turn came, she smiled, then put one foot in front of the other, glad the dress covered her shaking legs. Her eyes met Willie's, and he nodded at her. His smile stirred up a whole flock of butterflies in her stomach.

It almost made her giggle to see Jesse standing so seriously beside his brother, dressed in a tuxedo. What was Jesse thinking?

Her brothers smiled at her, and she relaxed. After Christina, the maid of honor, took her place, the music changed again. Everyone stood and turned toward the entrance.

When Aubrey entered on her father's arm, Jeremy's eyes widened. The simple lines of her gown accentuated her elegant figure. Beneath the veil, Aubrey's blond hair was pulled back into a French twist, exposing her glowing face. Haleigh's breath caught for a moment when she noticed her friend's almost invisible limp.

As the wedding party turned toward the front of the church, Haleigh focused on the ceremony

"Dearly beloved," Pastor Pete began.

She looked past the bride and groom once and caught Willie's gaze, then quickly refocused her eyes back toward the pastor. Haleigh couldn't avoid Willie, however, as he escorted her out of the church and stood beside her in the reception line.

"Green may be your favorite color, but you look lovely in blue."

"You look nice too." She briefly met his eyes.

Haleigh had met many of Aubrey's and Willie's extended family in the past. Willie's Grandpa White had the bride and groom in stitches, but Haleigh couldn't quite hear what he said. "I'd forgotten your grandfather's sense of humor. It's where Jesse gets his craziness, isn't it?" She spoke so only Willie could hear.

Willie nodded, then kissed his grandmother's cheek and shook hands with his grandfather. "Grandma and Grandpa, you remember Haleigh Abbott."

"Yes, I remember Haleigh. It's nice to see you again." Grandma White kissed Haleigh's cheek. "You girls all look lovely in your gowns."

"Thank you. It's nice to see you again too, Mrs. White. I'm grateful Aubrey asked me to be a bridesmaid."

"Another Abbott, eh?" Grandpa White stood in front of her, his blue eyes twinkling, his lips twitching. "We can't seem to get away from them today, can we, Willie?" He looked from Haleigh to Willie and back.

Willie grinned at Haleigh, and heat rose in her face.

"The flowers are beautiful, Willie." Grandma White laid her hand on his cheek. "Aubrey is so pleased."

"Haleigh was my assistant. I couldn't have done them without her help."

"Thanks, Willie." She'd done her best, for Aubrey and Jeremy and for him.

As Willie's grandparents moved on, Grandpa looked back at them once and winked.

She'd be glad when the line of guests came to an end. Not only were her feet aching, but standing beside Willie, close enough to feel his body heat and smell his clean scent, became harder by the minute.

It may have been Jeremy and Aubrey's wedding reception, but for Haleigh it was a homecoming. Friends welcomed her back to Greenlawn, and not one mentioned the teenager who had left Greenlawn in personal turmoil. She talked with Katie and had her picture taken with Aubrey and Katie. Aubrey's brothers and Haleigh's brothers moaned about the Three Sisters being back.

After the buffet meal provided by the church family, Haleigh circulated around the reception hall, visiting with the guests. She and the other bridesmaids distributed the bridal cake when it was cut.

The four groomsmen whispered together and disappeared out the door, probably on their way to embellish the bride and groom's getaway car.

Haleigh sat down to rest her feet as she ate her piece, savoring the rich chocolate flavor.

A young man approached her with a smile. "It's a nice wedding,"

With dark blond hair and hazel eyes, he looked familiar to Haleigh.

"I wondered if those two would get together." He pulled out a chair and sat.

Haleigh nodded and smiled. "Yes." Only a year ago her brother and Aubrey had become serious, although they'd grown up together.

She pressed her fork into the crumbs on her plate. She didn't intend to miss any of the goodness. "Did you have a piece of cake?"

"Yes, it was really good." He watched the newlyweds, then turned back to Haleigh. "Are you living in Greenlawn now?" he asked. "I think you've been gone for a while."

"Yes, I just graduated from college. My family lives in Wellsburg now." Haleigh searched her memory for his identity. He apparently knew her, so she was embarrassed to ask his name. "I'll be staying here for the summer." She stood and brushed a crumb from her dress.

"Excuse me, Chad. I need Haleigh." Katie grabbed her arm and pulled her away before the name registered to Haleigh's memory. "Come on, Haleigh, Aubrey's about to throw her bouquet!" Katie nearly dragged her to join the group of single women. "You should try to catch it."

"No." Haleigh held back. "You catch it." The bouquet would be wasted on her. She had no plans to marry, and she didn't want anyone thinking otherwise. She and Willie were just good friends.

The groomsmen reappeared just as Aubrey threw the special bouquet Willie made for this purpose. Many waving arms reached for the bouquet, and Katie tried her best, but Christina caught it.

Looping her arm through her friend's, Haleigh whispered in her ear. "Christina and her fiancé have a fall wedding planned."

Jeremy and Aubrey changed out of their wedding finery. Amid a shower of bird seed, they drove away in Jeremy's carefully decorated car, hardly recognizable with its balloons, streamers, 'just married' sign, and a string of cans tied to the bumper. Haleigh admired the careful handiwork of the groomsmen.

Most of the guests left. Haleigh changed out of her gown and helped clean up the reception hall. She collected her personal belongings and rode back to the cabin with Jason and Carmella.

THE WHITES and Abbotts met at the log home for a couple of hours to unwind and share memories of the day. As Haleigh leaned against the porch railing, most of the other family members were yawning. Her father, especially, appeared fatigued.

"I'm sorry to leave so early, but I'm ready to drop." Mrs. White embraced Mom. "We've been friends for a long time, Elizabeth, but now we have a family connection."

"Oh, Annette, what a beautiful wedding! You and Aubrey did a fine job planning it. Everything came together so well." Mom turned toward Willie. "The flowers were absolutely stunning, Willie."

Willie put his arm around Haleigh's shoulder and pulled her against him. "Don't forget my talented assistant." Haleigh warmed at his praise and touch.

Mom nodded. "Haleigh told me how much she's learned from you. You both did well."

"I'm glad I have only one daughter to give away. This old heart can't take doing that very often." Mr. White placed his hand on his chest.

"I think I know what you mean, Jim." Her father laid his hand on Haleigh's head. His voice held a slight tremor.

Mr. White took his wife's hand. "Do you young people have plans?"

Willie looked at Jesse. "Jesse and I will be home later." Jesse nodded.

After Mr. and Mrs. White said good night and drove away, Mom and Dad went indoors. Jason and Carmella had gone in earlier.

"Do you want to take a walk with us, Haleigh?" Willie asked.

"Good idea. I'm still wound up from all that's happened today. A walk will be good."

"We won't be long," she called to her parents.

They strolled toward Main Street, one White brother on either side of Haleigh, their way dimly lit by streetlights. The humid night air held the sweet fragrance of flowers.

"Jess, are you excited about going in the Air Force?" Haleigh hadn't had time to talk to Jesse about his career choice since the night she learned he joined.

"Some days I can hardly wait, and occasionally I wonder if it's the right choice."

Willie looked at his brother over Haleigh's head. "You said you prayed about it, Jess."

"I did, Wills, but aren't you ever afraid that maybe you made the wrong choice, that you're not following God's will?"

"There was a time when I would have said God's will didn't matter."

Haleigh stared at Willie. This must have been the time his mother had spoken about.

"In high school after you left, Haleigh, I fell into a 'slough of despond.' So many bad things happened, I wondered if God really cared. But Jesus wouldn't let me go. He's been so good to me. He honored my desire to become a florist, and I love my work."

"I remember that time." Jesse shook his head. "You weren't very nice to be around."

Haleigh turned her attention back to Jesse.

"Once in a while I wonder, but I'm pretty sure the Air Force is the right place for me. I've considered going into the military for a long time, and flying is exhilarating. There's nothing like the feeling you get when you're behind the controls and take to the skies."

Haleigh touched his arm. "Have you thought about being sent to a war zone?" She shuddered at the thought.

"Yeah. Might very well happen." He shrugged. "But it's a chance I'm willing to take."

Security lights illuminated the interiors of closed shops along Main Street, including Floral Creations. A group of teens stood outside Pizza Land, and others filled the tables inside. Willie and Jesse greeted several couples out for a stroll. Haleigh didn't recognize any of them.

"How about you, Haleigh?" Willie's voice broke into their silence. "What do you want to do?"

"Me?" She looked up at the stars. "I guess I would have to say, to find God's plan for me. The one Gram always told me He had, but I've never been able to find."

"Is that why you came back, to find God's plan?"

She held out her hands, palms up. "Almost everyone in college seemed so focused, so ready to go out into the world and get the right job. They seemed to know exactly what they would be: teachers, computer technicians, pastors, missionaries, secretaries. Some of them knew who they would marry. And then there was me." She laid a hand on her chest. 'What will you be doing, Haleigh?' 'Uh, I'm not sure yet.' Do you know how dumb I felt?"

Jesse walked backward, facing her. "I don't think it's dumb, Haleigh. You're just being honest. I've met people who jumped into careers, sometimes even Christian work, because they felt pressured to do it, rather than really knowing if it was God's will."

"You could do a lot of things." Willie walked with his hands in his pockets and his eyes on her. "You can keep working for me. You're good with flowers, and we make an awesome team."

"Thanks. I do enjoy working at Floral Creations, and I've learned a lot from you."

"You could train therapy dogs." Jesse turned to walk beside her. "Maybe even have a kennel and raise dogs. You sure had a special touch with ol' Sunshine."

Willie touched her arm. "You get along well with the elderly. You could work with senior citizens or in a nursing home, maybe as a program director, like Mrs. Evans."

She stopped and looked from one brother to the other. "I don't know." When she continued walking, they fell into step beside her again.

"You can use your gift of encouragement to help others." Willie's hands went back into his pockets. "Aubrey and Katie always said how much you helped them by your support. Remember where the name 'Three Sisters' came from?"

"Yes." Haleigh nodded. "You told us the story from the Iroquois about the corn, beans, and squash they grew. They called these plants the Three Sisters."

"I didn't know this." Jesse nudged her arm with his elbow. "Tell me."

"Corn was the big sister," Haleigh began, "Tall and strong, she looked after her younger sisters, Squash and Beans."

"In the Iroquois garden, those three crops were grown together." Willie took up the story. "The corn stalks supplied a support system for the other two. The squash provided ground cover and ran helter-skelter over the ground. The beans, the little sister, needed corn and squash for support, and yet benefitted the other two because it was a legume and enriched the soil."

Jesse nodded. "That really does sound like the three of you."

"Katie was the lively one, with bright-colored hair, Aubrey was the oldest and tallest, and had blond hair, like corn silk, and I was the little sister." Haleigh twisted her mouth. "My brothers called us Goldie, Red, and Beanie."

Willie and Jesse burst into laughter.

"Don't you try it! My brothers stopped calling me Beanie very fast." Her narrowed eyes were probably lost on them both because of the dim lighting. Would she be sorry she told them?

"Wouldn't think of it," Willie said. "But I've heard Jeremy call Aubrey 'Goldie.'"

Both brothers stopped laughing, although they couldn't suppress a few more chuckles.

"You cheered for them and encouraged them, and you were enthusiastic about what they did." Willie pulled his hands from his pockets. "You listened and sympathized with them and tried to help them solve their problems. Maybe you should become a counselor or psychologist."

"A long time ago we did that for each other." It was what made the Three Sisters friendship special. Haleigh sighed deeply. "I don't know. I have trouble dealing with my own problems, and I don't think I've helped people much." She'd cut herself off from her friends when they probably needed her the most. "How can I help anyone?"

"It's still a possibility." Willie could be right. He usually was.

"You could do what Katie does, have one job that pays the bills and work in a church ministry." Jesse faced her again, walking backward.

That appealed to her, but Haleigh shook her head. "I just don't know. I never knew I had so many options." They'd given her a lot to think about. Returning to Greenlawn had been the first step in finding her way.

"Well, this is where I leave you." Jesse stopped at the corner. "I'm going home to hit the sack. Remember, kids, tomorrow is

Sunday. Don't stay out too late." Jesse turned toward the White home.

AT FIRST WILLIE had welcomed Jesse because Haleigh relaxed more with Jesse than with him. They'd been together for most of the day with other people around. Now he preferred this time alone with her.

Tired of fighting his feelings for her, he draped his arm across her shoulders, to have her close. When she didn't shrug it off, he left it there.

"I guess it's just the two of us, Halo."

She didn't respond, probably thinking. He wanted her to talk to him.

"I really meant what I said, Haleigh. You can continue to work for me. I don't regret hiring you. You know flowers, and you're a valuable employee. The offer stands."

"Thanks, Willie. You're a good friend."

He wanted to be much more than a good friend. When would Haleigh realize that? Should he tell her now?

Or was there someone else, a possibility he hadn't considered before he met Stuart?

He'd better get her home. The day had been long for them both. He loved the sweet scent of newly mown grass and flowers that permeated the warm evening air. Party sounds came from a nearby house, and an occasional car passed by. A dog barked, and another down the block answered.

Willie dropped his arm and broke the silence that had fallen between them. "So, tell me about Stuart Webber."

"What?" Haleigh turned to face him, then shrugged and began to walk again. "There's not much to tell. We dated once in college, but once was enough."

"I hope I didn't cause a problem by showing up at Pizza Land when I did." Willie had used the excuse of asking Haleigh about the list so he could meet Stuart.

"No. In fact, I'm glad you came in."

"Why is that?"

"Stuart is ... well, not a person I want to spend a lot of time with."

"Oh?"

"Look, Willie, I'd rather not talk about Stuart. If I never see him again, it won't matter." Haleigh waved her hand as though brushing Stuart Webber away.

He stopped and grasped her arm, forcing her to look at him. "He didn't hurt you?"

"No, he didn't." She shook her head. "But he has a reputation for being possessive, and he didn't want to be just friends. I have no intention of encouraging him." She gently removed her arm from his grasp and continued walking.

Was she offended he'd asked? He stuffed his hands in his pockets. He only wanted to protect her, as he'd always done.

"You know, you were my sister's friend, but I had fun when you were around."

Haleigh laughed. "You were such a tease, but you were like a brother and one of my best friends."

Maybe he had to be satisfied with being friends. He didn't want to jump into a more intimate relationship than God intended them to have.

"I could hardly stand it when you left Greenlawn, Halo. You hurt so much, and I couldn't do anything to help you." His arm tingled when it brushed hers. With much more to say, he waited for her to look at him.

"You did more than you think." She looked up at the lights of a jet passing over instead of at him.

Willie sighed and focused forward. "Are we just friends, Haleigh?" Was she listening?

After a moment, not looking at him, she asked, "Are you seeing Tia?"

Now, why did she say that? "Tia? Tia Merino? Of course not! Whatever gave you that idea?"

"Tia said ..."

He'd wondered about the tension between the two young women. To be honest, he felt a little flattered to think he might be the cause. "Is that what causes the sparks to fly between you?" The corners of his mouth twitched, and he rubbed his upper lip to hide his smile.

"Actually, I think Tia is jealous because you hired me for the job she thought she should have. But she did hint that there was something going on between you."

Willie shook his head. "No, Tia's just my employee. She's a good worker and I like her, but we've never dated, and I don't plan to in the future. She doesn't share our faith in Jesus Christ."

"Oh."

They walked on in silence.

He took a deep breath. "When I first saw you two weeks ago, I felt like I'd been waiting for you to come back. Haleigh, I—"

"Isn't that a shooting star?" Haleigh pointed to a bright streak in the sky that winked out after a few seconds.

Willie sighed. She cut him off again. Did she do that on purpose?

The moon lit their silent way back to the cabin. He sensed a new tension between them.

"I've lived with fear for a long time," Haleigh said. "I'm afraid of letting people down, and they'll leave me. When the Sousas' cabin needed a sitter, Mom and Dad thought I should come back and try to settle some issues. They understand me better than I thought, perhaps even better than I know myself."

Maybe she did hear him. "And are you? Settling the issues, I mean."

Haleigh shrugged. "Maybe. I've talked with Aubrey and Katie. And with you, it's almost like I never left, like we've been in touch the whole time."

Their reconnection had happened quickly, and he wanted her

to stay, even as a friend. Before he risked his heart, he had to know she'd be willing to give hers.

The porch light glowed in the dark surrounding it. Jason and Carmella's car was parked in the driveway next to the Abbott parents' mini-van, Haleigh's Toyota on the lawn.

Haleigh sat down on the top step, and Willie joined her.

"When everything fell apart, you were strong and stable and dependable." She leaned her elbows on her knees and rested her chin on her clasped hands as she looked straight ahead. "I missed you when I left, but I hurt too much to communicate with anyone in Greenlawn. Totally selfish. I never answered Aubrey's or Katie's letters. I figured you'd be mad about Aubrey's accident."

Finally, she trusted him enough to open up about the past. She looked at him. "I'm still afraid, Willie."

"Of what?"

"Of the past. I've made so many mistakes. What if ..."

"I'm not planning to leave, Halo." He took her hand.

She looked at their hands, and he waited for her response.

Stars twinkled in the sky. An airplane passed overhead with a low rumble. Up the road a dog barked, breaking into the quiet, and a woman's voice called out to it.

Haleigh shifted on the step and moved her hand to her lap. "Have you ever met the people who live at the end of the road?"

"Can't say I have." She didn't follow up on his promise. A dark cloud of disappointment shadowed his hope for a breakthrough, and he rubbed his hand on his pantleg.

"On my first day here, I walked up to the end. At the bungalow next to the woods, there was a little boy playing with his dog." Haleigh paused. "A black dog that reminded me of Sunshine."

"Maybe you'll have another dog one day."

"I'd like to have another one, but not until it doesn't hurt so much to think about Sunshine."

He didn't want to talk about shooting stars, dogs, or the

neighbors. He wanted to say so much more. He loved Haleigh, but she wasn't ready for a declaration from him. Something from the past still shadowed her. Maybe it was too soon. She'd returned less than two weeks ago.

Normally a patient person, he knew he needed God's strength to remain patient with Haleigh. Maybe it was time for a man-to-man talk with Dad.

"I think it's time for me to go, Halo." He stood and stretched. "See you at church?"

Haleigh yawned. "Unless we all oversleep."

Pulling her to her feet, he resisted the urge to hold her in his arms. He bent toward her and kissed her forehead. "'Night, Halo."

"'Night, Willie."

He strode away. Maybe once she 'settled the issues' and overcame her fear of failure, she'd be ready to hear him out.

He turned to look back once. She stood where he left her. He waved. She waved back and went into the house.

10

On Sunday afternoon, Dad opened the door and stepped out on the porch. "I'm going for a walk, Haleigh. Do you want to come with me?"

"Sure, Dad." Haleigh jumped up from the rocking chair.

Their last father-daughter chat had been quite a while ago. Since Christmas, Dad hadn't been his vibrant self. On Friday, she credited his fatigue to the wedding and all the related activities. She'd forgotten about it until last night, when she noticed Dad's pale features and Mom's worried look.

Jason and Carmella planned to leave early this evening, her parents tomorrow morning.

"Have you been by the old house?" her father asked as they strolled toward Main Street.

"Once, with Aubrey last week."

"Have you and Aubrey worked things out?"

"We talked. I think we're okay now."

"And Katie? I spoke with her at the reception. She appears to be doing well."

"We have plans to have dinner on Thursday night." Haleigh shook her head. "I-I think a lot of the problem was me, Dad. I could only see me, and I lost all those years with my friends."

"Ah, the college years added some wisdom and perspective." Dad put his arm around her shoulders. "You've learned to take responsibility for your own actions." He released her and tucked his hands into his pockets. "Change can be hard, and for you it seems to be especially difficult. It doesn't necessarily get easier as you grow older, but you learn to accept it when you have no control over the situation. God has a way of working things out."

"I felt so secure and happy with what I had as a girl, I didn't want it to be different. Gram was right. I should have been glad that Aubrey and Katie could use their God-given talents Instead, I thought only about me."

"Your grandmother was one of a kind. We both still miss her."

Haleigh squeezed her dad's arm. Then she smiled. "How does it feel to be almost a grandpa?"

Dad grinned. "Great! It's hard to believe that Jason is old enough to be a father. I can remember how I felt when I knew your mother was expecting, and when I first held your brothers."

"I can't wait to spoil my niece or nephew, or maybe one of each." Twins—that would be fun!

Dad chuckled. "Twins are a possibility. Your mom's inside with Jason and Carmella now, talking about the baby. Jason told us that he and Carmella wanted us to keep quiet about it until after Jeremy's wedding. But your mother's thrilled she can now tell everyone she's going to be a grandmother."

A man and a boy played catch in the yard of their former home, and a woman pushed a girl on the apple tree swing. They waved but didn't stop to talk. Haleigh knew Dad had something on his mind.

A few minutes later, they entered Rose Hill Cemetery and headed toward Gram's grave. The pink geraniums bloomed beautifully, and a single red rose lay on the ground in front of the gravestone.

"That's from you, isn't it, Dad?"

"Yes." She sat beside him on a grassy knoll not far from her grandmother's grave and waited for him to speak. Birds sang from nearby trees. A couple of gray squirrels scampered to and fro, searching in the grass and playing tree tag.

"I have some news."

Haleigh's chest tightened as she watched her father's profile.

"I'm not sure how to tell you this, to make it easier for you." He took a deep breath. "But ... Haleigh, I have a heart condition."

Not Dad too. Haleigh pulled up the grass beside her and made a neat pile as he spoke.

"I've been feeling tired for a while and have experienced some pain." He continued. "I had tests, and apparently there's blockage. I'll have to have surgery. I have an appointment with the heart surgeon, who will explain what has to be done."

"When?" Haleigh whispered.

"The surgery is scheduled for the end of June. I wanted to wait until after your graduation and Jeremy's wedding."

"I noticed you and Mom seemed worried about something, but I thought it was because of the wedding. Why, Dad? Why you ... now?" She laid her head against his chest.

His arms encircled her. "Oh, Haleigh, I know."

As she cried, she heard her father's heartbeat and the rumble of his voice.

"I don't expect to die, not yet. The doctor is optimistic that I'll be better in no time."

Haleigh pulled away from her father and wiped the tears from her face. He handed her a clean handkerchief.

"Thanks. I'm okay, Dad." At least she hoped she was. "When I lost my best friends, my life seemed to fall apart. Gram helped me get Sunshine, and it was the best thing she could have done. Therapy dogs are supposed to help draw the sick and elderly out of loneliness and depression, but Sunshine did that for me."

Her father rubbed her back.

"My heart broke when Gram died. Then I was sick, and we moved away. When Sunshine died, it hurt so bad." She wiped her face and blew her nose. "Why do we have to lose the people we love? Why does it hurt so?" Haleigh crossed her arms against her chest and hugged herself. "I don't want to lose you too. I'm scared, Dad."

"By God's grace, we'll get through this together." His Adam's apple bobbed as he swallowed.

He laid his arm across her shoulders and pulled her close. "I'm glad you came back to Greenlawn, Haleigh. Your mother and I hope you'll get some things straightened out, find peace with the past. She and I prayed for a long time before leaving Greenlawn six years ago, and we decided you needed the opportunity to begin in a new place. We didn't like to see you alone so much and hoped you'd make new friends."

"Maybe I needed the time to grow up." She wiped her eyes with the corner of her blouse, then remembered the handkerchief in her hand. "Maybe moving away was the best thing, even though I resented it. I think I caused a lot of my own trouble. When I drove into Greenlawn two weeks ago, I felt like I came home."

"And how are you and Willie doing?"

Haleigh's eyes widened and her mouth dropped open. "W-What do you mean, Dad? Willie and I are friends, of course, and I work for him." In her heart, she knew she had a stronger connection to Willie. She felt so alive when they were together, and she heard it when he spoke to her. But she wasn't ready for anything more than friendship. And she didn't want to discuss it with her father.

"Your Mom and I have been watching, and we thought –"

"I'm not sure I'll ever get married, if that's what you're thinking."

Her father's forehead wrinkled. "Why? You're such a loving, caring person, you'd bring much into a marriage."

Haleigh bit her lip. "I hurt the people I get close to, or else they die and leave me. I don't think I can trust anyone that much. I don't think I trust myself."

"I'm sorry, Haleigh. I think I know why you're saying that, but I don't agree with you. I think your trust problem goes much deeper. You don't really trust God."

"Maybe you're right, Dad." She gazed thoughtfully at her father. "But He has taken away so much. I know He loves me, but that doesn't keep the hurt away. I've seen marriages break apart in divorce or because of death, and I'm not sure I can handle it."

Dad put his arm around her and pulled her to him. "I hope you change your mind. However, it may be God's will that you remain single. And, if so, then that's that. Just remember that your mother and I will be praying for you."

"Thanks, Dad. I'll be praying for you too."

Haleigh and her father stood and fell into step as they strolled back to the cabin, chatting about work, family, and friends. She didn't talk about Dad's heart trouble, fearing if she did, she might break down again.

HALEIGH USED time alone on Monday evening to clean the log home. Finally satisfied that the cabin sparkled, she put on a sweatshirt and sat on the top porch step. She breathed deeply of the cooling air as she opened her journal.

A not-so-busy day at Floral Creations. Willie and Jesse are working late on a landscaping project, and Katie is working evening shift at the Senior Home. Mom and Dad left this morning, so I cleaned the cabin.

I love listening to the spring peepers. Blue jays are scolding and flitting through the trees. The sun is just above the horizon, so the trees are casting long shadows across the road. In a tree across from me, a robin is singing his heart out. It reminds me of a camp song we used to sing, "Said the Robin to the

Sparrow." I hear kids laughing and dogs barking, and cars on Main Street.

Haleigh stopped writing, propped her elbows on her journal, and rested her chin in her hands. She loved evenings like this. In the two weeks since arriving in Greenlawn, she'd become accustomed to the cabin's night noises.

I can hardly find words to describe Saturday. Magical, wonderful. I think it was the happiest day for me since before the Three Sisters broke up. Aubrey looked so beautiful, and my brother so happy. I'm glad they found each other. I'm ashamed of the grief I caused them when I refused to talk to Aubrey. And it was wrong for me to stay away so long before trying to make things right here.

It had been easier to box up her guilt and grief and stay away from Greenlawn.

Dad was right. I don't like change. But the changes that have taken place since I came home to Greenlawn have been good. Aubrey and Katie forgave me, and we're friends again. I have a job I enjoy at Willie's place. Until I came back, I didn't realize how much I missed Willie. It's like those six years apart never happened. He's a good friend.

Willie made her smile and gave her confidence. The memory of his hands holding hers and the warmth in his eyes made her shiver. Better get back to writing.

Jason and Carmella are so excited about their baby. Is it a boy or a girl? Or maybe one of each? Will they be able to wait until the baby is born to find out? My bet is they won't wait.

Ugh! Dad's heart surgery. I knew something was up, but not this.

I don't think I could stand it if he died. Mom and Dad say they're trusting God for the outcome. I believe they are. Trust is hard for me. Maybe Dad is right: my trust problem is with God and not people or myself.

Jeremy and Aubrey are on their honeymoon, Jason and Carmella are planning for their baby, and Mom and Dad are home safely. They have each other. I'm the only one alone.

How I miss Sunshine! She helped me through the bad times.

Haleigh sniffled and wiped tears from her eyes.

Heavy breathing and the thud of running paws reached her. She looked up to see a black dog galloping toward her on gangly legs. Haleigh stood quickly, setting her journal on the porch railing.

"Sit." She put out her hand with the palm down. Surprised, the dog sat on its haunches, his tongue lolling out of the side of his mouth, his tail stirring up a cloud of dust. He had no collar.

Laughing at the dog's attitude, she said, "What are you doing here, fella? Does your master know you're here?" She stepped down and patted the dog's head. He took that as an invitation to stand and circle around her legs. "I suppose I should take you home."

Checking to be sure the cabin door was closed, she snapped her fingers and said, "Come."

The dog gamboled merrily around Haleigh, ran up the road toward the bungalow, and bounded back to her. A blue collar attached to a chain lay next to the doghouse in the yard of the bungalow. She rang the front doorbell, trying unsuccessfully to get the dog to sit. A young woman opened the door. She wore blue jeans and a red T-shirt, with her hair pulled back in a ponytail,

"Oh, hello."

Haleigh smiled. "I think this is your dog." She gestured with her hand at the dog sniffing around the steps. "He paid me a visit."

"Oh, no! He must have slipped his collar. We didn't know he was gone. I'm sorry he bothered you, but thank you for bringing him back."

The boy she'd met before came to the door, dressed in pajamas and a robe. "Hi. You're the lady who used to have a black dog like King." The dog bounded up to him and licked his hand.

"Yes. I'm Haleigh Abbott. I'm staying in the log home up the road for the summer."

The woman stepped outside. "I spoke to the Sousas a couple of times before they left, and they said someone would be house-sitting for them. I'm Nancy Morgan, and this is my son, Timmy. You've already met King."

"Timmy." Nancy turned to her son. "You'd better put King's collar back on him." Timmy came out and Nancy shut the door.

Timmy held the dog's face between his hands. "King, you're not supposed to run away." After slipping the collar over King's head, he stood with his hand under the collar. King sat quietly beside him.

"Let me show you something." Haleigh knelt in front of the dog. King took that as an invitation to kiss her cheek. She rubbed her cheek with the back of her hand. "If you tighten the collar one hole, no, two holes, it won't slip over his head." She helped Timmy adjust the collar. "See, you can still put your fingers through it, and it's not too tight. As King gets bigger, make the collar bigger, too, so he can breathe, and it won't cut into his neck."

"Okay, I can do that." He slipped his hand back under the collar "Did you know my dad's a soldier?"

Nancy nodded and sighed. "My husband, Sam, planned to leave the army, but decided to reenlist one more time. We found this house, which we could rent with the option to buy, so Sam helped Timmy and me move before he went back."

"Are you from around here?"

Nancy shook her head. "No. Sam has an Army buddy who knows the owner of our house, and when we came to look at the house, we liked the area."

"Living in a new place without your husband must be lonely for you."

"Yes, it is. I have to get a job because Sam's not here. I'm an LPN, and I applied at the nursing home today. Do you know anything about it?"

"Greenlawn Senior Home has a good reputation for both living and working. My grandmother lived there for several years after she had a stroke. A friend of mine is a nurse there."

"You're from Greenlawn?"

"I lived in Greenlawn until my junior year in high school. I've come back to house-sit for the summer. And my brother got married on Saturday, so I came back for that too."

Nancy looked down at her son, who sat on the step stroking and talking softly to his pet. "Time for bed, Tim."

"Aw, Mom."

"That's right, to bed. You may take King in with you, but he stays on the floor."

Haleigh knelt to look Timmy in the eye and tried to avoid King's slurpy tongue. "If you ever want help training your dog, I'd be glad to teach you."

"Really? What was your dog's name?"

"Her name was Sunshine."

"That's a nice name. My dog is King."

"Okay, Timmy, no more delays." His mother opened the door. "I'll be in in just a minute."

"Good night, Haleigh." He gave her a big smile and disappeared inside the house with his dog.

"Good night." Haleigh stood and brushed the dirt off the knees of her jeans.

Nancy watched her son for a moment, then turned back to Haleigh. "Timmy tries hard to be helpful since his father left.

Sam wanted him to have the dog, and King means the world to him." She stepped back inside. "Well, I have to make sure Timmy's in bed. I'd like to get together with you sometime, though."

"I'd like that too. I hope you'll get the job. Good night."

Haleigh hopped down the steps and headed back home. King's exuberant spirit and swishing tail had swept away her low spirits. Sunshine, her companion and friend, was no longer with her, but if she helped Timmy train his dog, maybe she wouldn't miss her so much.

She and Nancy both knew what it meant to be lonely. Maybe they could be friends.

11

"Whew!" Haleigh reached the top of the stairs and knocked on Katie's door on Thursday after work.

Katie opened the door with a big smile. "You're late!"

"I'm sorry," Haleigh said. "I had to go home before coming here, and it took me longer than I expected. I brought dessert." She lifted the lid on the cake saver she held.

"Oh, Haleigh, you remembered! I just can't resist a person who brings homemade chocolate cake with fudge frosting! Please, come in." They giggled together as Haleigh entered the apartment.

In the living room, beige walls and light brown furniture made the room warm and inviting. The curtains and throw pillows in bold orange, red, gold, and blue stripes added vibrancy.

"This is nice, Katie."

"Thank you. I had fun decorating. The apartment is small, but it's home. Would you like to see the rest of it?"

"Of course." Haleigh handed the cake to Katie and followed her into the kitchen. Bright sunflowers accented yellow walls. "This is cheerful. It's vibrant, like you."

Katie had decorated her bedroom with muted greens and coral.

"Restful, so I can sleep in it," she said. "Especially when I work nights and sleep days."

When they returned to the kitchen, Haleigh sniffed. "Whatever you're cooking, it smells wonderful!"

"I tried to remember what you liked, but I couldn't. So, I decided to make something I like and hope you do too. It's chicken and rice casserole with broccoli. We have fresh fruit salad, and your chocolate cake."

"Perfect!" Haleigh lifted a plate from the table. "I love your sunflower dishes! Where did you get them?"

"Mom and Dad found them for me at Dunn's Department Store at the mall."

"Dunn's Department Store. That stirs up memories."

Katie set the casserole and fruit salad on the table. They sat, and as Katie said the blessing, Haleigh silently thanked God for allowing her to reconnect with Katie. The years of lost friendship could never be recovered, but she had the present to start building it again.

Haleigh took a forkful of casserole. "This is delicious, Katie. I'll have to get your recipe." Her grandmother Hart had given her a cookbook last Christmas. Now that she lived alone, she should start collecting recipes.

"Thanks. I'll gladly share. It's easy to make, and it fits well with my work schedule."

"Do you like nursing?"

"I love it. The residents at the home are so sweet, and it's a good work environment."

"Gram liked living there. Mr. Evans came to Floral Creations the other day for his flowers."

"Speaking of flowers, what a beautiful wedding! I loved Aubrey's gown. And you and Willie did a great job with the flowers."

"Thank you. It was fun, and Willie is a good teacher."

"It's a perfect job for you."

"For now, anyway. I don't want to work there forever."

After putting away leftovers and washing and drying dishes, they sat in the living room with their dessert.

Katie sighed. "Life has turned out so different from what we expected, didn't it? I thought I'd become a world-famous actress, but here I am, still in Greenlawn."

"Don't you like Greenlawn? Before we moved away, I never imagined living anywhere else." Haleigh took a sip of tea.

"Greenlawn is a wonderful place to live. I love my work, both as a nurse and as drama director at church." Katie set her glass and plate on the coffee table. "But I sometimes wonder how things might be different if I'd made different choices. Only one time I let my guard down and let Nathan have his way. After I became pregnant, he dumped me really fast."

Haleigh's eyes burned. How much had her choices affected her family and friends as well as herself? She could have chosen to support Katie and Aubrey and remained friends with them.

"It was awful, Haleigh!" Katie's face crumpled as tears pooled in her eyes and spilled down her cheeks. She pulled a tissue from the box on the coffee table. "I was pregnant, and you moved away, and Aubrey was in that accident."

Haleigh pulled in a shaky breath, not sure what to say.

Katie's voice lowered. "I couldn't keep him, Haleigh. I couldn't keep my baby. My dad was furious about my pregnancy, and he and Mom were talking divorce. Nathan left town. I had to let him be adopted. He needed a mother and father to love him and care for him. I signed away all parental rights."

Setting down her plate, Haleigh put her arms around her friend.

"It's hard to talk about him, but I want to tell you." Katie's words were broken by sobs. "He's with a loving family. We had an adoption ceremony when I gave him to them. But it still hurts!"

"You don't have to say any more." Tears ran down Haleigh's

face as well. "I'm sorry I didn't try to help you. I didn't think it would matter. To be honest, I didn't know what to do. And I was pretty wrapped up in myself."

Katie went to her bedroom and came back with a photograph of a little boy, a toddler who looked like her, with red curls and big green eyes.

"He's beautiful, Katie," she whispered.

Pressing the photo to her chest, Katie nodded. "I'm not sure I should keep it, but it's the only remembrance I have of him. His parents sent me this picture through my lawyer several years ago. I hope that one day, when he's older, he'll want to meet me. Then I can explain why I couldn't keep him and tell him I love him. I hope he'll understand."

"I don't usually talk about that time in my life." Katie wiped her eyes and blew her nose. "Only the people closest to me remember, because I stayed with my grandmother until his birth. Thank you, Haleigh."

Haleigh frowned. "For what? I haven't done anything. Remember, I left when you and Aubrey were in trouble."

"You've come back, and you're here now, and I can talk to you."

Haleigh shook her head. "I should have been there for you and Aubrey. I could have written or called, even after we moved away." Her eyes stung with unshed tears. "How can I help anyone? I don't think I can ever make up for the mistakes I've made."

"Isn't it good that God forgives our past and our mistakes and lets us start over, gives us another chance?" Katie smiled and sniffled. "We're so blessed because God never gives up on us when we belong to Him. We can be confident 'that He who has begun a good work in you will complete it until the day of Jesus Christ.'"

"That's Philippians 1:6, isn't it?" Was God still at work in her to make something good of her life?

Katie took a forkful of cake and closed her eyes. "This cake is so good! Maybe you should open a bakery and make chocolate cake with fudge frosting your specialty. You'd have at least one customer."

What an outrageous suggestion. Haleigh laughed. "I assure you, my baking skills are basic. This cake is an exception."

Katie became serious. "Nathan is coming around again."

Alarm signals sounded in Haleigh's brain. She'd never trusted Nathan, and she'd warned Katie about him, but Katie hadn't listened.

She set down her plate. "Oh?"

"He's different. He's more mature and caring. And now he's a Christian as well."

"Are you going to marry him?"

"Probably not. Because of our history, I'm not sure I can trust him again. But he is different."

"Please be careful, Katie." Haleigh laid her hand on her friend's arm. "I didn't like or trust Nathan before, but a lot of that was because he stole my friend away. I really can't say anything about him now, because I don't know him anymore. But I don't want you to get hurt again."

"Will you pray for me, for us? I wanted to tell you before someone else said something, or you saw us together."

"I'm glad you did. I might have come to the wrong conclusion. I'll pray."

"Pastor Pete suggested I shouldn't carry bitterness in my heart toward Nathan. Forgiveness is an act of obedience for a Christian, and forgiving Nathan would allow me to move forward with my life. It wasn't all Nathan's fault. I made a few wrong choices. I knew what I was doing was wrong."

Haleigh arrived home that night after eleven o'clock. Getting up for work in the morning would be a struggle, but she and Katie had a lot of catching up to do.

She listened to Willie's voicemail message about what he

wanted her to do at Floral Creations on Friday. He and Jesse had a landscaping project in the morning, and they probably wouldn't finish until after closing time.

12

The middle of June came, and Haleigh had been in Greenlawn for six weeks.

Life had settled to a comfortable routine, but one big issue plagued her: what would she do next?

Three Labrador retriever puppies, one yellow, one chocolate, and one black, watched her from the calendar hanging from the wall by the kitchen dining nook as she readied for work. As grateful as she was for her renewed and new friendships in Greenlawn, she still longed for Sunshine's companionship.

One day she'd have another dog, but it was too soon and her life journey too uncertain right now.

"Haleigh, are you going to the game fellowship Friday night?" Katie asked during their standing Tuesday lunch at the café.

"I don't know." Haleigh shrugged. "Willie mentioned it, but since I'm not good at volleyball, I'm not sure I'll go."

Her friends had pulled her back into involvement at church, but she avoided active participation in sports.

"Go anyway. You don't have to play. You'll have fun and can cheer us on. I'm going to drop by before I go to work at eleven."

"You're working the late shift?"

"Uh-huh. Starting tomorrow. Not my favorite hours, but someone must do it."

Haleigh laughed at Katie's martyr tone.

"The pay's a little higher, too, so that's an added incentive."

"I don't know. Maybe. I'll see." Haleigh bit her lip. "You know, maybe I'll invite Nancy to come. She would probably enjoy a night out."

"And Nancy is ...?"

"My neighbor, the one with the little boy, Timmy. Her husband is overseas with the military right now. She doesn't go out much."

"Oh, I remember now." Katie's curls bounced when she nodded. "You told me about the dog's visit."

"Nancy just got hired as an LPN at the Senior Home. Haven't you met her yet?"

"Not yet. I think she's on day shift in another unit."

Haleigh held her sandwich. "Nancy works so hard and is a good mother. I told her I'd watch Timmy for her if she needed me on weekends. I'm not working on Saturdays right now, and I'd love to take Timmy to Sunday school on Sunday."

Katie tipped her head. "You know, there are several women in the church who are day care providers. Will she need a place for Timmy when school is out for the summer?"

"I hadn't thought about that. I'll ask her." Haleigh finished her sandwich and drank her iced tea.

"I guess you have to get back to work." Katie motioned to the waitress. "I'll be spoiled by the time you leave Greenlawn. Meeting for lunch is more fun than going to the mall when we were kids." At least as much fun.

They paid for their food and left the café.

She'd miss Katie—and others—when she left at the end of the summer.

"Are you busy Friday night?" Haleigh asked Tia in the shop that afternoon. "The young adults at church are having a game night, and I wondered if you would like to go."

"No, I'm busy Friday night. Maybe another time." Tia didn't make eye contact with her. What was she hiding?

"All right." Haleigh finished a funeral arrangement of daisies, carnations, and a red rose, with ferns. She didn't know the grieving family, but she said a prayer for their comfort, remembering her grief when Gram died. She looked at the name on the card and wondered if this was someone's grandmother.

After work she walked to the Morgans' bungalow. She rang the doorbell, surprised Timmy wasn't out in the yard playing with King. She heard a "woof" as Nancy opened the door.

Dark rings formed half-moons beneath Nancy's eyes. "Hi, Haleigh."

"Are you all right, Nancy? You look tired."

"I am. Please come in. Timmy has a cold, so he and King are watching the kids' special on TV."

Haleigh sat on the sofa in the living room. King greeted her, resting his muzzle on her knees, his tail making crazy circles. She scratched the top of his head and behind his ears.

"Hi, Haleigh." Timmy sat on the carpeted floor and turned toward her. "I have a cold."

"Your mom told me. I hope you feel better soon."

With a nod, Timmy turned his attention back to the television program. King sighed and flopped down beside him. Nancy sat in the platform rocker across from Haleigh.

Haleigh leaned forward. "If you're not busy Friday night, would you like to come with me to a game night at church?"

"What's a game night?"

"It's a young adults' event. "Usually there's a game of basketball or volleyball, snacks, lots of talking, and a short devotional."

"What about Timmy? I'd have to get a sitter."

"A lot of parents bring their children and share the childcare. Timmy would have fun too."

"I'm not big on church, but I need to get out. Let's see how

Timmy and I feel by then, but I'll say yes for now." Nancy said she was tired, not sick.

"It's not a church service, and very informal."

"Timmy and I are going to have some lemonade. Would you like a glass too?" Nancy stood up on a forward rock.

"I'd like that, thank you." The nature program on the television, about black bears, caught Haleigh's attention for a moment. Timmy hopped up from the floor and lifted a framed photograph from the end table.

"This is my dad." He proudly showed her the photo of a man dressed in military camouflage.

"Why, Timmy, you look just like him!" She glanced from the photo to the boy. "He must be a good soldier."

Timmy nodded. "He is. I'm going to be a soldier someday." The boy gazed at the picture. "I miss him a lot."

"I'm sure you do." Haleigh put her arm around him. "Even though I'm a grownup, and my father lives just a few hours away, I miss him sometimes."

He'd have his heart surgery soon, and she'd go to Wellsburg to be there for him.

Replacing the photo gently in its place, Timmy sat next to his dog on the floor.

Nancy returned with three glasses of pink lemonade on a tray.

"Thank you." Haleigh lifted a frosty glass from the tray.

"Yeah, thanks, Mom," Timmy said.

"You're welcome, both of you." Nancy sat again, and the three of them sipped lemonade.

"Timmy showed me the picture of his dad." Haleigh pointed to the photo. "They look a lot alike."

"Yes, he's quite proud of his dad. They're very close, and Timmy misses Sam so much. We try to video chat once a week when Sam can do it." Nancy sighed. "But it's still hard having him away, especially knowing where he is."

Haleigh tried to think of something encouraging to say, but

she didn't have a loved one on duty in a war zone. Instead, she asked, "How is it working at the nursing home? Do you like it?"

"Sometimes it's hard. The residents in my unit need extra help. Some of them have to be fed, and the mobile ones have to be watched carefully. I'm glad I have this job, especially because Sam is in the service. I love the residents I care for."

"I knew most of the residents of the Senior Home when Gram lived there. She knew everyone, and they all knew her." Haleigh finished her drink and set it on the tray. "I have to get going. Thanks for the lemonade. I can pick you up at six fifteen on Friday."

"Okay, Haleigh. I'll let you know if we won't be able to make it."

Timmy jumped up to give Haleigh a hug. King, too, demanded his share of attention, his tail wagging furiously. Haleigh held the young dog's head between her hands and looked into his eyes. "You smile, just like Sunshine did." She swallowed hard, and King kissed her cheek with his tongue.

THEY RODE TOGETHER in Willie's van on Friday night, Jesse in front with his brother. Haleigh sat in back with Nancy and Timmy. The little boy had never ridden in a large van before.

"It's almost as big as a school bus!" Haleigh and Nancy smiled at his enthusiasm.

"Almost." Willie peered at him in the rearview mirror. "I like having a van so I can take other people places."

"Like us," Timmy said.

"Yes, especially like you, Sport."

"My name is Timmy." The boy thrust out his chin.

Willie grimaced. "Sorry, Timmy. My dad used to call me Sport as sort of a nickname."

"Oh, it's okay then. Did you know my daddy's in the war?"

Jesse turned to look back at Timmy. "Haleigh told us. Did you know I'm going into the Air Force soon?"

"You mean you'll be flying airplanes?" Timmy bounced in his booster seat as much as the safety belt allowed.

"That's right. In fact, I have a pilot's license and can fly small airplanes now."

"Wow! Mom, can I go flying with Jesse? Can I, Mom? Please?"

"We'll see." Nancy placed her hand on his leg. "Jesse didn't invite you, but I'd have to think about it for a while if he did."

"Oh, okay." Timmy's shoulders sagged, but when Jesse grinned at him, he grinned back.

Willie turned the van into the church parking lot. "If it's all right with your mom, you can go with us to our next T-ball game. T-ball teaches kids your age how to play baseball. Jesse and I coach, but you can sit and watch with Haleigh."

"Can I, Mom?"

"I don't see why not. As long as you listen to Haleigh."

"I promise." Timmy made an X across his chest with his fingers.

"Okay. Haleigh will let you know when we'll pick you up." Willie caught her eye in the rearview mirror and Haleigh nodded.

Haleigh and Nancy sat in the bleachers as sides were chosen for volleyball. Willie and Jesse, as captains, chose their teams quickly. Willie picked Katie to be on his team, and what the spirited redhead lacked in skill, she made up in enthusiasm. Haleigh cheered for Willie's team, jumping up when they scored and yelling out encouragement.

Nancy chuckled. "You're quite a cheering section."

"I don't usually play. I'm almost a klutz when it comes to sports, but that doesn't mean I can't cheer."

Willie came over for a drink from his water bottle. "I always wanted Haleigh on my side because she was a good cheerleader." He winked at her and returned to the game.

Would Willie's wink and comment give Nancy the wrong impression? "You look tired again tonight, Nancy. Is everything all right?"

"Yes and no." Nancy's voice trembled. "I'm pregnant."

"How wonderful! Except Sam isn't here. I'm sorry. I didn't think."

"That's okay, really. I found out just after Sam left. It's a little hard without him."

"Does Timmy know?"

Nancy shook her head. "You're the first one I've told outside our families. I'd rather he didn't find out yet. I'm not quite ready for the secret to go public."

"I won't tell anyone until you're ready. But how can I help you?"

"Just be my friend for now. I may need extra help with Timmy, I'm not sure. I've been having some nausea, and I tire quickly. If I need your help, I'll let you know."

Haleigh nodded, wishing she could say something astounding that would make everything right for her friend. She didn't have much confidence in her ability to give good advice. Her stomach clenched. This was the right time to ask her new friend an important question.

"Nancy, are you a believer? Do you know Jesus Christ as your Savior?" Sharing her faith had never been easy for Haleigh.

"I don't go to church, if that's what you mean. I went to Sunday school as a child, and we did a lot of fun things. But Sam and I haven't been back to church since our wedding. We've been too busy." Haleigh couldn't tell if Nancy was interested or irritated.

"If you'd like to go, I'd be glad to pick you and Timmy up on Sunday morning." Haleigh wanted to do everything right this time.

Nancy shook her head. "Not right now. Maybe one day I will."

Although disappointed with Nancy's declaration, she

wouldn't press her now to change her mind. However, she wouldn't fail with Nancy as she had with Leanna.

On the way home that night, as Timmy told Willie and Jesse about his dad, and Haleigh chatted with Nancy, her serenity was shaken when a red Mustang convertible turned the corner ahead of them.

Willie offered to go with Haleigh when she returned to Wellsburg at the end of June for her father's surgery.

"You and Jesse have that big landscaping project lined up for this week. You can't take time off now." If she brought him home with her, her family might get the wrong idea about her relationship with Willie.

"It's a long drive, and you'll be thinking about your father. I want you to be safe."

"Remember, I drove here by myself in May. I'll be careful." He didn't have to know she asked Katie to go, but her friend had to work. "I'll be fine, but thank you for your offer."

He shrugged and went back to his office. Haleigh almost changed her mind. Willie meant well, and she'd enjoy his company on the trip. She knocked on the doorway to his office. He looked up from his desk.

"Will you pray with me for my dad?"

His face lit up with a smile. "Of course, I will, Halo."

Pushing up from his chair, he held out his hands. For a moment she hesitated, then laid hers in his. He prayed, asking

God to give skill to the surgical team, strength and healing to her father, and comfort and strength to the family.

Only after she released his hands did she realize how tightly she'd grasped them. Their warmth remained for several minutes.

DAD LAY in the hospital bed, pale and ill, like Gram after her stroke. The monitoring machines attached to him emitted regular beeps.

Stifling a sob, Haleigh stepped back from the doorway and leaned against the wall in the hallway, her body trembling. Her stomach somersaulted. She couldn't go in there like this. Taking a deep breath and whispering a prayer for self-control, she pushed away from the wall and entered the room.

"Hi, Dad."

He opened pain-filled eyes and smiled weakly.

She curled her fingers around his hand. "I love you, Dad." Her lips wobbled when she smiled.

"I love you too," he whispered before his eyes closed.

Five minutes later she returned to the lounge, where her family waited, and lowered her shaking body into a chair next to her mother. She pressed her hand against her mouth, and Mom's arms came around her as she sobbed.

"It's okay, Haleigh. Have your cry. I did. We all did. But just remember that your father is in God's hands."

Haleigh pulled back from her mother and nodded. Someone handed her a box of tissues. "Thank you."

For the next couple of days, Mom went to the hospital each morning and stayed until visiting hours were over. Haleigh and her brothers took turns staying with Mom during the day so she would never be alone.

Haleigh's relationship with her mother had an added dimension. Still mother and daughter, they were two women, two friends, sharing a difficult time.

On the third day after the surgery, the J brothers and their wives stayed at the hospital to be with Dad, and Haleigh brought Mom home at noon for company and to make sure she rested.

She took a dish of beef stew from the refrigerator, heated it in a pan on the stove, and set the kitchen table for two.

With tired lines etching her face, Mom sat at the table as Haleigh stirred the stew. "I'm glad you came home for this, Haleigh. You and your brothers. Your dad appreciates having you here, and so do I."

"How could we not come, Mom? We love you and Dad, and we're in this together. You've been so strong, like a rock, holding all of us up."

"So often I asked God why it had to be my husband, why it had to be us." She shook her head. "It's been hard seeing your dad go through the pain and experience the uncertainty. I've tried to be strong for his sake, tried not to be anxious. Many, many people have been praying, and your dad has shown such faith. God is truly our strength."

Haleigh set the stew on the table between them and sat across from her mother. She thanked God for the food and prayed for her dad, then let her mother serve herself first. They ate in silence. Haleigh appreciated the quiet of her parents' home after the bustle and lack of privacy in the hospital.

"I think I needed to get away from the hospital for a while." Mom sipped her tea. "Your dad has a long road to recovery ahead of him. I don't want to wear myself out at the beginning. Thank you for bringing me home."

"Mom, do you ever expect God to tell you why?" Haleigh set down her fork. "There's so much suffering in the world, why doesn't God stop it? Dad's been faithful to God just like Gram was, and they both experienced a lot of suffering. I don't understand."

Mom held out her hands across the table. Haleigh laid both her hands in her mother's, and their eyes met.

"God never promised life would be perfect. We live in a

world of suffering because of sin. Just because we're Christians and serve God doesn't make us exempt from pain or suffering. In the book of James in the Bible, the author reminds us that trials produce patience and mature our faith. Think about the missionaries and Christian workers you've known whose difficulties made them trust God more."

Haleigh nodded as her heart soaked in her mother's words.

"Try to trust God. Believe He wants the best for you—for all His children. Your father has a long, uphill, physical battle to fight, but God has provided him with a strong spirit and good doctors. God takes care of him and us, no matter what."

The telephone rang, and they both stood. Haleigh hugged her mother. "Thank you, Mom." The phone continued to ring. "I'll get it. You go get some rest."

"Thank you, dear." As Mom gave her a hug, she whispered, "I'm thankful God gave you to me as my daughter."

"Me too." Now more than ever.

Haleigh answered several phone calls during the next two hours, some of them inquiries about her father, a couple of them telemarketers, and a wrong number. She packed sandwiches and snacks to take with them to the hospital. After she washed and put away dishes, cleaned the kitchen counters, and vacuumed the living room carpet, she drove her mother back to the hospital.

THE NEXT MORNING, when Haleigh came downstairs, she heard Aubrey and Carmella talking in the kitchen. They stopped when she walked in.

She looked at one then the other. "Good morning."

Neither of them looked directly at her as they returned her greeting. What or who had they been talking about?

The knit top Carmella wore revealed her expanding

midsection. She pulled out a chair and sat at the table. Aubrey leaned against the counter.

Haleigh peered out the window over the sink. The back yard basked in the sunshine. "I think it's going to be a nice day. What time are you guys leaving?"

"We'll go to the hospital first, then leave from there." Carmella leaned her elbows on the table. "Jason and I both have to get back for work, now that we know your dad is recovering."

"We'll be leaving then too." Aubrey rested one arm on the counter. "Jeremy has a staff meeting at church, and I have an interview for a teaching position for next year. Your dad is improving, so Jeremy feels comfortable about going home."

"Did Jason and Jeremy go out for their run?" Both had been members of the track team in high school and college. When at home together, they used running time to stay in shape and talk in private.

Aubrey nodded. "Yes, they wanted to get in one last run. Your mom hasn't come down yet. I hope she's getting some extra sleep."

"I think she's able to rest easier now that Dad's recovering." The doctor's assurance that he would get better eased some of Haleigh's worry about his weakness.

Carmella yawned. "When do you have to go back to Greenlawn?"

"Willie said to take as much time as I need."

"I don't think I've told you how much I appreciated your work on our wedding flowers. Everything was beautiful." Aubrey gave her a quick hug. "Willie said he couldn't have had a better assistant."

"Willie's a good teacher and loves his work. I'm not sure I want to do it forever, but I enjoy working at Floral Creations for now."

"Are you going to stay in Greenlawn?" Carmella asked.

"Well..." Greenlawn had welcomed her back. She had friends,

she had a house, and she had a job. She wanted to stay but couldn't commit yet. "At least for the summer. The Sousas said I can use their house until next May, when they return from their sabbatical."

Aubrey smirked. "I know there's a certain person who wants you to stay."

The corners of Carmella's lips turned up.

She'd been set up! Haleigh opened the refrigerator door to cool her face. "How about some French toast for breakfast?" She'd been right not to let Willie come.

"Baby Abbott says, 'Yum'!" Carmella patted her stomach.

"I'll make the coffee." Aubrey pulled the coffeemaker from the back of the counter.

RIGHT AFTER SEEING Dad and learning he would be released to go home the next day, Haleigh's brothers and their wives left from the hospital.

Haleigh helped Mom bring Dad home and get him settled, then she went shopping, picked up medications from the pharmacy, and ran errands. She made sure her mother had the names and phone numbers of church members who had volunteered to help if needed.

The day after his release, Haleigh packed her suitcase and drove back to Greenlawn.

14

*A*n almost perfect evening.

Haleigh's sides hurt. She hadn't laughed this much in a long time, and it was wonderful to be together again.

Jeremy and Aubrey had returned to Greenlawn to pick up some of Aubrey's things from her parents' house. They'd be returning to their apartment tomorrow afternoon.

Along with Katie, Willie, and Jesse, the newlyweds had joined Haleigh at the cabin for a Friday evening cookout, Haleigh's first opportunity to host a party.

She refused to let the knowledge that it would end soon dampen her spirits.

The sun went down, and the light faded. They sat in the darkness together on the front porch with only the starlight and a dim glow from a streetlight on the corner. Lights shone from the windows of the neighbors' houses. She could turn her porch light on, but that would attract bugs.

Calmness and security surrounded Haleigh like a blanket. "The sky is so beautiful tonight. We can see the Milky Way."

She and Willie sat side-by-side on the top step, close enough that their shoulders touched. For some reason, she didn't feel the need to pull away.

"Isn't God good?" Willie's breath tickled her ear and sent a chill down her neck. "He gave us beautiful things." Haleigh felt Willie's gaze but refused to turn her head.

She leaned back. "Jeremy, Katie and I were wondering if we could borrow Aubrey for a little while tomorrow morning, before you leave."

"I don't know. This could be dangerous, and I'm not sure I could survive having her away from me." Jeremy drew Aubrey close as they sat along the porch railing.

"We just want her for a couple of hours, that's all." Katie looked up from the bottom step where she sat beside Jesse. "We want to go to the mall."

"Can we come too?" Jesse asked.

"No!" Haleigh and her friends responded together.

"Oh, no," Willie moaned. "The Three Sisters are back."

"Well, okay, but you'd better not be long," Jeremy said. "This is only a temporary loan. You'll owe me, Haleigh."

Reaching behind Willie, Haleigh tapped Jeremy's leg.

"Aubrey, Haleigh hit me."

"I didn't hurt you, Bro. I want you to be able to carry your bride across the threshold tomorrow."

"You mean, like this?" Jeremy jumped off the railing and lifted Aubrey into his arms.

"Put me down, you goof! We've already done that, you know." Aubrey laughed so hard she nearly fell when Jeremy put her down.

Willie hopped off the step, startling Haleigh, and jogged to the shrubbery in the side yard. He returned with his hands cupped. "Here, hold out your hands."

Everyone else was watching as she obeyed. His hands hovered above hers, and she felt a flutter between her palms. He quickly pressed her hands together and held them.

"Look, Haleigh." His voice was soft and intimate, his hands warm.

She peeked between her thumbs. A light blinked. "A firefly!"

He dropped his hands and stepped back with a smile. She watched the firefly blink several times, then she opened her hands and released it.

The yard filled with tiny, blinking lights. Awed voices whispered, "Wow!"

"Remember when we used to catch lightning bugs when we were kids? We'd see who could catch the most." Jesse lunged for one in the grass but missed it.

Katie stood. "Do you have any jars, Haleigh? Let's see who can catch the most."

"I think I saw some canning jars in the basement. I'll check. Just a minute."

Willie called to her as she opened the outside basement door. "Need help?"

"No, thanks. I can handle it." The light switch was just inside the door. She found the box of jars right where she remembered seeing it, and it wasn't heavy.

For the next half hour, six young adults chased fireflies. She hoped the neighbors didn't mind the noise.

"I don't remember it being so hard." Jesse panted.

"I think it's in the way you flick your wrist." Jeremy suggested and Aubrey laughed.

"Right," Katie said.

"I got it!" Haleigh and Willie yelled together, reaching for the same firefly. They came up empty-handed and bumped heads.

Haleigh rubbed the spot but forgot about the pain when she discovered Willie's face just inches from her own. She straightened and stepped back, glad the darkness hid her blush.

"Who won?" someone asked.

They all counted.

"I won. I got twelve," Katie announced. "I guess I haven't lost my touch."

Releasing the bugs from the jars, they watched the light show for a few minutes more.

Jeremy stretched and yawned. "I think it's time to call it a night. Some of us have to work tomorrow, and some of us will have miles to travel before reaching home."

"Just put the jars in the box. I'll wash them in the morning." Haleigh wished the party could last longer.

When Katie said good night, Haleigh joined her as she walked to her car.

"This was so much fun, Haleigh!"

"I know, but we'll probably never do it again."

"Maybe not this group, but there will be other times and other friends."

"I know." Change wasn't always bad.

"See you in the morning."

Haleigh watched her car until it turned the corner.

Standing by the porch, Willie and Jesse finished a conversation with their sister and hugged her.

"Walk us to the van, Haleigh." Jesse held out his hand.

"All right."

Instead of taking her hand, Jesse put his arm around Haleigh's waist. Willie cleared his throat and placed his arm across Haleigh's shoulders from the other side. They had sometimes walked this way as kids, but now, squished between the two men, she sensed tension between the brothers as she walked the brief distance with them.

The fireflies continued their light show, the air heavy with the scent of honeysuckle, as Haleigh returned to the cabin. Jeremy and Aubrey had already gone inside. She paused at the door, reliving the intimacy of the lightning bug moment with Willie.

"THIS IS AMAZING! I didn't think we'd ever do this again." Haleigh savored a bite of her cinnamon roll.

The Three Sisters had been shopping and laughing at the mall for the last hour and a half. Though it would soon be time to leave, they sat in a booth at the food court, snacking and drinking tea.

"I feel so bad because of all the years of your friendship I missed." Haleigh wiped her hands on her napkin. "It was my fault. I was too immature to see past myself."

"We all made mistakes. And have been forgiven." Katie tapped the tabletop with her index finger. "Without Jesus, I'm not sure where I'd be today."

"I made a poor choice by getting into Derek's car that night. After the accident, I wished I'd died instead of Leanna." Aubrey stirred her tea. "I realized then how much I missed both of you and the bond we had."

Haleigh reached out a hand to each of her friends. "You guys are so good to me. Thank you for accepting me back. We've changed, and our lives will never be the same. We won't be together in Greenlawn, but we can still be friends."

"What we've shared in the past can keep us together, no matter where we live." Aubrey squeezed her hand. "After Jeremy finishes seminary, we don't know where we'll be living. Let's not lose touch again. We all have computers and cell phones."

"Maybe we can plan on having a reunion of the Three Sisters from time to time," Katie suggested.

"Friends forever?" Haleigh put up both hands.

How good to share her friends' high-five again!

WILLIE SAT ALONE with his father in the back yard of the Whites' house a few nights later.

"Dad, I don't know what to do. I love her, but she has put up some sort of a barrier. Or maybe it's God stopping me."

Dad leaned forward, resting his arms on his legs. "When Haleigh returned to Greenlawn, your mother and I saw how much she means to you. You'd been waiting for her."

Willie nodded.

"It's obvious to most people how you feel about her, except maybe Haleigh herself."

"I sometimes think she knows, but she denies it to herself. I don't want to push her away by speaking out too soon, but I don't know how much longer I can wait. We're friends, but I want to be more. Every time I try to talk about our relationship, she talks about shooting stars or the neighbors. I'm afraid if I lose her this time, I'll never have another chance with her." And what would he do if she left Greenlawn, left him, again?

"Willie, your mother and I both love Haleigh, and we'd be thrilled if you married her. And Glenn assured me that he and Elizabeth feel the same. But this is between you and Haleigh. Be patient, show her how you feel, and we'll pray that one day soon she'll be ready and willing to accept your love and return it, if that's God's will for you."

"Will you pray with me now, Dad?"

15

The brim of Haleigh's straw hat bounced as she walked down Main Street. Her backpack contained her lunch, water, sunscreen, and a small first aid kit, the things she thought she'd need for the hike to the fire tower.

A red Mustang convertible passed her and turned at the corner of Main and Elm. What business did Stuart Webber have in Greenlawn?

She shrugged. She'd looked forward to this hike for several weeks now, and Stuart wouldn't ruin it for her.

Soon after Haleigh arrived at the church parking lot, Jesse came jogging up. Nineteen young adults gathered around Pastor Pete and Amy. Katie couldn't come because she had to work.

"Willie will come later, after he closes the shop. He said he'd pick up any stragglers," Jesse told Pastor Pete. "Nice hat," he whispered to Haleigh.

Accustomed to his teasing, she wrinkled her nose at him. "It keeps the sun off my face."

Amy checked her list. "I think everyone else is here who said they were coming."

"Okay." Pastor Pete clapped his hands. "Let's get loaded up."

Haleigh and Jesse got into a van belonging to Courtney and

127

Doug, a young couple who recently moved to Greenlawn. Haleigh had met them at the young adult game night. Anita and Caitlin, two young women Haleigh had seen at church but didn't know, sat in the back seat.

"Tia called in sick this morning," Jesse said in a low voice to Haleigh.

"That's unusual." Haleigh frowned. "So, why didn't Willie call me?"

"He didn't want to ruin your day off, and Mom was willing to work."

"Is Will your brother?" Courtney looked over her shoulder at Jesse. "I'm trying to figure out relationships."

"Will is one of my brothers. My oldest brother, Mike, is married and doesn't live in Greenlawn."

"Are you Jesse's sister, Haleigh?"

"No." Haleigh shook her head. "Jesse's sister, Aubrey, and I are friends. Aubrey is married to my brother, Jeremy."

"Oh, that wedding took place the first weekend we were here. I always see you with Jesse and Will, so I thought you were related."

"No, just friends. Our families have been close for many years, and I work for Will at Floral Creations on Main Street."

"I'll remember that when I want to get my wife flowers," Doug said. Courtney gave him a sweet smile.

"Do you have a girlfriend, Jesse?" Anita pushed a few hairs back from her face as Caitlin gave her a pouty look. The two must have been discussing Jesse.

"Ah, no." Jesse raised his eyebrows at Haleigh, and she gave him a weak smile.

"Didn't I hear you're going into the Air Force?" Doug peered at them through the rear-view mirror.

"That's right, in the fall. I'm looking forward to going." He liked to tease and flirt with girls, but the Air Force was his focus now.

Anita shrugged. "Oh, I didn't know."

"Have you and Caitlin lived in Greenlawn very long, Anita?" Courtney asked.

"I've lived on a farm outside Greenlawn all my life." Caitlin answered first. "I took a secretarial course in college, and I'm looking for a job."

"I'm working for my aunt at her bed-and-breakfast for the summer." Anita fluttered her eyelashes at Jesse. "I'll be in my second year at the community college."

"What's your major?" he asked.

"I'm not sure yet. I'm taking general studies that will prepare me to transfer to a four-year school."

"How about you, Haleigh?" Anita eyes traveled from Haleigh's face to her hat and back. "Are you going to college?"

"I graduated in May."

"You're a college graduate? You look about sixteen." It wasn't what Anita said but the sneer in her voice that made Haleigh blink.

She bit back a defensive reply and faced forward, choosing to believe Anita didn't intend to offend.

Other people said that to her, mostly in fun. And she didn't mind. Not really. She hoped when she reached thirty, she'd still look younger than her age.

Jesse frowned, indicating he recognized the put-down, but she gave her head a small shake to keep him from saying anything. An uncomfortable silence followed. Haleigh looked out the window as they drove into the parking area.

"I think we picked a great day for a hike." Jesse broke the silence. "I haven't been to the fire tower for a couple of years. I hope you guys brought plenty of insect repellant."

Following Jesse, Haleigh jumped out of the van with her backpack. The men and women formed pairs or small groups as they started up the trail, grateful for the shade offered by trees along the way.

Haleigh stopped to shift her backpack to a more comfortable position. She watched as Anita, Caitlin, and a girl named Lori vied for Jesse's attention. He laughed and joked with them, but Haleigh could see that he didn't favor any one of them. Sooner or later, they'd get the hint and either leave him alone or enjoy his friendship. In the meantime, she'd step into Aubrey's big sister role and keep her eye on him.

Although she didn't participate in sports, she loved hiking. She'd looked forward to this outing ever since Amy had mentioned it to her.

What a perfect, summer day—the sun, a soft breeze, and low humidity. Watching for rocks or roots in the path, she picked her way after Jesse up the trail, pacing herself so she wouldn't tire.

"I haven't taken the opportunity to welcome you back to Greenlawn, Haleigh." A young man walked up beside her.

Her eyes widened as she recognized him from Jeremy's wedding.

"I guess you don't remember me. I'm Chad Young. I graduated with Mike White, but I played soccer and was on the track team with your brothers."

Haleigh nodded. "I remember you. You came to Jeremy's wedding." Now she remembered seeing him at soccer games and track meets, but she'd never met him or talked with him.

"That's right. I hear you're working for Will White."

Haleigh laughed. "In a small town, word gets around." She shifted her backpack again.

"May I carry your pack for you?"

"Thanks for the offer, but I'll carry it. I'm a little out of practice, but I'll be okay." She wasn't a helpless female, after all.

"So, where have you been for the past six years?" He'd started this conversation at the wedding reception.

"I graduated from college in May."

"That's what Jeremy said. I'm sorry you lost your dog. What kind did you have?"

"A black lab mix." He'd been talking to her brother about her?

"My mother raises beagles."

Interested, Haleigh opened her mouth to ask Chad about the beagles.

"Haleigh Abbott, I heard you moved back to Greenlawn" A female voice interrupted. "Where have you been keeping yourself?"

Haleigh turned her head toward the young woman who'd spoken to her, an attractive blue-eyed blonde with perfect figure, perfect make-up, and her hair pulled back into a perfect knot at the back of her head. The man beside her was also blond and well over six feet tall.

Hurrying ahead, Chad caught up with Jesse.

"Oh, you're Cheryl. Cheryl Nelson." Haleigh detected a resemblance to Leanna in Cheryl's face. Haleigh hardly knew Leanna's younger sister, so she was surprised at Cheryl's friendliness.

"Yes. Have you met my fiancé, Lars Olsen?"

He engulfed her hand in his huge one.

She had to look up, way up, to meet his smile. "It's nice to meet you, Lars."

"You work at the flower shop on Main Street, right?" He put his arm around Cheryl. "Do you make the flower arrangements?"

"Most of them right now. I know why you seemed familiar, Lars. I remember the arrangement you ordered." And the big man who ordered them.

"You mean she made that gorgeous arrangement you gave me for my birthday? I didn't know you could arrange flowers, Haleigh."

Haleigh didn't know why Cheryl would know. "My grandmother taught me a lot about flowers, and Will hired me to work in his shop. I work with Tia Merino."

"I'm surprised Tia didn't mention that, though I don't see her very often right now. We both seem to have other interests. I just started an interior decorating business. And there's Lars." Cheryl smiled at her young man and took his arm.

Her co-worker probably wouldn't have anything nice to say about her anyway.

"For a while Tia could only talk of Will White this and Will White that. Of course, Will is one of Greenlawn's most eligible young bachelors. But a couple of times she has talked about a mysterious rich guy with a red Mustang convertible, Stuart Walton, or Webber, or something."

"Stuart Webber. I've seen his Mustang around town a few times." Now Haleigh knew why. She whispered a prayer that Tia knew what she was doing.

Cheryl liked talking about her work, and Haleigh decided she liked her, even though she was chatty. As they hiked along, Lars picked a wild snapdragon and handed it to Cheryl. How sweet.

Long ago, Leanna Nelson had come on a youth group hike with Aubrey. Haleigh resented Leanna's presence. If that wasn't enough to make her miserable, Katie had brought Nathan. Katie adored him. He was a drama club star, often paired with Katie. Haleigh didn't trust his charm and good looks. He did his best to embarrass her in front of her friends, and Katie didn't try to stop him.

Popular because of her athletic skill, Leanna attracted followers like a magnet. Aubrey and Leanna became best buddies, but Haleigh didn't fit into Leanna's circle.

Goofing off for her audience, which included Haleigh's brothers, Leanna had slipped on some loose gravel during their hike. She'd slid off the path and down a shallow embankment. Haleigh thought Leanna deserved to fall, since she was always trying to be the center of attention. She didn't want anything really bad to happen to Leanna, just prayed she'd go away. When Leanna did go away, guilt weighted Haleigh down.

"I'm sorry," she whispered.

"Sorry about what?" Cheryl asked.

"Oh!" She'd forgotten Cheryl and Lars walked beside her. "I'm sorry about Leanna." She bit her lip. What if Cheryl didn't want to be reminded of her sister's death?

"Thanks. My family has adjusted pretty well, but we all still miss her." Cheryl's voice caught.

Lars placed his arm around her.

Tears shone in Cheryl's eyes. "She was so smart, and a basketball star."

"I don't think we ever stop missing those we love." Haleigh spoke in a quiet voice. "Saying goodbye is hard."

Cheryl shook her head. "I didn't really get to say goodbye. She went to the game and never came home. I started going to church occasionally after she died. But I never could understand why God let her die. Nobody has ever been able to explain it to me." Cheryl's tone conveyed bitterness

Haleigh wished she could explain.

"It seems unfair that everybody isn't able to leave a mark on the world, make his or her own contribution, so to speak, before dying." Cheryl seemed to be talking to herself. "Leanna didn't have time, she died so young. Derek made sure of that. And I didn't get to say goodbye."

Haleigh touched her arm. "I was angry at God when my grandmother died. Gram was wonderful, and she left me a legacy that I hope to live up to one day, but I still miss her a lot. I didn't know Leanna very well, just that she was a good basketball player. I'm sorry." She kicked a small stone in front of her. "She was your big sister. You must have many good memories of her."

Cheryl stopped walking. "I do. Leanna was a fun person and a good big sister. She taught me to go for what I wanted. That was her legacy. Thanks for reminding me."

Would Cheryl be thanking her if she knew the truth about her relationship with Leanna? Cheryl had told Tia that her sister didn't like Haleigh. Had she forgotten, or had Tia made it up?

Maybe God was giving her a chance to correct her mistakes through Cheryl.

As Haleigh began walking again, she noticed Jesse enjoying attention from Anita, Caitlin, and Lori. A couple of times she caught his eye and raised her eyebrows, but he just winked at her and continued flirting with the girls. She shook her head. Jesse enjoyed having an audience.

When they arrived at the summit, they divided into groups of four to climb the stairs to the top of the tower. Cheryl, Lars, and Chad joined her. The breathtaking view from the fire tower and the refreshing breeze on the mountain top made her tired leg muscles worthwhile, even though they'd be sore tomorrow.

She leaned against the metal rail and inhaled.

Beside her, Chad grasped the rail. "What a view! The rangers can spot smoke or fire for miles in any direction."

"It gives me the sensation of being on top of the world, but I don't think I'd enjoy staying in the ranger's cabin alone." She moved over and pointed to the small cabin standing between the tower and the woods.

"When I was a kid, I wanted to be a forest ranger."

"Really? What do you do? I mean, where do you work?"

"I'm a security guard. I work for an agency that hires out security for businesses."

Haleigh nodded and moved to where she could see the head of the trail. Was Willie on his way up yet? Trees and rocks hid most of the trail.

Cheryl and Lars appeared to be involved in a deep discussion with each other. That was probably why Chad followed her around. She didn't mind. He was nice enough, and her brothers' friend.

"The church youth group used to hike up here every summer. I made the trek every year when I lived in Greenlawn." She looked over the railing. "They're signaling us to come down so the next group can come up."

When Haleigh returned to the ground, she sat under the spreading limbs of a huge oak tree, where she could watch the trail. She pulled off her backpack. Cheryl and Lars chose a spot within talking distance. Jesse waved to her as he tossed a frisbee with Anita, Doug, and Courteney. Other hikers, like Haleigh, found comfortable places to sit and wait for lunchtime.

She expected Chad to ask to sit with her, but he walked over to sit with Caitlin and Lori.

Her stomach growled as she watched groups of four climb up and down the steps and find places in the shade of the trees. The last group descended the stairs.

Would Willie close Floral Creations in time to join them today? She hoped so.

"Hi, everybody, I'm here!" Willie called out from the top of the trail. He breathed heavily, as though he'd hurried, and beneath his baseball cap, his face was flushed.

Several called back their welcome. He stopped to speak to Pastor Pete and Amy. Jesse handed him a brown bag from his backpack.

He scanned the area and smiled when his eyes met Haleigh's. A thrill passed through her. Had he been looking for her? She waved. He must have taken that as an invitation because he headed toward her and lowered himself to the ground beside her. She would have been disappointed if he hadn't.

"A busy morning at the shop. I wasn't sure I'd make it in time. Tia called in sick. It's the first time she's done that."

"She told me she couldn't come on the hike because she had something else planned for this afternoon."

"She sounded awful on the phone. Mom came in and ran the cash register."

As he caught his breath, he reached over and squeezed her hand where it rested on her knee. He held it while Pastor Pete gave thanks, the warmth of his grasp flowing up her arm. After the amen, he let go.

Reaching for her backpack, she glanced around to see if anyone noticed he'd held her hand. Everyone, even Cheryl and Lars, laughed and chattered as they prepared to eat.

Willie joined in, and the music of his voice and laughter reached her heart.

Haleigh removed her lunch bag from her backpack and unwrapped her sandwich. Her arm tingled when Willie's shoulder brushed hers. A whiff of his aftershave invaded her sense of smell.

"What's in your sandwich?" His breath close to her ear sent a chill down her neck.

After she finished chewing and swallowing, she turned to face him. He grinned and took a bite of his sandwich. His green cap shaded his eyes, giving him an air of mystery. The outdoors had tanned his muscular arms to a golden shade. She'd never been so aware of him. What had changed?

He'd asked her a question.

"Oh, uh, turkey and cheese."

"Mine's ham and cheese." He leaned toward her. "Is everything okay? You're quiet today."

She couldn't tell him he distracted her. "I'm fine. I have chocolate chip cookies, and I'll share."

"You made them?"

"Yes, I did."

He pulled a sandwich bag of brownies out of his lunch bag. "I'll trade you a chocolate chip cookie for one of my mom's brownies."

"Ooh! One of your mom's brownies is worth two of my cookies."

"I won't refuse."

Haleigh had just returned her empty lunch bag to her backpack when Pastor Pete stood and took a deep breath.

"I love coming up here," he said. "I'm glad all of you came today." He paused and made eye contact with some of them.

"God is so good. Look at all this beauty." He turned slowly in a circle.

Haleigh picked out the village of Greenlawn, the state park, and the lake. She couldn't find the log home, hidden by the trees, but she found the church spire.

"When I see this, I can't help but praise God. Did you know He's the creator of all this? He takes care of the whole universe, and yet He cares about each of us as individuals.

"He knows what you are struggling with—illness, a bad relationship, the death of a loved one, work problems. He knows. And He cares. Listen to this verse: First Peter chapter five, verse seven, '… casting all your care upon Him, for He cares for you.' He wants to help you with your problems. He wants you to trust Him. He loves you so much."

Haleigh took a deep breath. Trust. Dad had suggested she didn't trust God enough. For a long time, she'd held on to anger at God for taking Gram away. And she'd blamed God for the broken friendship with Aubrey and Katie, until she accepted her own responsibility.

"God showed us His love when He gave us His Son, Jesus Christ, to take the punishment for our sins. You and I are sinners. Romans three verse ten says, 'There is none righteous, no, not one.' We've all disobeyed God, whether by a little white lie, or by robbing a bank, or by showing self-righteous pride, or something else. Jesus, who never sinned, shed His blood to pay for our sins, so that you and I may be forgiven and have life forever with God."

How many, like Cheryl and Lars, searched for answers? Who among them might need a word of encouragement or prayer as they struggled with everyday challenges? Maybe Anita, Caitlin, or Lori needed a friend.

God, if I have the opportunity, let me speak to one of them today. Don't let me make the same mistake I made with Leanna.

"So, the God who made all this," Pastor Pete gestured with his hand, "cares about you, and how you live your life, and where you'll spend eternity. Will you listen as He speaks to you now? Will you accept His invitation to become one of His?" He prayed and encouraged anyone in the group who had a need or questions to speak to him.

Willie stood first and brushed off his jeans. He held out his hand, and when she took it, he pulled her up. She reached for her backpack, but he tugged on her hand. She looked up. Her eyes met his, and the world stopped.

"I'll get that." When he broke eye contact to pick up the backpack, it left her a little dizzy. "I'll carry this for you."

She shook her head. "No, it's light. I can carry it." She held out her hand, but he helped settle it on her back.

He didn't offer to take her hand again. She couldn't decide if she wanted him to.

As they started down the trail, Willie walked beside Haleigh. "I had hoped Derek would come with us, but he didn't show up, and he didn't answer his phone."

"Oh." The hike would have been spoiled if Derek had come.

"I know most people aren't comfortable with Derek and don't want him around. But he needs to know that people care, and that God cares."

Could Willie read her thoughts? She nodded, humbled by his attitude. "You're right."

"Hey, Willie!" Jesse beckoned to him, and Willie jogged ahead to speak with his brother.

Cheryl and Lars caught up with her. "I'm glad we came today," Cheryl said. She looked at Willie, then at her. "Are you and Will together?"

"What do you mean?" Haleigh shifted her backpack.

"I mean, are you living together? Are you getting married?"

Haleigh blushed and took a deep breath, which she let out slowly. "No, we're just friends. And we're not married, so we don't live together. He still lives with his parents."

"Lars and I do—I mean, live together. We plan to get

married soon, but in the meantime, we're giving ourselves time to find out if we're compatible."

"And we are." Lars smiled down at his companion.

"I-I don't believe in living together before marriage. I don't believe it's what God intends for us." Haleigh bit her lip and held her breath. She hoped she didn't come across as self-righteous.

Cheryl's face registered surprise. "But everyone does it today."

"I know a lot of people who don't. I believe in making a public and legal commitment before living with anyone as my husband. I-I don't mean to offend you."

"No, it's okay. No offense taken. I asked. It is a kind of old-fashioned way of looking at things. Lars and I are very happy together."

Uncertain how to respond, Haleigh nodded. They looked happy. "Well, I'm glad you and Lars came today. Do you attend church?"

Lars answered this time. "We go sometimes. We're very busy, and Sunday is usually the only time we have the whole day to spend together."

Ahead of her, Anita, Caitlin, and Lori flirted with Willie and Jesse. Chad joined their group. The young men laughed at something one of the girls said. Why did Haleigh find that so upsetting?

She remembered the couple beside her. "You're welcome to come to Greenlawn Bible Church any time." She answered Cheryl's smile with one of her own. "Maybe you could come tomorrow."

"We'll see.' Cheryl looked at Lars. "Thank you for the invitation."

Willie had stopped and waited for them to catch up to him. Cheryl and Lars greeted him, then walked ahead to talk to Courtney and Doug.

"You seemed to be in a deep discussion with Cheryl and

Lars." Willie matched his stride with her shorter one, obviously expecting a reply.

She pushed a lock of hair behind her ear. "We were discussing ... living together before marriage." She didn't mention Cheryl's inquiry about her relationship with Willie.

Willie nodded. "Lars and Cheryl do."

"I know. They told me they were very happy. And I told them I don't believe God wants a couple to live together before they made a public and legal commitment."

"And how did they react to that?"

"Cheryl said it didn't offend them, but I'm not sure my words had any impact."

"Probably more than you think. You only spoke the truth, and they're a couple who are searching for the truth. You and I need to pray that they'll find it."

You and I. Willie made her feel important and whole. Significant. With his great spiritual insight, he'd make a good pastor or missionary one day.

It didn't matter how he made his living. He cared so much about other people and went out of his way to help where and when he could. That was the reason for the missions trip he planned to take in October. He would always help others. Now he included her. *You and I.*

"What are you thinking about?" He peered under the brim of her hat.

His grin made her heart flip-flop in time with her hat brim. It broadened when heat rushed into her face. She shook her head. Let him think as he wished.

When they arrived back at the parking lot, Pastor Pete gathered them and made sure everyone had a ride home.

"I'll take Haleigh and Jesse with me." Willie opened the door for Haleigh to get in the front seat, while Jesse hopped in the back.

Three pairs of disappointed female eyes watched as Willie's van slid by.

17

When Haleigh arrived at work before Tia on Monday morning, Willie waved his greeting from his office and turned his attention back to the computer screen.

Willie and his family hadn't been in church yesterday. They'd left early to attend worship with his aunt's family and go to a birthday party.

Although disappointed, Hailey had more time to figure out what had changed in their relationship on Saturday. Today he acted as though nothing had happened. Maybe it was her imagination.

She started toward the office to say good morning to him when Tia rushed in, out of breath.

"Sorry I'm late."

Tia had parted her hair low on the left side, so it flopped over the right side of her face. Haleigh tried not to stare at her co-worker's thickly applied eye shadow and the dark blush on her cheeks. She glanced toward Willie, but he was glued to his computer. Should she or shouldn't she speak to Tia?

Unable to hold back any longer, she stepped toward her co-worker. "Tia, are you all right?"

Tia busied herself opening the cash register and counting the money in it. "I'm fine."

Were those bruises on her wrists?

"Are you sure? You ..."

"I'm okay!"

Haleigh read through her work orders for the day. She had to make several arrangements, and Willie wanted her to work in the greenhouse. Tia sniffed and wiped the side of her face, smearing mascara.

Haleigh paused in choosing blooms for the first arrangement. "Tia, are you...?"

"Just leave me alone, will you?"

Haleigh's mouth dropped open. Tia ran to the rest room and slammed the door. Willie looked up.

"Is there a problem, Haleigh?" He walked up to the front counter.

"Tia said she's all right, but I know there's something wrong." What should her next step be—try to help Tia or leave her alone?

"Maybe she's still sick. Tell her she can go home if she needs to."

A customer came into the shop, looking for a potted plant. The telephone rang. Haleigh waited on the customer while Willie took the call in his office. After a few minutes, a more composed Tia returned to run the cash register. She'd repaired the smeared mascara, but she wouldn't make eye contact with Haleigh.

The red Mustang. Tia had admired Stuart the day he came into the shop. Cheryl Nelson said Tia talked about him. Did Tia go out with Stuart? He tried to be controlling, but would he stoop to physical abuse? Stuart was bigger than Tia. Did he ...?

Haleigh shook her head, but the thought wouldn't go away. She had to try again to talk with Tia. She'd try a different approach. "We had a good time on our hike on Saturday. I'm sorry you were sick. Willie said if you're still feeling sick, you may go home."

Tia shook her head.

Looking around to be sure no customers were in the shop, Haleigh decided to be direct. "I saw Stuart's Mustang around town this weekend." Her co-worker wouldn't look at her or respond. She reached out and laid her hand on Tia's arm. "Tia, did you have a date with Stuart? Did he hurt you?"

Tia yanked her arm away and glared at her. "What's it to you? It's really none of your business."

"I suppose you're right. It's just that I introduced you to Stuart. And if he hurt you, as your friend ..."

"Who said you're my friend?"

Haleigh's head jerked back, Tia's words like a slap in the face. She persisted. "Okay, but I'd like to help you."

"I think I do feel ill. I'm going home. Tell Will for me, will you?" Tia grabbed her purse from under the counter and fled out the door.

What should she do? Haleigh had to talk to Willie.

"What's the matter, Haleigh? Did Tia decide to go home?" He continued to type at his computer when she entered the office.

"She told me she felt ill and went home, but ..." She choked up on the words and trembled.

Willie looked up. "Are you okay? Are you not feeling well?" He got up and came around his desk.

"I'm fine, but I'm not sure about Tia. Willie, I ..." She couldn't stop shaking.

He guided her to sit in the chair placed for customers, then sat on the corner of his desk and waited.

Finally, the words came out. "Willie, I don't think Tia is sick. I think she's hurt."

"You mean, you think she had an accident?" He frowned.

"No." She shook her head and bit her lip. "I mean someone hit her."

Willie stood. "Why do you think that?"

"You didn't get a good look at her when she came in. She's wearing her hair over her face to hide a bruise on her cheek, near her eye. Both her wrists had bruises. And she's so upset." Tears filled her eyes.

"Who do you think would do such a thing to her?" Willie laid his hand on her shoulder, and she barely kept control.

"I'm not sure I should name anyone since I don't really know." She hesitated. "I don't want to start rumors." She also knew that Willie's sense of chivalry might step in and cause him to confront the person.

"But you do have someone in mind?"

Haleigh nodded, then looked up at him. "She wouldn't let me help her, Willie. She won't let me be her friend."

"All you can do is keep trying and keep praying. You can't force someone to listen to you."

"This time I tried."

Willie raised his eyebrows. "This time?"

"Last time I didn't ..." Haleigh shook her head. "Never mind." She would handle this on her own. "I've got a lot of work to do, and Tia's too." She stood and headed toward the front counter.

If she'd been kinder and tried harder with Leanna, Leanna might be alive today. She'd written an apology to Leanna, as Amy had suggested. The nightmare about the accident hadn't returned since her reconciliation with Aubrey and Katie, yet she still wrestled with the thought that she was somehow at least partially responsible for Leanna's death.

Giving up wasn't an option. She had to keep trying with Tia.

"O-KAY." Willie shook his head.

He watched her from the office doorway as she began

putting together an arrangement. "If you get overwhelmed, let me know, and I'll see if Mom can come in for a few hours."

"All right."

At his computer, though needing to finish the landscaping plans, he swiveled around to watch Haleigh, absorbed in her work.

With a sigh, he leaned his chin on his hand. He'd followed his instincts as well as his heart in hiring her, and she'd proven to be an invaluable employee. She obviously enjoyed arranging flowers and caring for the plants in the greenhouse. Uncertain at first about her own ability to work for him, she had no problems waiting on customers and making floral arrangements.

And he loved having her nearby.

Her working relationship with Tia was cordial, although he knew it frustrated her because Tia wouldn't accept her friendship. What happened the 'last time'?

He shook his head as he turned back to the computer screen. He couldn't force Haleigh to talk. If she only understood his frustration over her not trusting him enough to take him into her confidence. Something still bothered her, something from the past, something that stood in the way of the deeper relationship he wanted with her.

Didn't she know there was nothing that would keep him from loving her?

18

The hot summer sun struck Haleigh's head and shoulders as she walked to the Morgans' bungalow on her Saturday off. Willie had a meeting, so Tia and Jesse ran the shop until noon. Haleigh would look after Timmy while his mother worked the eleven-to-seven shift at the Senior Home.

She'd already taught Timmy some simple commands for King, and the boy handled his dog well. However, the rambunctious young dog needed more discipline. Otherwise, he'd become too hard for the boy to handle, or he'd get into some other trouble. Today was the day Haleigh chose to begin more serious training.

After she and Timmy shared a lunch of peanut butter and jelly sandwiches, apples, and cookies, they rested with King under the red maple in the Morgans' yard. Haleigh had brought out bottles of water for Timmy and herself, a big bowl of water for King, and an abundant supply of sunscreen. King lay stretched out on his side in the cool grass beside his master.

Timmy gently stroked King's soft fur. "He's learning to sit and lie down when I tell him. I only have to tell him once now."

"That's good, Timmy. You must be working hard and spending a lot of time teaching him." She knew her 'well done' encouraged him to work harder. "We'll work on getting him to come to you right away when you call him."

Timmy shook his head. "He's not too good at doing that."

"King has to know you're his boss and be willing to obey you right away." Haleigh smiled. "You have to keep trying. It's very important, and it will keep him out of trouble as he gets older."

"I know. Did your dog, did Sunshine, obey you?"

An edge of sorrow hit her. She swallowed and licked her lips. "We had to work on it, but Sunshine got so she was pretty good at it. She had to be because I took her into places with sick people."

"King will do good." Timmy stroked his dog. "Maybe King and I can help people too." King wagged his tail.

Haleigh stood and stretched. "Let's try walking him on his leash first."

"He doesn't like that much." Timmy got up and snapped the leash to his dog's collar. "He likes to go where he wants."

King got up and yawned and stretched.

"I know what you mean." Haleigh patted King's head. "Once Sunshine learned to not pull me around, we had fun taking walks together."

Timmy showed Haleigh how quickly King obeyed the commands to sit and lie down. After about ten minutes of walking and stopping and sitting, King began to understand what was expected.

"Look, Haleigh, he's not pulling! He's just walking along with me." Timmy patted his dog's head. "Good dog." King licked his hand. "Can we see if he'll come now?"

A black and white cat came out of the woods. It stopped when it saw the threesome, one paw in the air, then bounded toward Main Street. Curious and ready to play, King lunged against his leash and pulled it from Timmy's grasp.

"King, come back!" The boy took off after his dog.

"Come, King!" Haleigh started running. "Timmy, wait for me!"

King paused just long enough to glance back at them, then chased the cat again, his leash flipping around wildly. The cat reached Main Street and arrived safely on the other side. King dashed after the cat. He didn't know he had to stop for the minivan coming toward him.

Timmy ran at top speed to catch his dog. "King!"

"No!" Haleigh screamed as Timmy followed his dog into the street, in front of an oncoming car.

Screeching brakes! Two thuds, and more screeching brakes!

Haleigh froze. It couldn't be real. The boy and his dog both lay in the street. Timmy lay ominously silent, and King's cries tore at her heart.

"No, God! Please, no," she whispered and charged toward them.

"Oh, Timmy, why didn't you listen to me?" Kneeling beside the boy, she laid her hand on his chest and heaved a sigh. He was breathing. He had a gash on his forehead and a badly scraped arm. His right leg lay twisted at an abnormal angle. He moaned, although he remained unconscious. She gently stroked the hair back from his forehead. "I'm so sorry. I'm so sorry. I'm so sorry."

She heard shouts as people ran toward them. "Call 911," she screamed.

A middle-aged man in a business suit ran up to them. "I-I couldn't stop! He came too fast. I wasn't speeding or anything." He pulled out his cell phone and called for help.

"I know." She had to restrain herself from gathering Timmy in her arms. "Somebody needs to call his mother. Nancy Morgan. She works at the Senior Home." She should do it, but she was too shaken. Her shell-shocked brain struggled to control the fear and sorrow along with the scream eddying in her throat. She must be strong for Timmy and King.

A few feet away, a young woman leaned over King.

"How is he?" Haleigh asked.

"He's hurt, but he's still alive. I'm so sorry. He ran out in front of me. I couldn't stop." Tears ran down the woman's face.

Haleigh acknowledged the woman's words with a nod. It had to be a dream. This was worse than her nightmare. What if Timmy died? Would Nancy ever forgive her?

Failure, failure, failure, echoed through her mind.

Screaming sirens approached. Curious spectators gathered.

Haleigh trembled as she pulled out her phone. Willie had gone to a meeting in preparation for his upcoming missions trip. She called the first number she thought of, the Whites'. With sirens and shouting in the background, she tried to talk to Mrs. White.

"What's wrong, Haleigh? Where are you? What's all the noise?"

"T-Timmy's been h-hit by a car! K-King ran away, and Timmy ran after him. I-I couldn't stop them!" Haleigh managed to tell her where they were.

"I'll be right there."

The sirens died away as the paramedics arrived with the ambulance. Police cars blocked Main Street at either end of the accident scene.

The ambulance driver and one paramedic pulled out equipment as the second paramedic knelt beside Timmy. Haleigh tried to explain what happened. They worked for several minutes before she remembered King.

The dog lay in the road, whimpering and trembling. The young woman had removed a blanket from her car and laid it over King. Haleigh thanked her and knelt beside him.

Haleigh spoke softly to King as she ran her shaking hand across his body, searching for injuries. When she reached his right back hip, he growled a warning. "Okay, boy," she said, "this must be where you're hurt."

A paramedic approached her. "Are you the boy's mother?"

Haleigh stood up. "No, I'm his babysitter. Can you tell me how he is?"

"He's stable at the moment, but he has to be transported to the hospital."

"His mother works at the Senior Home. Her name is Nancy Morgan. I think somebody called her. His name is Timmy."

The paramedic asked a few more questions about Timmy and the accident, then took a moment to examine King.

"Haleigh," Mrs. White called.

Relieved to see a familiar face, Haleigh ran into her arms.

"The police will want to talk to you as an eyewitness." The paramedic eyed Haleigh. "Are you all right?"

Haleigh nodded, and the paramedic walked back to the ambulance.

"Do you think they'll let me see Timmy?"

"We can try." Mrs. White took her hand and walked her over to where Timmy lay, pale and quiet, under a blanket and strapped to a gurney. The paramedics had placed him on a backboard with a cervical collar. An IV was attached to his arm, and an oxygen mask covered his nose and mouth.

A police officer approached her as Timmy was being loaded into the ambulance. "I understand the boy was in your care when the accident happened. I'll need a statement from you."

Haleigh's stomach clenched, and she stammered as she relived the events of the accident and gave the officer the information he requested about Timmy.

The ambulance pulled away, it's siren warning everyone to clear the way.

"I don't know what to do." Haleigh wrung her hands. "I can't let Timmy go to the hospital alone, but King needs help too."

"I can transport the dog to the animal hospital in the squad car, if someone will come and give the vet the necessary information." The police officer closed his notebook. "I have a dog and kids myself at home."

"Oh, thank you. I know Timmy would like that. He loves his dog."

Mrs. White put her arm around Haleigh's shoulders. "I'll take you to the hospital so you can be with Timmy, then I'll take care of King. Write down the information about King on the way, so I can give it to the vet."

"I'm so glad you're here. I can't think straight. I-I hope I didn't take you away from anything important."

"Nothing I can't do later."

Haleigh and Mrs. White helped the policeman place King on the blanket and lay him on the back seat of the squad car. He whimpered.

"It's okay, boy. You'll be okay." Haleigh said the words for herself as much as for King.

Still trembling, Hailey was overwhelmed by grief and guilt as they followed the ambulance to the hospital. "How will Nancy ever forgive me? She has so much going on, she really doesn't need this."

"You can be there for her at the hospital. With her husband away, she'll need a friend nearby." Mrs. White pulled into the emergency room parking lot.

The ambulance stood outside the hospital's emergency entrance. They'd already taken Timmy in.

"If she wants to be my friend," Haleigh said. She blew her nose on a tissue from a box in the car. She pulled out several more.

"Haleigh, accidents happen. I don't believe you were negligent. You love Timmy too much. Puppies and boys are impulsive. Take it from one who knows." Mrs. White shook her head.

Haleigh got out of the car. "Thank you." Willie's mother had been through accidents and boys, and she tried to believe her assurances. Her stomach roiled. Oh, no, she couldn't be sick!

Why did this happen, God? Are you punishing me?" Timmy had to live!

Alone, Haleigh waited in the emergency room waiting area. Timmy was somewhere behind the closed door, and she couldn't get information about him because of the healthcare privacy laws. They told her he was stable, whatever that meant.

Even though Nancy would need support when she came in, Haleigh doubted Timmy's mother would accept help from her. She was supposed to take care of Timmy, keeping him out of harm's way.

Nancy rushed in through the sliding glass doors, dressed in her work smock. Haleigh immediately got up to give her a hug.

She grasped Haleigh's shoulders. "How's Timmy? What happened?"

Shaking her head, Haleigh gulped, unable to speak.

Nancy went to the window and identified herself, then took her health insurance card from her purse. She signed some forms and the receptionist directed her to sit in the waiting area.

Haleigh approached her. "Nancy, I'm so sorry. King got away from Timmy, and Timmy ran after him. They both ran into Main Street. I couldn't stop them."

"You were supposed to be watching them, Haleigh. I trusted you. How could you let this happen?" Nancy's angry words sliced through Haleigh's heart like a knife. "So much for your God who lets little boys get hit by cars!" Nancy spit out the words and turned away.

A nurse opened the door. "Mrs. Morgan, you may see your son now. The doctor needs to speak with you."

Ignoring Haleigh, Nancy went with the nurse. The door clicked behind them.

How could Haleigh make things right with Nancy? Would she even be allowed to see Timmy? She sat down in a chair to wait. She leaned forward and covered her face with her hands.

More people came into the emergency room. One man moaned as he held his middle, a little girl whimpered on her mother's shoulder. A security guard came through the door of the exam area. Haleigh went to the check-in window, but the receptionist refused to tell her anything. Nancy wouldn't give permission for Haleigh to see Timmy.

What good would it do to stay at the hospital any longer?

She'd walk the two-and-a-half miles back to the log home. She patted her pocket. At least she had her house key.

Sorrow, like a stone, weighted her chest as she walked out the door and across the parking lot. Lifting her legs became a chore and time meaningless as she trudged along the road. When someone honked, Haleigh paid no attention.

"Haleigh, do you need a ride?" A familiar voice called out. Willie, back from his meeting.

She turned toward the van, relieved he was there but not sure she could talk to him. She'd rather go home, lock herself in, and curl up in bed.

Willie pulled over and waited. She crossed the road and climbed in.

<h1 style="text-align:center">19</h1>

With one look at her blotched face and trembling lips, Willie turned the van off.

"What's wrong, Haleigh?"

She burst into tears.

Releasing his seatbelt, he turned sideways. He leaned toward her and drew her head against his chest. He held her and stroked her hair as she cried deep, heart-wrenching sobs. How could he help her if he didn't know what was wrong? When her sobs had quieted somewhat, he held out a box of tissues.

'Th-thanks, Willie, y-you're a g-good friend." She drew back and pulled out a tissue. "I'm sorry. I got your shirt wet." She wiped her eyes, blew her nose, and took a deep, shaky breath.

"My shirt is fine. I'm concerned about you." He waited a minute, fingers tapping the steering wheel. When she said nothing more, he asked, "Do you want to talk about it?"

"I-it's all my fault!" She started crying again.

He handed her another tissue. "What's all your fault?" He wished she wouldn't blame herself for everything.

"That Timmy and King got hurt, and now Nancy's mad at me!" She bit her lip as more tears trickled from her eyes.

"Are you on your way home?" He buckled his seatbelt.

When Haleigh nodded, Willie started the van and pulled out into the street. Haleigh fumbled with her seatbelt and finally managed to secure it.

He would have to ask for more information. "How did Timmy and King get hurt, and why is it your fault?"

Haleigh took a deep breath. "Timmy was teaching King to … Oh, King is at the animal hospital with your mom. I need to go there."

"My mom is at the animal hospital with King?" Why was Mom with King?

"Y-yes." She took a deep breath. "A cat came out of the woods, and King got away from Timmy and ran after the cat. Then Timmy ran after King. They both ran into the street, and I couldn't stop them. And they got hit. I called your mother." Haleigh leaned back. "I-I'm glad you're here. I'm having a hard time thinking."

"Is Timmy in the hospital?"

She nodded. "Your mother drove me there so I could be with Timmy, and she went to the animal hospital so I wouldn't worry about King."

"Okay. We'll go there and see how King is doing." He would do whatever he could to help her, even if it meant crossing the ocean or traveling to the North Pole.

She loved that boy and his dog. Training King was healing her from losing Sunshine. He prayed both Timmy and King would survive.

WILLIE OPENED the door to the animal hospital and let Haleigh enter before him. Mom met them inside.

"I was just on the way to the hospital to check on Timmy and to pick you up, Haleigh. Did Nancy get there? How is Timmy?"

"I don't know." Haleigh shrugged and shook her head. "They

wouldn't let me see Timmy, and Nancy is so mad at me she won't speak to me. They took Timmy somewhere, and Nancy went with him, but I don't know what the doctor told her." Haleigh swallowed hard. "She blames me."

She put her arm across Haleigh's shoulders. "I'll go see what I can find out. Willie, take Haleigh home. I'll let you know what I learn. And I'll give Nancy Dr. Payne's card so she can contact him about King's care."

"What about King?" Haleigh asked. "I want to see him. Will he be all right?"

"His back right leg is broken, but the vet can't do anything without Nancy's approval, since she's responsible for him and will pay for his care."

"Willie, I need to see King before I go home. Please. He must be so afraid and lonely. And Timmy's not here."

Even if her eyes hadn't pleaded with him, he'd wait with her. "Of course. We'll wait for you to see King and talk to Dr. Payne."

"I'll go see how Timmy is." Mom gave Haleigh a hug.

"Thank you." Haleigh grasped her hand. "And thank you for helping with King."

Mom gave Willie a look full of meaning. He nodded. She expected him to take care of Haleigh, which he had every intention of doing. He had nothing more important to do right now.

His mother left, and Haleigh told the receptionist her reason for being there.

"Just a minute, I'll get Dr. Payne." She went through a door down the hall from the reception desk.

Willie pointed to the chairs. "Let's sit down while we wait."

She chose a seat and stared down the hallway. He sat beside her. She'd probably forgotten he was even there. He sat back and stretched out his legs. Being with her now mattered, and he would do whatever he could to help her.

"It was awful, Willie. I couldn't stop them. I don't understand why God allowed this to happen."

She hadn't forgotten him after all, but she watched the hallway as she spoke.

"God has His reasons, Halo, but I don't always understand them either." He'd asked why, after Aubrey's accident and Leanna's death. He'd been in a tailspin for a while.

The door down the hall opened. The receptionist came out, and a woman with a pet carrier. A cat peered out as the woman stopped at the reception desk.

Dr. Payne, the veterinarian, walked toward them. The Whites brought their cat to him for a checkup and shots every year, so Willie knew him. They shook hands and Willie introduced Haleigh.

"King has a break and multiple fractures along his right femur, Haleigh, and his pelvis is bruised. He needs surgery soon for it to be the most effective. I can't proceed until I get the owner's permission."

Haleigh ran her tongue over her lower lip. "Will King heal all right if he has the surgery? Timmy, the little boy who owns him, will need him because he got hit by a car, too, and is in the hospital."

"I think King has a good chance of a full recovery. He's young and healthy. And with the encouragement of his family, the dog should recover well."

"If I say I'll be responsible to pay for his treatment, can you do it right away? Nancy, Timmy's mother, has a lot on her mind right now, and her husband is in the military overseas."

Willie laid his hand on her arm. "Are you sure you can afford this, Haleigh?"

"Yes, I think I have enough in savings."

"Tell you what," the vet said. "Since the father is in the military, I'll be willing to reduce the charge. I know military families often suffer economic hardship, and I feel this is something I can do to help a soldier on active duty. Annette took my card to give to Mrs. Morgan, so as soon as I hear from her, I can proceed."

"I don't have my checkbook with me now. It's at home. I'll be back in a little while and pay you."

"Do you want to see King now? I think he'd like a visit from someone he knows."

"Yes. Definitely. Thank you."

THE SCENE of the accident had been cleaned up, except for some dark spots, maybe blood stains, on the pavement. Traffic moved normally.

When he pulled into the parking space beside Haleigh's car, Willie turned off the van. Leaning his left arm against the steering wheel, he waited for her to look up at him. The pain and sadness in her eyes broke his heart. When her family left Greenlawn six years ago, she'd been like this.

"Are you sure this is the right thing to do? Maybe Nancy won't like it that you made this decision for her."

"Do you expect me to let King die?"

"No, Haleigh, but I know you don't have a lot of money, and you're very upset right now. I want you to be sure you're doing the right thing."

"It's what I have to do." Haleigh took a deep breath and blew it out. "If it weren't for me, Timmy and King wouldn't be hurt. I have to help somehow."

"Why don't we pray together." Willie held out his hand

Grasping his hand like a lifeline, she bowed her head.

He prayed for Timmy, King, and Nancy. "And please give Haleigh peace about her decision, Father. She feels responsible. Help her to accept Your forgiveness and peace. In Jesus' name, amen." He squeezed her hand and let go.

"Thanks, Willie, for everything. You're a good friend."

He started to get out.

Haleigh opened the door and jumped to the ground. "I'll drive myself back to the animal hospital. You haven't even been home yet. Oh, I forgot to ask you how your meeting went."

He'd forgotten about the meeting. "Good. The meeting was good, and I'm excited about going. I wish you could go too. I'll tell you more another time." Haleigh had too much on her mind right now to hear any details, although he wanted to tell her.

With a nod, Haleigh pushed the door closed. Willie started the van and backed out. He preferred to stay with Haleigh since she was so upset. But she needed some space and time alone to sort things out. He would keep his eye on her, though. As her good friend.

SHE SHOWERED, changed, made herself a sandwich, and checked her mail. Before she left home, she walked to the bungalow and gathered the blanket, water bottles, King's water dish, and the remnants of their lunch, which ants had discovered. She set the house key Nancy gave her on the kitchen table.

By the time she arrived back at the animal hospital, King was out of surgery, his leg in a cast.

"Hi, boy." She stroked the dog as he lay on his side in a crate. The wag at the tip of his usually active tail encouraged Haleigh. "I'm so sorry you got hurt. Will you forgive me?" King's ear twitched. "I'll take you home with me, at least until Timmy gets out of the hospital, unless Nancy doesn't want me to. Okay?" A sigh and another tail wag.

Haleigh went to the hospital next, stopping at the reception desk for Timmy's room number. He was alone when she walked in, and her chest tightened as she looked at the little boy with a bandage on his head and a cast on his leg. He appeared to be sleeping.

"Timmy, are you awake?"

Timmy's eyes fluttered open, and he gave her a weak smile. "Hi, Haleigh." His eyes closed again.

"Haleigh, what are you doing here?" Haleigh cringed at Nancy's angry tone.

She stepped back from the bed. "I-I came to see how Timmy is, and to let you know King is being cared for. The vet said he should be okay because he's young and healthy. His leg should heal well. I figured Timmy would like to know."

"His leg? Oh, that's right. The vet told me when I called him."

"He has a broken leg and a bruised pelvis from being hit by the van. I'll take him home with me on Monday if you want."

"How can I afford this?" Nancy shook her head. "Timmy loves that dog, so I can't have him put down. But veterinary care is so expensive."

"I'll take care of it for you, Nancy. Don't worry. Dr. Payne is reducing the fee because Sam is in the military. So, don't worry." *Please let me help.*

"I really can't worry about King right now. My son is my main concern. Do what you want."

At least Nancy would allow her to help. Haleigh blew out a sigh.

Opening his eyes again, Timmy shifted restlessly. "Haleigh, how is King? Is he okay?"

Haleigh smiled. "King looks like you, with a cast on his leg. He wagged his tail. I think he'll be fine. Especially when he sees you at home."

"Good." The little boy's eyes fluttered closed. "I'm tired."

Nancy didn't speak to her again. Haleigh stood back when a nurses' aide came in to take Timmy's vital signs, followed by a nurse a couple of minutes later. That was her cue. She left the room.

She leaned against the wall around the corner from Timmy's room. The tightness in her chest made it hard to breathe. She pulled in air and released it. Wiping her eyes with her fingers, she headed for the elevator and home.

20

"**I**'m late!"

Haleigh hurried into church just as the congregation stood to sing. She slipped into the pew between Willie and Jesse.

Jesse leaned toward her. "You're late."

She had no response for his teasing. It took too much effort this morning to do anything but the essentials. After the events of yesterday and staying awake for half the night, she almost didn't come to church. She would have accepted an offer of a ride this morning.

Focusing her attention on the music and words of praise to God reduced her fatigue. If she could only stay awake for the rest of the service.

After the singing, Haleigh leaned back in the pew and waited as Pastor Pete came to the pulpit.

Willie squeezed her hand. "Are you all right, Halo?"

His whisper in her ear sent a chill down her spine. The tenderness in his eyes spoke caring and something more.

"Just tired."

He nodded and released her hand.

The pastor included the Morgans and King in his prayer this

morning. Haleigh had thought of little else since the accident, and now her mind bubbled with everything she had to do to prepare for King's release from the vet's tomorrow morning. She wrote reminders in the margins of her sermon notes, and once Willie nudged her, awaking her from a doze.

When the service ended, Willie leaned toward her. "Mom wants you to come over for dinner."

She breathed in his scent. Everything about him was familiar and comforting.

"I can't. I have too much to do."

"Yes, I saw your to do list. You can do it all after we eat." He grasped her hand. "You could hardly stay awake during the service. You're tired, and you had a hard day yesterday. If you don't eat with us, you'll probably skip eating altogether. Mom always prepares plenty. Please come."

"All right." She hadn't planned a time to eat.

"Do you need a ride?"

"No, I have my car." She turned to leave.

"Just remember." The touch of his fingers on her arm pulled her attention back to him. "If you don't show, I'll find you."

She nodded.

EARLY MONDAY MORNING, Willie drove Haleigh to the animal hospital to get King. Willie arranged the seats in his van so Haleigh could sit beside King to keep him calm during the trip. Jesse came along to help carry the dog to the van then into the cabin, using a blanket as a stretcher. The cone fastened around King's neck, to prevent him from chewing at the bandage, made handling him more difficult.

"Thank you for helping me lay the carpet piece on the floor last night." Haleigh led the way to the laundry room. "Chad's mother was kind to send it over."

"Chad said she keeps things like this to use with her beagles in an emergency." Jesse backed into the room carrying one side of the blanket. "Sometimes they need something softer and less slippery to rest on after an injury or surgery."

As they laid him gently on the floor, King whimpered.

"Sorry, fella." Willie scratched him behind his ear.

Haleigh taped Dr. Payne's home care instructions to the door. It wouldn't be easy. However, King hadn't reached his adult weight yet, so Haleigh thought she could handle him.

"I think this room is best. It gives King enough space, it will be easier to clean up messes, and it's close to the back door when he has to go out."

The guys stood, and Jesse stepped out of the room as Haleigh knelt on the floor beside King.

"Mom will send dinner over for you tonight, Haleigh. She knows you won't have much time to cook, and she wants to be sure you have a good meal."

"Just like a mother." She didn't usually skip meals, but she might opt for something quick and comforting rather than healthy. Haleigh looked up at Willie. "I'm so grateful for all your mom's help."

She opened her mouth to call him her good friend, but something in his gaze prevented her from saying it.

Her stomach growled and her face heated.

"Have you had anything to eat yet?" Willie crouched beside her.

"No. I forgot." She stroked King, avoiding Willie's eyes.

"Haleigh, please promise you'll take care of yourself. It won't benefit anyone if you get sick."

"I will." She glanced up, and her heart beat double time at his tender expression. He was so close she could lean against him, as she had yesterday when he held her as she cried. Or caress his cheek.

He touched hers and stood, then reached down to help her up.

"Jesse and I have to go now. We'll check on you and King

throughout the day. If you need anything, please call. Pastor Pete said he could come if you needed him, and there are a couple other men from the church who said they'd be available to help."

In the living room, Haleigh faced her friends. "Thank you so much, both of you. I couldn't have done it without you."

"Glad to help." Jesse grinned. "Call if you need me."

"I will." She gave him a hug. He went out the door whistling, and Haleigh turned to Willie.

He placed his hands on her shoulders. "I think you need some rest, Halo. Knowing you, you probably didn't sleep much last night from worrying. Eat first, then take a nap. If you need more help with King, be sure to ask. That's what friends are for." He kissed her forehead and left, closing the door behind him.

She stared at the door. He didn't wait for his hug.

Was Willie only a friend? Something more than friendship brought him to her side whenever she needed help.

King. She'd better check him. When she entered, the dog looked up at her and whined. His tail thumped. She sat beside him, stroking his side. He sighed and laid his head down.

"Are you okay, King? I'm sorry you got hurt. I'll try to take good care of you."

He whined and thumped his tail again.

"You miss Timmy, don't you? I do too. He'll probably be home in a day or two." That was only a guess, because she hadn't heard from Nancy. "Then you can go home too." She kissed his head.

Laying a thrift store blanket over him, she stood and read over the home care instructions. Pain meds weren't due for a couple of hours yet. His closed eyes and soft snores showed he'd fallen asleep.

Aching with exhaustion, she inhaled and exhaled slowly. Had it been less than twenty-four hours, and not a lifetime, since the accident?

She'd promised Willie she'd eat, so she fixed herself a cup of green tea to go with a bowl of cereal, a slice of toast, and a banana.

After eating, she checked on King again. He still slept. Time for her nap.

Whispering thanks for friends to help her through this traumatic time, she lay on the sofa, covering herself with the crocheted throw she kept there. If King needed her, she wanted to be close so she could hear him. Her eyes closed and she drifted to sleep.

AFTER GOBBLING UP HIS FOOD, King looked up at Haleigh with hopeful eyes.

"No, King, you've had enough." Haleigh patted his head and moved his dish. "You don't want to get fat." She didn't tell him she'd mixed his pain medication with his food. Not that he'd understand anyway. She had to talk to somebody, and King was the only one present.

"You're such a good boy." She held his face between her hands. He licked her nose, and she laughed as she wiped it with the back of her hand. "Someone will be here soon to help you go out."

Maybe Willie would come and bring the promised meal from his mother. She hadn't seen him since this morning.

"Haleigh, are you here?" Willie.

King woofed and Haleigh jumped up. "Just a minute."

Excitement bubbled inside her. She handed the dog a chewy bone to keep him busy and hurried into the living room, smoothing her hair and straightening her shirt along the way.

Willie peered around the door, and his grin set a whole swarm of butterflies frolicking in her stomach,

"Come in." She opened the door wider and stepped back.

He entered carrying a large basket, followed by Jesse.

"I knocked, but you didn't answer, so I was concerned. Are you all right?"

"I'm fine. I was in with King. He ate, and he's waiting to go out." She closed the door.

"I'll go see my buddy." Jesse slipped around them.

"Mom sent you a feast, Halo. A casserole, salad, homemade bread, and dessert. She thought you wouldn't take time to fix yourself good meals, so she made enough for leftovers."

"Your mom is wonderful. Please thank her for me." A second hand 'thank you' wouldn't be enough. She'd have to do it in person soon. "Set the basket on the kitchen table, please. I'd like King to go out before we eat."

"Anything for you, Halo."

"Thanks, Willie."

The words "You're a good friend" stalled in her brain at the look he gave her as he set the basket down.

"I hope you don't mind that Jesse and I invited ourselves to eat with you. I thought you might like to take a walk with me later. Jesse can stay with King."

"I don't mind. And a walk will be wonderful." The food, the company, and the walk were all welcomed after most of her day alone with a dog, even a sweet dog like King.

After taking him out and then showering him with plenty of attention, they left him chewing his bone.

"Where are your dishes, Haleigh? I'll set the table." Jesse opened the cupboard door Haleigh pointed to.

Willie lifted the food from the basket as Jesse set the table and Haleigh made a pitcher of iced tea. The food aromas made her mouth water.

After giving thanks for the meal, Willie filled Haleigh's plate. While she ate, she listened to the brothers talk about their latest landscaping project.

"That was delicious." She pushed her empty plate away.

"Want some more?" Willie reached for the casserole dish. "There's plenty here."

She shook her head. "No, thanks. I've had enough."

Jesse stood and collected the plates. Willie passed her the container of his mother's brownies.

"I love your mom's brownies. Mine never come out this good." She leaned her arms on the table. "Jesse, I want you to know how thankful I am for your help with King today."

"Glad I could do it." Jesse sat and reached for a brownie. "King's a good dog."

"I'm sorry I couldn't get away again the way I planned." Willie leaned back. "I had some business to take care of. Jesse said Pastor Pete came with him in the morning and at noon, and Chad helped this afternoon."

"You have a business to run. Jesse and his crew provided King with the care he needed." Although she'd been disappointed when Willie didn't show up, he was here now.

Jesse washed dishes, Willie dried, and Haleigh put away leftovers. She placed Mrs. White's clean serving dishes in the basket and put the other dishes where they belonged.

"Have you heard from Nancy yet?" Willie leaned against the counter.

"No. She'll probably call to let me know when to take King home after Timmy is released from the hospital. She's been upset with me since the accident. Her car has passed by a couple of times, but she hasn't stopped or called. Maybe tomorrow." Nancy hadn't responded to her text messages either.

"She can't hold an accident against you forever." Jesse pulled out a chair and sat.

"Timmy and King were hurt on my watch." Tears filled her eyes.

"Give Nancy some time." Willie's arm came around her shoulders, comforting her. "Are you ready for that walk?"

"I want to check on King before we go." She led the way to the laundry room, where King lay snoring.

Jesse slid to the floor beside King and stretched out his legs. "I'll stand watch. You go."

Nodding her thanks, she followed Willie to the front door, which he held open for her. They walked down the steps and turned toward the Morgans' bungalow.

Conscious of Willie's nearness, she breathed in the scent of his aftershave. He didn't offer to take her hand as they sauntered along. If he hadn't stuffed his hands in his pockets, she might have slid hers in his.

Refreshed by cooler outdoor air, Haleigh listened to the chirping of birds and breathed in the scent of the woods.

"I hope Nancy will forgive me. I hope she knows I would never purposely put Timmy in danger." She took a shaky breath, and tears pooled in her eyes.

Willie put his arm around her and pulled her closer. "I'm sure Nancy knows that."

She leaned against him, drawing strength from him, and wiped her face with the sleeve of her T-shirt. "What I'm really afraid of is that Nancy won't give God a chance now. She said she couldn't understand how a loving God could let a little boy like Timmy get hit by a car." Haleigh couldn't quite understand that either.

"Give God time to work, and give Nancy time to get past the shock of what happened to Timmy." He released her and took her hand, intertwining his fingers with hers. The gesture felt natural and comforting. Haleigh didn't try to pull away.

Except for birds chirping in the red maple tree and a couple of rabbits watching them from the side yard of the bungalow, the place gave off an air of emptiness—no lights in the windows, no dog and boy playing in the yard. Haleigh took a trembling breath. She tightened her hold on Willie's hand.

"Nancy's working, or she's at the hospital. I wonder if Sam will come home when he hears about Timmy."

"I don't know how it works with the military, but I believe they help the soldiers during family emergencies."

"She's going to need help."

Willie squeezed her hand. They turned and walked back toward Main Street.

"I only wanted to help Timmy train King. They were doing so well, until that cat showed up. Everything happened so fast, and I couldn't stop them." Haleigh's voice broke.

"I know you feel responsible but try to let it go. Let God take care of it."

"Timmy could have died. What if he's crippled for life?"

Willie stopped and turned her to face him. "Haleigh, Timmy didn't die, and no one has said he'll be crippled for life."

She sniffled and nodded. "I know." But why did God allow the accident to happen?

They reached the corner of Woods Road and Main Street. The scene of the boy and dog lying in the street flashed before her. "I don't want ..." She choked on her words.

"The memories are still raw, aren't they?" Willie tugged her hand and they turned back.

She needed something else to think about. Willie said he came to tell her about his trip. "When are you leaving on your trip?"

They passed the log home and headed toward the bungalow again.

"The last week in September. It's a good time. Business will be slow then. I'll be gone about a month, but I'll be home in time to see Jesse off."

"What will you be doing? You said something about helping with gardens."

Without further encouragement, Willie explained to Haleigh the missions team's goal, to teach the people skills that would help them become self-supporting. Using his plant knowledge and business background, he would help people establish vegetable gardens to feed their families and provide an income.

She watched his face and caught his excitement as he talked, wishing she were going.

A whole month without Willie. The thought gave her a

sinking feeling in the pit of her stomach. Love made life more complicated.

Love? Where did that word come from?

For so long she tried to ignore her true feelings, especially where Willie was concerned. Maybe the truth had sneaked in through her broken heart. Or maybe she was no longer afraid of the truth. She'd released her guilt and fear from its box, faced it, and the past no longer held her captive.

"SOMEONE'S AT THE DOOR, King. I wonder who it is." Giving him one more pat on his head, Haleigh rose from her knees and hurried to answer the door.

"Katie!"

As usual, Katie's sparkle brightened Haleigh's day. Not that the day had been bad, just uneventful.

"Come in." She pulled her friend inside and gave her a big hug.

"I'm sorry I didn't call first."

"That's all right. I can't go anywhere, and it's just King and me here. Friends are always welcome." Although she liked dogs, she couldn't have a two-way conversation with King.

"I hope you haven't had lunch yet." Katie held up a white paper bag. "We usually have lunch together on Tuesdays, so I stopped at the café and bought sandwiches for both of us."

"Thank you. King had his lunch, but I couldn't decide what I wanted. You rescued me from having to decide."

"How is King?"

"Improving. He loves having visitors. Let's put our sandwiches in the kitchen, and I'll take you see him before we eat."

Ten minutes later, seated across from each other, they bowed their heads while Haleigh thanked God for their food and for Katie's visit.

"Have you been to the hospital to see Timmy? How is he today?" Katie sipped her iced tea.

"Nancy finally texted me this morning. Timmy is coming home today. She wants King home at three. I didn't try to visit Timmy at the hospital again. Nancy made it plain she doesn't want me around. I decided I could help best by staying here and caring for King."

Katie reached across the table and touched Haleigh's hand. "I'm sure Nancy doesn't mean it. She's worried about Timmy more than anything."

Haleigh sighed. "I know." She picked up her napkin and laid it on her lap. "I guess I'd be mad at me too. Timmy and King got hurt when I was responsible for them."

"Don't let this discourage you. Accidents happen."

"Timmy was so proud of his dog. You should have seen him. We were working on King obeying the command to come when called but didn't expect a cat to show up and King to take off after it. Timmy was so concerned about his dog, he forgot to be careful. Why is life so hard, Katie?" Haleigh rubbed her forehead. If she could only wipe away bad memories.

"I'm not sure."

After they finished their sandwiches, Haleigh brought a plastic container to the table. "I have a treat for you." She lifted the lid.

"Ooo! I haven't had any of these for a long time. They're Mrs. White's brownies, aren't they?" Katie chose one and took a bite. "Mmmm."

"Mrs. White provided dinner for me last night, and Willie and Jesse ate with me. We used Willie's van to bring King home from the vet's yesterday, and Jesse brought someone with him every few hours to take King out. He and Chad left a few minutes before you came."

"I wanted to come yesterday, but I had to work. After everything else I had to do, there wasn't time."

"I understand. You called yesterday, and you're here today. I think I needed you more today."

"Then I'm glad I came today."

They finished eating, and cleanup took only a few minutes.

"I have to work later today, so I can't stay." Katie pulled her car key from her pocket.

Haleigh followed her into the living room. "Thank you for coming. You made my day brighter."

"Before I go, may I share some verses with you that help me when I'm struggling?" Katie lifted Haleigh's Bible from where it lay on the end table. Haleigh sat on the sofa while her friend turned the pages.

"The first one is Psalm 55, verse 22, the first part of the verse. 'Cast your burden on the LORD, and He shall sustain you.' The other one is First Peter 5, verse 7. 'Casting all your care upon Him, for He cares for you.'" Haleigh finished repeating the verse with Katie.

"I suppose if life was easy, we wouldn't have a reason to trust God." Haleigh hugged her friend. "I know those verses, but sometimes I need to remember God still cares, even when we have problems."

She closed the door behind Katie.

The humid air made the laundry room stuffy. Haleigh turned on the small box fan in the window to air out the room then refilled King's water dish. She sat and held King's head on her lap.

"Timmy's coming home." His tail thudded against the carpet. "In fact, he's probably home now. And soon you will be too." She stroked his muzzle. "I'll be sure to visit you. And when you get better, we can work on getting you to come when you're called." *If Nancy allows it.*

Leaving him to chew on his bone, she retrieved her journal from her bedroom. Writing about the last four days would relieve some of the stress.

JESSE DROVE THE VAN, arriving with Chad just before three o'clock, and they pulled up next to the bungalow right at three.

Haleigh knocked on the door, her stomach clenching. Had Nancy forgiven her yet? Would she be allowed to see Timmy? The door opened.

"Oh, hello, Haleigh. You can bring King into the living room. I've set his crate up in there." Nancy pointed in that direction.

No smile, no "I'm happy to see you," no "Thank you." Haleigh's heart sank.

She turned and signaled to the men. They carried King in and settled him in his crate.

"Nancy, you know Jesse, and this is Chad, a friend who has been helping."

"Nice to meet you." Her lips turned up, but her eyes remained cold.

Jesse pointed to the door. "We'll wait in the van."

"Okay." They were traitors to leave her to face Nancy alone, but she'd probably do the same if the situation was reversed.

Taking a deep breath, she handed the care instructions to Nancy. "These are the vet's instructions for King's home care." She held out a bag she carried in her other hand. "This is a small bag of puppy food Dr. Payne recommended."

"We have plenty of food for King." She didn't take the bag.

"I didn't have his food at my house. This came from the vet, so it's yours."

Careful not to touch Haleigh's fingers, she accepted it.

Nancy didn't thank her or ask if she wanted to see Timmy.

"May I say hello to Timmy? Please?" She held her breath.

Nancy paused, maybe trying to decide on an excuse to say no, then she turned. "All right. This way."

Propped against pillows, Timmy sat on his bed, his leg in a cast stretched in front of him with a small pillow under his knee.

A coloring book and crayons lay beside him, and he held a toy truck. He looked up when she walked in.

"Hi, Timmy." She didn't want to cry.

"Hi, Haleigh, did you bring King home? How is he?"

Nancy spoke. "I'll take you out to see King in a few minutes."

"Oh, okay. Haleigh, will you sign my cast? The nurses and doctor at the hospital did."

"I'd love to." She took a step toward the bed.

"Haleigh has other things to do, so she has to get going now." Nancy's meaning was obvious.

"Maybe another time. Bye, Timmy, and get well." She didn't have anything more important to do, but she wouldn't contradict Timmy's mother.

Nancy's aloofness sliced through Haleigh's heart, but she'd have to wait until she got home to cry.

When Haleigh returned to work the next morning, she forced cheerfulness as she reported on Timmy and King to Willie and Tia. "King is moving much better on his own. I don't know who was happier to see whom, Timmy or King." She didn't mention Nancy's cool reception.

Sadness lay heavy on her chest and tied her stomach in knots. If only she could do Saturday all over again and undo the bad.

In a shallow, round dish she placed three small plants in soil. Timmy might find these interesting because of their shapes and colors, and they'd be easy to care for. To this dish garden, she attached a bumble bee balloon with the words 'Get Well Soon' printed on it. She'd take it to him after work and hoped Nancy would allow her to see Timmy and King.

In place of Nancy's car, an unfamiliar car sat in the driveway. Probably Nancy hired someone to care for Timmy and King today while she worked. Haleigh shook her head. It was her fault Nancy had this added expense.

King's chain lay on the ground by the doghouse, and the yard quiet and empty. She knocked on the door and waited.

The woman who opened the door looked familiar to Haleigh, although she knew they'd never met.

"Hi, I'm Haleigh from up the road. This is for Timmy." She held out her gift.

"How nice. I'm Timmy's grandmother, Nancy's mother. I'm here to help for a few days. Nancy went to work." *Nancy's mother. That's why she looked familiar.*

"How are Timmy and King doing? Are they allowed visitors?" The knots in her stomach tightened.

"I'm not ..." Her smile disappeared and her eyes narrowed. "You're the young woman who was with him when he got hurt." She shook her head. "No, I don't think Timmy is up to having visitors today. Maybe another time."

Tears burned Haleigh's eyes, though she willed them to stay there. What had Nancy told her mother? Her heart broke all over again, and she struggled to take a breath. "Will you give this to Timmy and tell him it's from Haleigh?"

"Yes, I'll see he gets it." She took the dish garden from Haleigh's hands. "Another time would probably be best for a visit." She shut the door.

Shoulders drooping, feet dragging, Haleigh walked down the steps and to the road. She kicked at a stone and missed. The grandmother's face had said it all. She'd messed up again, big time! This time a little boy and his dog got hurt. She would never have another opportunity to talk to Nancy about becoming a Christian or to help Timmy train his dog.

Haleigh had told Willie she'd work for him for the rest of the summer, and she would fulfill that promise. But then it would be time to move on or to move back to Wellsburg.

A dark cloud of guilt pressed down on her mind, body, and spirit.

Without eating, she went to bed early then tossed and turned throughout the night.

Dragging herself out of bed in the morning, she prepared for work, tempted to call in sick. Then Willie would know, and she didn't want him to know. He would try to make her feel better, and she just wanted to be miserable.

She managed to choke down a bowl of cereal and a glass of orange juice before leaving.

The warm, fresh air and the blue sky with a few puffy clouds didn't matter, nor did the singing birds or the colorful flower gardens. She didn't want to enjoy the beauty of the day, so she drove to work.

"Hi, Tia." 'Good morning' wasn't in her vocabulary this morning.

"Mornin'." Tia's usual greeting.

Haleigh put away her purse and went immediately to the greenhouse. When Willie hurried in a few minutes later, she waved to him and continued to water the flowers. He didn't have time to stop and chat because he had a late summer landscaping project.

At least she didn't have to face Willie this morning. She didn't want any questions.

Tia watched her closely. Haleigh had no intention of confiding in her co-worker and kept her distance as much as possible. She did her best to be cheerful with customers.

When he returned unexpectedly to the shop before noon, Willie caught her putting together an arrangement. "You look tired, Haleigh. Are you all right?"

She nodded. "I'm fine."

Probably because he was tired from landscaping, or he had a lot on his mind preparing for his missions trip, he didn't question her further. Several times she discovered him watching her from his office.

After a better sleep that night, by morning a glimmer of hope lifted a little of her heaviness.

NANCY SENT Haleigh a check in the mail, reimbursing her for King's veterinary care. That Nancy didn't try to contact her otherwise continued to make her heart ache.

While Timmy's grandmother's car remained in their driveway, Haleigh stayed away. She longed to see the boy and his dog, to see for herself they were recovering. She ordered a puzzle book and a book on dog care for Timmy online.

Nancy's car stood in the driveway of the bungalow on Monday after work, so Haleigh knocked on the door. Nancy opened the door, an apron tied around her expanding midsection.

Haleigh smiled. "Hi, Nancy."

"Oh, hello, Haleigh." Nancy didn't smile back.

"I bought these books for Timmy. I thought he'd like them." She held them out, hoping to be invited in.

Nancy took the books. "That's thoughtful of you. I'll make sure he gets them." She started to close the door.

"Is—is he ...?" Haleigh clasped her hands. "Is Timmy up to having visitors yet?"

"My son is taking a nap." Nancy's blunt tone tore her heart.

"How is he? And how is King?"

"They are both getting better, everything considered." Nancy avoided meeting her eyes.

"Nancy ..." Haleigh reached out her hand. "Nancy, I'm sorry. I didn't mean for them to get hurt. You know I love Timmy."

"Well ... yes." A bell dinged inside the house. "I have to go now. My cake will burn." Nancy shut the door.

Haleigh kicked a stone in the road in front of her. She followed its crazy path along the road, back and forth, kicking it again and again.

When does the punishment end, God? I've asked for forgiveness, but I'm still overwhelmed by guilt. Why don't I feel forgiven? I'm such a failure. Is it time to leave Greenlawn?

With one final hard kick, the stone disappeared into the grass at the side of the road.

Maybe she should call Katie. No, Katie had her own life to live and didn't need to hear about all Haleigh's problems. Willie would listen, but with his business and the missions trip, he had other, more important things on his mind. She didn't want to become dependent on him.

Some things she had to work out by herself. Wasn't that what it meant to be an adult?

A nightmare about Timmy and King, the squeal of brakes followed by thuds, woke Haleigh up that night, not for the first time. She picked up her phone to dial Pastor Pete but put it down. She'd cry if she tried to talk to him.

HALEIGH AWOKE to a cloudy sky and a stuffy head. That, along with worry about Timmy and King, her relationship with Nancy, and her father's illness sapped her energy.

"Mornin'." Tia was placing money in the cash register when she walked in late.

Responding to Tia's greeting with only a nod, she put her purse away and returned to the work counter. Maybe if she made the flower arrangements first, her head would clear. She always enjoyed this part of her workday best. She'd start with an anniversary bouquet: roses, carnations, lilies, greens.

Choosing a vase the right size and shape, she placed the greens first, then carefully positioned each flower. Only one more, a rose for the center. Picking up the bloom she wanted, her elbow connected with the vase.

"Oh, no!" Haleigh froze.

The vase crashed to the floor, shattering into pieces and scattering flowers across the floor. Her head throbbed.

"Oh, my. Here, let me help you." Tia crouched down and picked up some flowers.

"No! I'll take care of it. It's my mess."

Without another word, Tia dropped the flowers and backed away.

Haleigh closed her eyes and sucked in air. She'd never barked at Tia that way before.

First laying the flowers and greens on the counter, she swept the ceramic pieces into the dustpan and dumped them in the trash then mopped the floor, all the time counting the cost of her clumsy move. She'd have to tell Willie. And apologize to Tia.

Her co-worker stood by the cash register with her back to Haleigh and flinched when Haleigh touched her shoulder.

"I'm sorry, Tia. I shouldn't have yelled at you. Please forgive me."

Tia shrugged.

"Thank you for trying to help."

When Tia turned, Haleigh felt worse because she'd been crying. "I forgive you." She snickered. "You sure made a mess."

"I did. It was a clumsy move."

Willie breezed in. "Good morning, ladies. Sorry I'm late." If he noticed anything amiss, he didn't say so. He strode to his office. His morning must be great.

Haleigh returned to her work and started over.

"I have news." Haleigh peered over her shoulder as Willie approached the front counter waving a paper. "I have the schedule and itinerary for the missions trip. Four weeks from Monday, I'll be leaving."

Could the day get worse?

On top of everything else, Willie would be thousands of miles away for a whole month.

Stay or leave? And if she left Greenlawn, where would she go and what would she do? Leaving like this would be another failure, but staying would be impossible now. Why did life have to be so hard?

A visit home might be good. Time away in Wellsburg might help clarify her thinking. She shook her head. No, she didn't want her parents to worry or fuss.

She called Katie and left a voicemail. "Katie, I'm really busy today and won't be able to meet you for lunch. I'm sorry." She skipped lunch and drank a glass of iced tea and ate crackers after work, her appetite gone.

DURING THE NIGHT, Haleigh awoke, rolled over and moaned. Swallowing didn't lessen the soreness in her throat. Coughing didn't relieve the heaviness in her chest. Her whole body ached.

"Oh, no, I can't be sick!" This had happened to her after Gram died.

She sat up and waited for her eyes to focus on her alarm clock. Two fifty-five. She moaned again and lay back, praying it was only a bad dream, and dozed.

A dog barked from the woods up the road. "Sunshine!" Haleigh sat up again, her head throbbing. The bark turned into a cry of pain. "Sunshine, I'm coming! Hold on!"

Rolling out of bed, she nearly collapsed to the floor. Shoes—where were they? She needed shoes to help Sunshine. Slipping her bare feet into her sneakers, she ran to the closet for her raincoat, shoelaces flapping. The long coat covered her pajama-clad legs. She struggled with the buttons.

In a hurry, she pulled back the deadbolt lock and opened the door. The screen door banged shut behind her, and she thought she heard her mother call out, "Don't slam the screen door!" Sunshine cried again. She had to hurry.

"I'm coming, Sunshine. Hang on!" As she cut across the grass towards the woods, she tripped over her flapping shoelaces and landed with a whop, face down on the ground. Stunned, she lay there until she could breathe again.

Shivering, she sat up and pulled her coat around her. Why was she here? The dog. *That's right, Sunshine needs me!*

But Sunshine was dead.

Why did life have to be so hard?

Tears streaming down her face, her body aching, she pushed herself up from the ground and limped back home. She'd left the door open. Dropping her coat in a pile on the floor, she collapsed on the sofa and pulled the throw around her. *S-so c-cold!*

If only Mom was here.

Turning on the lamp beside her, Haleigh reached for her phone. "I think this is right," she muttered as she punched in the number. Mr. White's sleepy voice answered.

She struggled to hold the phone. "This is Haleigh. I'm ... Can you help me?" She coughed.

"Hold on, Haleigh. We'll be right there." Haleigh heard a click on the other end of the line. She clicked off the phone and dropped it beside her as her eyes closed.

"Haleigh! Haleigh, dear, it's Annette White." Haleigh felt a cool hand on her forehead. "She's burning up! We'd better get her to the hospital. She's wearing sneakers, and there's dirt on her pajamas. I wonder what's been going on here."

"Sunshine. I heard Sunshine. Needed help," Haleigh muttered.

Strong arms lifted her. She opened her eyes. "Willie?"

"You've got dirty hands again."

She sighed and relaxed, her head resting against his chest. He whispered in her hair, "Why didn't you ask me for help sooner, Halo?"

"Such a good friend," she murmured.

22

*H*aleigh awoke covered by a white sheet and a thin white blanket. Her left arm rested beside her, taped to an IV. The striped beige curtains at the window and the antiseptic smell—she lay in a hospital bed. She turned her head at the swish of the door as the nurse, Katie's mother, entered her room.

"Mrs. Mann? Where am I?"

The nurse checked the IV bag. "In Community Hospital."

"Oh. How long have I been here?"

"You came in early this morning. Don't you remember?" She stuck a plastic-covered thermometer into Haleigh's ear and took it out at the beep. "Still 101, but better than the 104 you came in with. How are you feeling?"

"Yukky! How did I get here?" She moved and moaned. Her right knee hurt and her shoulder ached.

"The Whites brought you in. Willie and his mother stayed around until they knew you'd be okay."

Haleigh let that sink in. "I-I think I must have been sleep-walking. I remember hearing my dog, but she's gone, and I remember waking up on the ground."

"Are you thirsty? Mrs. Mann lifted a cup of water with a straw to Haleigh's lips. "You should try to drink a little."

Licking her dry lips first, Haleigh took a long sip, then a second. She lay back on the pillow and closed her eyes.

"Call if you need anything, Haleigh."

When she opened her eyes a while later, a small, yellow, smiley-face balloon tied to a bouquet of multi-colored Shasta daisies in a vase stood on the sunny windowsill. She wanted to sit up, and she needed to use the bathroom. Her hospital gown was damp with sweat, her mouth felt dry, and her stomach rumbled. She found the call button clipped to the bottom sheet.

A half hour later she sat up in bed, washed and in a clean gown, the IV removed. She sipped water several times while waiting for the arrival of a late breakfast tray and ate hungrily. The hospital food tasted good this morning.

Feeling much better but very tired, she leaned back and closed her eyes, trying to remember the events of the day before. Yesterday began badly.

"Haleigh Abbott, what are you doing here?"

She opened her eyes at the greeting. Katie. She struggled to shake the lethargy from her mind and body.

"My mom called and said you came in early this morning." Katie handed her a card and set a vase with a single yellow rose with baby's breath and a fern on the windowsill. She sniffed the daisies. "I see Willie's been at work."

Haleigh nodded. "I think it's Willie. I haven't read the card yet."

Katie handed her the florist card.

It was signed simply 'Willie.'

Last night he had teased her about her dirty hands.

"So, what happened?" Katie sat on the foot of the bed.

"I woke up in the night, not feeling well at all. I must have fallen back to sleep because I heard Sunshine barking and then crying from the woods. I thought I had to help her, so I ran out and fell down."

Katie wrinkled her forehead. "You're a sleep-walker? I didn't know."

"I'm not usually. But when I'm sick, I get weird dreams. I must have been dreaming. Or maybe I did hear a dog. I know Sunshine is gone. Somehow, I got back to the cabin and called the Whites. I don't remember much else, until I woke up here earlier this morning."

Willie had held her so gently and securely. Her face heated.

If Katie noticed her blush, she chose not to comment. "Do you need anything from home?" Katie removed a pad of paper and a pen from her purse "I have to work later, but I have time to stop by your house." She made a list of the things Haleigh said she needed.

After Katie left, Mrs. Mann encouraged her to make out her lunch and supper menus. Haleigh had fallen asleep again when the bedside telephone rang. She fumbled to pick it up. "Hello."

"Hello, Haleigh, this is Mom."

A wave of homesickness washed over her at the sound of her mother's voice. "Oh, Mom." She tried to hold back the tears. "I'm sorry."

"For what?"

"For getting sick and making you worry. You have enough to do."

"Haleigh, listen. Stop feeling guilty. You didn't get sick on purpose. You have nothing to apologize for."

Haleigh shook her head. She'd brought this on herself. "But, Mom, I—"

"It's okay. Dad and I want to know how you are."

"I'm better than I was." Haleigh sniffled. "The Whites brought me to the hospital. The doctor said I picked up a virus, and I'm dehydrated." She didn't add the part about stress and not eating. "Gail Mann is on duty today."

"You're in good hands then. Please tell her hello from us. Your father and I are sorry we can't come right now."

"I'm a big girl, Mom. It's okay. How's Dad?"

"God is good, Haleigh. Your father is getting stronger every day. The doctor said he can work at home from his computer, but he can't go to the office yet. I sent him to get a half gallon of milk—the fat-free kind. He still has to be careful, and we're trying to adjust to a new diet." Her mother's cheerful tone comforted her.

"The little boy, Timmy, and his dog got hit by a car when I was their caregiver. They both have broken legs, and I feel terrible. His father's overseas, and his mother is struggling." Haleigh couldn't remember how much she had already told her parents.

"Yes, you called and told us. We've put them on our prayer list. Life isn't easy for military families with a loved one gone. Are they believers?"

"No. I've spent a lot of time with Timmy, and Nancy comes to our young adult functions when she can. Now Nancy blames me for the accident, and I don't think she wants to have anything to do with God or me. And, Mom, she's pregnant."

"It must be tough for her. We'll keep praying. Now, how are you doing, other than being in the hospital?"

Haleigh forced cheer into her voice. "I'm doing fine, Mom. I enjoy the work at Floral Creations. I'm involved in church. Katie and I spend a lot of time together." She wasn't fine, but she didn't want her mother to worry. She didn't speak of her recent struggle. "Jesse is leaving for the Air Force at the end of October. And did you know that Willie is going to Africa on a missions trip soon?"

"Yes, Annette reminded me when she called to tell us you were in the hospital. It's wonderful to see young people using their talents for the Lord."

Haleigh remembered Gram's words from years ago.

"I think I'd better let you rest now," Mom said. "You must be tired from holding the phone and talking. Please call us, Haleigh, if you need us."

"I will, Mom." She yawned. "I'm ready for a nap. But please

don't worry about me. I'll be all right. Maybe I'll come home for a visit soon."

"We would enjoy that. I wish I could be there with you. I know you're an adult, but I'm still your mother."

"I love you too, Mom." Haleigh pushed the *end* button and let her arm fall back to the bed. She wished her mother could be here, but Dad needed her more.

Her sore throat and body aches reminded her it was time for her medication.

When she awoke from an afternoon nap, Katie had left a backpack of her things at the foot of her bed. She changed out of the hospital gown into her own pajamas and robe and sat back in the padded chair next to her bed. With her Bible, journal, and a library book in her lap, she tried to decide what to do.

A knock at the door made her look up. She saw a large pot of burgundy mums with Willie's grinning face behind it. Her stomach flip-flopped, and she pulled the front of her robe together.

"Special delivery, courtesy of your local florist. When I discovered this order was for you, I brought it myself." He squeezed the large pot between the two smaller vases on the windowsill and handed her the card.

"Thanks, Willie, you're a—"

"I know, a good friend." He sighed and sat on the edge of the bed.

"Did you do landscaping today?"

"Yes, probably our last one. And I have to get back or my brother will think I deserted him. I had to change my clothes before coming here, and see, even my hands are clean." He held them out for her to inspect.

"But you'll only get dirty again. You didn't have to do all that for me."

He took her hand between his. "I'd do anything for you, Halo." The warmth in his eyes matched that of his hands. He meant it.

"It's a gorgeous mum. I admired it in the greenhouse and wished I had the money to buy it." She read the card. "Oh, it's from my parents."

"Yes, they called the shop and asked Tia if we had a plant you'd like and could take home with you. She'd seen you looking at this one often."

She'd have to thank Tia. Perhaps there was hope for friendship between them.

"I'm glad you're feeling better today. You had me worried last night."

She lowered her eyes. "I'm sorry to be such a bother."

When he let go of her hand, she stared at it, feeling bereft.

"That's not what I meant, Haleigh. Please promise me you'll ask for help whenever you need it."

He stood. She looked up at him and nodded. He obviously cared about her.

"I have to get back to work now. Will it be all right for me to stop in again tonight?"

It was more than all right. "Sure, I'm not going anywhere. They're keeping me here until tomorrow morning." She leaned forward and touched his arm. "Thank you for rescuing me last night."

"My pleasure. See you later." He winked and left, and she stared at the empty doorway, missing him already.

THE KNOCK on her door startled her from a doze. Willie stepped in.

"Hey, Sleeping Beauty." He ambled toward her, his hands in his pockets, and stopped at the foot of the bed.

Tongue-tied by his presence, she couldn't break away from his gaze. His hunter green shirt complimented the red highlights glistening in his hair, and those arms held her last night. His smile broadened, and her body zinged fully awake.

"Hey, Willie." She wiggled into a straighter position against her pillows and tugged the front of her robe around her. "I see your hands are clean."

"I washed them before I came." He turned the chair and sat facing her. "They weren't presentable when I finished work." He leaned forward. "I want you to be honest with me. Are you all right?" His eyes communicated tenderness and caring, and her heart rate soared.

"I will be." She stretched her hand out to him, and he grasped it. "I should be out of here tomorrow. I'm tired, but my fever is gone, my throat isn't sore, and I'm feeling so much better." And she was, but her physical wellbeing probably wasn't all he meant.

He squeezed her hand and let go, then he pulled his phone out of his pocket. "The missions trip coordinator messaged some photos and information. I thought you'd like to see them, so you'll know a little more about where I'll be and who I'll be with."

When he sat on the edge of the bed, she leaned against his arm as he showed her the photos and explained them, aware of the man beside her and the change in their relationship.

When she awoke and opened her eyes, daylight peeked around the edges of the blinds at her window.

Willie—his kindness and compassion, his great faith, the strength and comfort she felt in his arms. How could she resist any longer? She loved him. How could she bear his absence for a whole month when he went to Africa? Life without him would be—empty? Lonely?

An aide arrived to take her vital signs, and a lab tech drew several vials of blood. Hearing the clatter of the food cart, she flipped back her bedcovers and padded to the bathroom.

Returning to her bedside, she sat in her chair and prepared for her breakfast tray.

Later, someone knocked. Haleigh looked up from the book she was reading. Nancy Morgan stood at the door, dressed in her nursing smock.

"Hi, Haleigh, I see you're awake. May I come in?" Nancy wasn't smiling, but she didn't look angry either.

"Please do." Haleigh closed her book. "I'm surprised to see you."

Nancy walked in and stood at the end of the bed. "How are you?"

"I've been sleeping a lot, but this morning I'm wide awake. I expect to go home today. I'm waiting for the doctor."

Nancy bit her lip and held her clasped hands to her chest. "I-I need to apologize. I haven't treated you very well since Timmy got hurt." She took a deep breath. "I blamed you, but it wasn't your fault. Timmy explained what happened. It was an accident and could have happened to me or anyone." She shook her head. "Timmy and King can be unpredictable."

Tears collected in Haleigh's eyes as weight lifted from her heart. "I felt so bad, and I wanted to help you. That's why I took care of King, so you didn't have to worry about him."

"Thank you for doing that. I had so much on my mind with Timmy's care. I'm forgiven, then?"

Haleigh closed her eyes and breathed a quick *thank you*. "Of course. You're my friend, and I don't want bad feelings between us." She'd lost too much already because she hadn't been willing to forgive.

"Good!" Nancy sat on the edge of the bed facing Haleigh. She drew a pink envelope from her smock pocket, which she handed to Haleigh.

Haleigh pulled out a card with a folded paper inside. She smiled at Timmy's drawing of himself and King with hearts filling the sky. "Thanks, Nancy. Timmy's drawing is sweet. Tell him I love it."

"He's so worried about you." Nancy shook her head, and tears filled her eyes. "I'm worried about him, Haleigh. He misses his father, and he blames himself that King got hurt. He thinks I'm mad at him, but I'm not. It's only ... he's my son."

Nancy's pale face and the dark circles under her eyes indicated the strain she'd been experiencing. What could she say to encourage Nancy?

Nancy frowned. "Why is God so cruel to let all this happen to an innocent boy and his dog? Why does life have to be so hard?"

"I've asked that question often," Haleigh said, "and I really don't know the answer. My grandmother always said we're imperfect people living in an imperfect world. I know God is here, and He loves me."

"Haven't you ever doubted?"

"Yes. Sometimes. Often." For six years.

"I have to get going. I dropped Timmy off at the sitter's, and I'm on my way to work. We'll see you when you get home, okay?"

Haleigh leaned forward. She wanted to continue their conversation about God but knew Nancy had enough for now.

"Thanks for coming." She held out her hand, and Nancy grasped it

After she left, Haleigh leaned back. "Father God, thank you for Nancy's forgiveness. Thank you for your love. Please help Nancy to see your love in all this."

A deep voice outside her door mingled with the voices and clatter from the hallway. The doctor knocked at her door. She sat up.

"Good morning. How are you feeling this morning?" Doctor Freeland's smile and pleasant bedside manner put Haleigh at ease.

"Much better, and ready to go home."

"Your temperature's down, your vital signs are normal, and your bloodwork came back clear. You can go home. The nurse will be in with your release papers and instructions for your care at home. Be sure to take all the medication prescribed. Do you have any concerns or questions for me?"

Haleigh shook her head. "Not right now." As he headed out the door, she added, "Thank you, Doctor."

After getting dressed, she looked around the hospital room to be sure she'd gathered everything. Then she sat in the chair and closed her eyes. Katie would be here soon.

Katie walked in, and Mrs. Mann followed her with the release papers for Haleigh to sign and reviewed at-home care procedures.

"Are you all set? I'll get the wheelchair." Mrs. Mann went out.

"And I'll drive my car around and meet you at the front door," Katie exited the room with the backpack and the pot of mums.

"Thanks, Katie."

When Mrs. Mann returned with the wheelchair, Haleigh sank into it, aware of her lingering physical weakness. In her lap she held Willie's bouquet, the balloon bouncing around and bumping her nose, and the vase with Katie's rose.

She was going home!

23

$\mathcal{H}$ad it been only a day and a half since she left? She opened the car door, already drained of energy.

Katie got out. "You go ahead, Haleigh. I'll bring your things in for you."

"Thanks, Katie. Let me carry at least one of the flower vases. And leave the mums on the porch please."

She unlocked the door of the log home and stepped inside. How good to be home!

After leaving her backpack in her bedroom, she plopped down on the living room sofa. Covered by the throw, she lay back on pillows and awoke two hours later.

"So, you're awake." Katie sat in the chair across from her, closing the book she'd been reading. "How are you feeling?"

"Better, but not quite ready for a marathon." Haleigh yawned and stretched. She sat up and pushed back the throw. "May I have some water, please? I'm thirsty." She licked her dry lips.

"Right next to you." Katie pointed to the end table.

Haleigh positioned herself to lean against the corner of the sofa, propped up by pillows. "What would I do without you?" She took a sip of ice water.

"Miss me." Katie counted off on her fingers. "Stay all alone in your cabin. Fix your own meals. ..."

"Okay, okay, I get the picture." Haleigh laughed. "You're good for me, Katie."

"That's what friends are for. It's getting toward dinner time. Any thoughts about what you want to eat?"

"I'm really hungry! I think they starved me at the hospital. Let's see—soup and sandwiches, pizza, barbecued chicken, steak, double cheeseburger and fries ..."

Katie laughed. "How about something light to begin with, say chicken noodle soup and a grilled cheese sandwich? That's within my cooking ability, and they say chicken soup is good for the soul."

Haleigh rubbed her stomach. "I'll settle for good for my tummy."

When Katie went into the kitchen, Haleigh remained seated on the sofa. She hated feeling so weak and dependent.

The phone rang as she got up to go into the bathroom. "Will you get that for me?" she called. When she returned with her hair brushed and feeling refreshed and awake, Katie brought a tray of food in from the kitchen.

"Just Annette White on the phone, checking up to see that you got home." Katie paused beside the sofa. "I assumed you'd rather sit in here to eat for today."

Haleigh nodded and gratefully accepted the tray. Katie brought in another for herself.

The simple meal satisfied her. She leaned back comfortably. "Katie, if you have something to do, I'll be all right."

"No. I promised your parents and Willie that I'd stay with you until I'm sure you're strong enough to be alone."

"You don't have to, you know."

"Yes, I do. I'm your friend, here to help you. You're weaker than you think. Your family can't be here, and it's too far for you to travel to Wellsburg right now. The doctor said you have to be careful for a few days, so you don't have a relapse."

"I'm sorry." Haleigh sighed. "It's just that I don't want to be a bother."

Katie leaned forward. "The truth is, Haleigh, you want people to know you can make it on your own." Katie stared her down.

Haleigh's eyes widened, then lowered. "How do you know that?"

"We've been friends for a long time. You always complained that your family looked on you as the baby. One reason you came back to Greenlawn for the summer is to prove you can live on your own."

Haleigh couldn't argue with her.

"I'm not moving in, just staying a night or two." Katie glanced out the front window. "Besides, you'll have a visitor in a minute."

The doorbell rang before Haleigh could ask who. Katie opened the door.

"Timmy!" Haleigh exclaimed when the boy hopped into the room on crutches. "I've missed you!" Nancy followed Timmy, and Katie shut the door.

"I miss you too." Timmy shyly handed her a box wrapped in floral paper. "So does King." Timmy licked his lips before saying more. "I'm sorry that I didn't listen to you, Haleigh. King and I are both sorry."

Haleigh held out her arms to the contrite boy. She hugged him. "You're forgiven, Timmy. I'm only sorry that you and King got hurt." Timmy sat next to her and cuddled against her side.

"Timmy has been so concerned for you, Haleigh. We hope you don't mind our visit tonight." Nancy lowered herself into the rocking chair.

"Not at all, but I'm not very good company."

"That's all right, we came to cheer you up. I get grumpy when I'm sick too," Timmy assured her.

Haleigh laughed and hugged Timmy, then opened his gift, a box of chocolate-covered cherries, and passed it around. The

Morgans didn't stay long. Haleigh considered getting ready for bed when the doorbell rang again. Katie opened the door.

"Hi, Willie, come in. Why am I not surprised to see you?"

Haleigh ran her hand over her hair and sat up straighter.

"I brought brownies to share." He held out the plate as he walked in.

"Then you're even more welcome." Katie laughed.

"Did you make them?" Haleigh sniffed the chocolatey fragrance that filled the room.

"No. Mom made them." He pulled back the foil covering the brownies. "And I shamelessly begged her to let me bring some over. She has a soft heart for you, Haleigh. She let me bring most of them." He stopped in front of her and held out the plate.

Haleigh sighed as she took a bite. "These are so good. You're a ..."

"I know, a good friend." He looked over his shoulder. "Is she being a good patient, Katie?"

"The best! I'll get some iced tea to go with them." Katie retreated to the kitchen.

Willie moved Haleigh's water bottle to the side then set the plate of brownies on the end table. He lowered himself to the sofa by Haleigh's feet. She pulled her feet back and ran her fingers over the throw, reluctant to meet his eyes. The memory of being in his arms triggered a desire to be there again.

The heat rose up her neck into her face. She reached for her water. If he noticed her blush, he didn't say anything. Good!

"I don't expect you to come back to work until you feel well. Take at least the rest of this week off."

She looked up. "But you're busy this week. I'm—"

"I've been so worried about you. Ever since Timmy's accident I've watched you lose weight and shut yourself away from your friends again. If you hadn't called for help that night, I would have confronted you the next day."

"I'm sor—"

He laid his hand over hers. "No, Haleigh, don't blame

yourself for anything." The warmth of his hand seeped into hers. "Mom will come into the shop until you're well. She's feeling empty-nestish, so I may hire her full time now that Tia is back in school. She and Dad agree working in the shop regularly might be good for her, and it will certainly help me."

Suddenly fatigued, Haleigh nodded, then yawned, "Thank you, Willie."

Katie returned with the tea, and Willie stayed long enough to finish his drink and a couple of brownies.

THAT NIGHT, Katie stayed again, then came in and out for most of the next day. She made Haleigh's meals and made sure she took her medication.

Haleigh envied her joy and confidence. She'd become a lovely young woman. Why was Nathan West the only man interested in dating her?

The second day after coming home from the hospital, Haleigh felt much better. The mild air held a hint of fall as she and Katie sat on the porch, sipping iced tea. Her pot of mums sat on the top step.

"I haven't seen Nathan around."

"He's been invisible all summer," Katie said. "I thought he wanted to work on our relationship, but I guess it's not important to him after all." She shrugged. "I don't think I'm interested anyway. I've put my past behind me, and I want it to stay that way."

Haleigh nodded. She kept her own opinions about Nathan to herself.

"Do you ever think about getting married?" She couldn't get Willie out of her mind. She shivered, remembering his strength and tenderness that night, when he lifted her in his arms.

"Sometimes." Katie leaned her elbow on the arm of the chair and rested her cheek against her hand. "I made a mistake once.

I'm not planning to make another one. I can truly say I'm content where I am right now. I love my life in Greenlawn, but that doesn't mean I'm opposed to having a special someone in my life."

"Aubrey is married to Jeremy, and they're happy together. You're content and just bubble over with life. I feel so ... I don't know." Haleigh sighed. "What does God want me to do?"

"He wants you to be you, Haleigh. Let Him direct you. Don't hold back so much."

Other people had told her that, but she hadn't listened to them. "But I'm afraid, Katie." The confession startled her, even though she'd once told Willie. "I'm afraid to take chances."

"You're too hard on yourself. You always were. You're special, with so much talent." Katie spoke with confidence. "Don't be afraid to try. Jesus promised to be with us always."

Haleigh, still unconvinced, shook her head. "But what if I fail? What if I can't do what God wants me to do? And what if I marry someone only to find out later it was a mistake?"

When Katie smiled at her last question, she wondered if she had said too much.

"Pastor Pete reminded me that God never fails." Katie rubbed her thumb against her glass. "He's there not only to pick up the pieces after our mistakes, but He's with us to complete His work. Philippians 1:6 says ..."

From the living room Katie's cell phone rang, and she ran in to answer it. She came out carrying her purse. "I have to go over to church and check out something about the next drama I'm directing. I'm on the schedule to go back to work in the morning, so I need to stay at my apartment tonight. I'll come back and check on you, but I think you're well enough to be on your own now."

"Thanks for everything."

After Katie left, Haleigh heard King bark from the Morgan's bungalow. Her thoughts turned to ways she could help Nancy and Timmy.

Remembering the conversation she and Katie started earlier, Haleigh turned to Philippians 1:6 in her Bible and read, "Being confident of this very thing, that He who has begun a good work in you will complete it until the day of Jesus Christ."

It all depends on trusting God.

NANCY AND TIMMY stopped by on the way home the next afternoon.

"Daddy's supposed to call us tonight," Timmy called out as soon as his car door cracked open. He grabbed his crutches before his mother got around to his door and moved with ease, his face no longer etched with pain.

"That's great! I'm so glad for you!" Haleigh watched as mother and son came up the walk. "I think he'll be pleased to know how much better you are."

Timmy leaned against the porch railing. His mother sat in the second rocking chair.

"Would you like some iced tea, lemonade, or cold water?"

Timmy looked at his mother, who nodded. "I'll have some lemonade, please."

"How about you, Nancy?"

"Some water will be good, thank you."

Haleigh brought their drinks out to the porch. "Timmy, why don't you sit in my rocking chair." Once he settled in the chair, she handed out the drinks then sat on the top step and leaned against the post so she could see them. 'Timmy, if it's all right with your mom, would you like to come here with King tomorrow afternoon?"

"Mom?" Timmy looked at his mother.

"Certainly, so long as Haleigh is up to it." Nancy nodded. "I think the exercise will be good for you and King. Do you want me to walk you over?"

Timmy thought for a moment. "Naw, I think King and me

can make it together. If we get stuck, we'll yell real loud so you can help us."

Both women laughed and Nancy ruffled his hair. "Okay."

"I have something special to show you," Haleigh told him.

"What?" Timmy's eyes opened wide with excitement.

"You'll have to wait until tomorrow." She pretended to zipper her mouth.

With a grin, Timmy finished his lemonade. "You know what, Haleigh?"

"No, what?"

"I'm getting my cast off in two weeks!"

"Wow! That's great. Must be you're getting better."

"I am."

Nancy finished her water and they left, eager to be home when their warrior called.

It was time.

Since her hospital stay, Haleigh discerned a new spirit within, as though she had inhaled a deep, cleansing breath of fresh, crisp morning air, and had exhaled the fear and uncertainty of past mistakes and guilt. The past no longer held her back. Her life lay open to explore new possibilities, ready to find and follow God's plan.

The scrapbooks she pulled from the storage container covered eight years of her life, the time she'd shared with her therapy dog. Sunshine had been her friend and companion, and the sweet dog had helped her through a difficult period in her life.

She sat on the sofa and began to leaf through the books. Those eight years might have been totally wasted if not for Gram, who kept her connected with God, and Sunshine, who kept her connected to people.

When she had handled her resentment by refusing to forgive her two closest friends and by closing herself off from other close relationships, she'd been the loser. Kids in high school and college had offered their friendship, and she chose to remain on the fringe, sentencing herself to loneliness.

Gazing at the pictures of her dog with the elderly in resident care and children in the hospital, she saw how God had used her through her self-imposed exile. Yet, she had missed so much more.

God had planned this time, her illness, for her to face her problems and work through them, continuing the work he had begun years ago, just as Philippians 1:6 said.

She waited for her guests on the porch, soothed by the rocking chair's rhythm. A few red and orange maple leaves mingled with the green grass on the lawn. A flock of Canada geese honked its way across the sky and circled back.

The aroma of freshly baked chocolate chip cookies wafted through the screen door. She heard children's voices from Main Street and knew Timmy would be home soon.

Nancy honked as they drove by, and soon boy and dog came limping toward the log home, side by side. King favored his one hind leg, and Timmy held King's leash as he maneuvered on his crutches.

A lump formed in her throat. One day she would have another dog. For now, she would help Timmy and King.

"Hi, Haleigh!" Timmy called out. "Me and King are here."

"So, I see." Haleigh stood and motioned for them to join her on the porch. Awkwardly, they managed to climb the steps. "Why don't you sit right here, and I'll bring you some chocolate chip cookies and milk."

Timmy nodded and licked his lips.

"And may I give a dog biscuit to King?" She pulled one from her pocket. "Sunshine always liked them."

Sitting in the second rocking chair, Timmy set his crutches on the floor. King circled and lay down with a sigh. He no longer wore the cone around his neck.

"Oh, yes, King loves dog biscuits. Mom doesn't let me give him very many. She said he won't eat his dinner, or he'll get too fat if he has too many treats."

"Your mother is wise." She handed him the treat.

"I know." Timmy scratched King's head. "King, sit."

His movements almost normal, King obeyed, his focus on the treat.

"Speak."

"Woof."

"Good boy."

King took the treat gently from Timmy' fingers, and with a couple of chomps and a gulp, it disappeared.

Haleigh set the plate of cookies and two glasses of milk on a TV tray between them and opened the first scrapbook.

As she showed Timmy the photos, she reminisced about Gram, Sunshine, and her family. Sometimes he commented on a photo or said something about his family.

"Haleigh." He rocked as she put away the last scrapbook. "You should get another dog. Then you could help the old people and the children feel better, and King would have someone to play with."

"I'm sure I will someday." When she found a home of her own.

"Are you still going to help me make King obey?" He stroked his dog's side. King's tail thumped on the floor.

"Of course, Timmy. As soon as you and King are both ready."

"Good. I thought you wouldn't because we didn't listen to you before."

"We all do things we're sorry for and need a second chance."

Timmy nodded. "We'll do better."

EVERY DAY after she came home from the hospital, Willie checked on Haleigh in person. She couldn't imagine life without him, yet she couldn't build up the courage to tell him.

When she returned to work on Monday, she breathed in the

familiar scent as she entered the shop. Willie greeted her from his office. Since she'd resumed classes, Tia worked only Tuesday and Thursday afternoons and Saturday mornings. Haleigh missed her presence.

After Haleigh put away her purse and jacket, Willie met her at the front counter. "No heavy lifting, and I want you to run the cash register today."

She could sit on a stool to do that. He let her answer the phone when he was busy with customers, and he finally allowed her to make an arrangement ordered for the afternoon.

By the end of the day, she appreciated his concern. Exhausted, she fell into bed early.

Her strength returned slowly. By Friday she thanked Willie for giving her Saturday morning off.

Nancy invited Haleigh to have supper with them on Friday night, and her stomach growled at the aroma of lasagna when she entered the house. Her mouth watered.

"Daddy is going to call tomorrow," Timmy told Haleigh. "I can't wait to tell him about King's new trick."

"What trick is that, Timmy?" his mother asked.

"He says please when he wants a dog biscuit."

Nancy looked at Haleigh. Haleigh shrugged. "I told Timmy that King needs to learn good manners. Instead of just grabbing a treat from his hand, a dog needs to learn to say please, just like a boy should."

Nancy raised her eyebrows. "Oh. And how many treats did King have, to learn this new skill?"

"Haleigh showed me how to break one into tiny pieces, so King gets lots of practice without eating too much."

"Good." Nancy smiled. "You take such good care of your dog. Daddy will be proud."

Timmy's chest swelled. He grinned and nodded. "May King and I go out to play now?"

"Yes, as long as you're careful. Please make sure your chair is pushed in. Then you may go."

Timmy obeyed his mother then hopped out the door on his crutches with his dog. Haleigh washed the dishes as Nancy dried them and put them away.

"Would you like a cup of tea, Haleigh?" Nancy asked as they finished. "We can sit in the living room and watch Timmy and King through the front window while we chat."

"That sounds great. Thank you for inviting me over tonight. I enjoyed the company, and your lasagna was delicious."

"It's my grandmother's recipe." Nancy turned on the burner under the teakettle. "Sam loves it, so I make it often for him. This is the first time since he left." Nancy stopped, and Haleigh could see she struggled to control her emotions.

"You miss Sam."

"Yes, I do. It's hard knowing he's halfway around the world and in danger most of the time." She finished preparing their tea, and they carried their cups into the living room.

Haleigh sat on the sofa. "Will Sam be able to get any leave?"

"He wanted to come home when Timmy got hurt." Nancy lowered herself into her rocking chair. "But Timmy ... Timmy knows if Sam comes home now, he won't be able to come when the baby is born. He told his father to wait." Nancy wiped a tear from her eye. "We're hoping he can stay until after Christmas."

"That would be wonderful for all of you. In the meantime, what can I do for you?"

Nancy sighed. "Just continue to be my friend. Timmy and I have talked about going to church the next time I have a Sunday off."

Haleigh wanted to stand up and cheer, but she smiled instead. "I was afraid you wouldn't give God another chance after I messed things up so badly."

"No, Haleigh, you didn't mess up anything. I needed time to accept the fact that it was an accident. And you stuck by us, despite my bad attitude, because you really care about Timmy and King and me."

"I do, Nancy, and God does too. I'm still learning how

faithful and good God is, even though I've been a Christian for a long time."

"That's another thing." Nancy leaned forward. "You're honest about your problems. You don't pretend you're perfect, or that you never doubt. Willie, Katie, Jesse, and your other friends from church have been good to Timmy and me. I've tried to explain it to Sam, but I can't wait for him to meet all of you. You're making me think seriously about a relationship with Jesus."

Haleigh couldn't stop smiling, inside and out.

Through the front window she watched Timmy and King. He gave King commands. When Timmy walked, King walked beside him. Timmy stopped, and King stopped and sat. Timmy walked away and turned toward his dog. King got up and walked to Timmy. He sat, and Timmy reached into his pocket and held up something. King woofed, and Timmy gave him the treat. Haleigh was proud of both pupils.

A short time later, Haleigh went home. She'd finished taking her medication, but her body still hadn't recovered its full strength and stamina.

"HALEIGH, have you finished checking our supplies? Halloween and Thanksgiving are just around the corner. I want to make the order today to be sure everything arrives before we need it." Willie stopped beside her.

In and out of the shop all morning, he'd spoken to her only once before now, when she first came in.

"Almost." She laid down the stem of daisies she'd been ready to poke into the foam base, distracted by his proximity. "As soon as I finish this arrangement, I'll get back to it."

"Good. And Jesse just brought in a vanload of mums. Leave some in the greenhouse and fill in displays with others." He didn't meet her gaze because his eyes were glued to his phone.

"Okay." Had she imagined they had more than friendship between them?

As though suddenly aware of her eyes on him, he looked at her. "Haleigh—" His phone rang, and he walked away as he answered it.

Willie had a lot on his mind and much to do to prepare for the smooth running of Floral Creations during his absence.

What if the four weeks without him ended in goodbye? She hadn't promised to remain longer than the end of summer, and he hadn't asked, but she'd stay until he returned. Beyond that, she didn't know.

Before her lunch break, she finished the arrangement and laid the completed list beside Willie's computer. Escaping the shop, she ate alone at the café.

In the afternoon, Jesse helped Haleigh arrange the mum displays. They placed several scarecrows and craft straw bales, along with pumpkins and squash Willie raised in his home garden, among the vibrant flowers. The shop took on a festive look.

"When are you leaving for boot camp, Jesse?"

"The first of November, right after Willie returns from his trip."

Another goodbye. She'd miss him—a joyous, fun-loving person, and like a younger brother to her. Would he be different when he returned?

ON WEDNESDAY AFTERNOON, the shop door opened, and Haleigh looked up. Oh, no! Derek! Willie had gone on a quick errand, Jesse had taken a late lunch break, and she was alone.

Taking a breath, she left the arrangement she was working on and stepped to the front counter. Trying to keep her voice steady, she said politely, "May I help you?"

Derek looked around and then at her. He hesitated before saying, "I want some flowers."

Well, that was reasonable. "What kind of flowers?" Did Derek have a girlfriend?

"I don't know. They're for my mother." He tapped the countertop.

Derek was buying flowers for his mother? "Does she have a favorite flower? Would she prefer a potted plant to cut flowers?"

Derek grinned. Haleigh saw the school-boy charm return to his face. "No plants. She kills them. I think her favorite is roses, but I can't afford those."

"How about a mixed bouquet of cut flowers, and we'll include one rosebud?" Haleigh stated the price.

Derek shrugged. "I guess so." He stood next to the counter and watched as Haleigh chose the flowers and wrapped them in green tissue. "My mother has had to put up with me for a long time. She never gave up on me. It's her birthday, and I want to get her something special."

Her heart warmed toward Derek. She relaxed and smiled. "I think she'll like these, especially because they're from you."

After paying for the flowers, he picked them up, then looked directly at her. "Why are you being nice to me? I've never given you anything but trouble."

Until now he'd always intimidated her. "You're a customer, Derek, and you haven't threatened me. In fact, I think it's great that you're getting these flowers for your mother."

He gave a small nod. "Will is always trying to help me too. Is he around?"

"No, he's out for the moment. Had an errand." She looked toward the door, hoping to see Willie. "Would you like to leave a message or come back later?"

"I'll come back later." Derek turned to leave. He stopped to look at a mum display, then turned back toward Haleigh.

"I'm sorry about the accident. I didn't want Leanna to die or

Aubrey to get hurt. I was just out for some fun, at least I thought I was."

Haleigh rested her hands on the counter.

"I guess it was expensive fun." Derek shook his head. "And, in the end, not fun at all, especially going to prison and knowing I killed someone. I go to AA, and it's helped me a lot. And going to church with my mother has helped too."

The confession surprised her. "I'm glad for you, Derek." And she meant it. "I respect you for what you said. I know the words were hard for you to say. But I also know that facing the truth is necessary for healing, so you can go forward with your life."

"Thanks," He raised the bouquet and left.

Haleigh went back to work.

A little later, Willie came into the greenhouse while Haleigh was deadheading some of the plants. "Haleigh, I want you to go home for a visit. Take some time off."

"W-what?" Haleigh paused, her hand suspended. "You already gave me time off."

"You still don't have your strength back, and business at the shop has slowed. I want you to go home and rest. And I know you want to see your father." He leaned against a support post with his arms crossed.

She continued her work. "They say he's doing well, but I'm afraid they're hiding something."

"So, you'll go?"

"Willie, you leave next week. And I'd miss your commissioning service on Sunday."

"I know, but I have to make sure you leave first, so I know you actually go. You're apt to change your mind." He raised his eyebrows.

Haleigh stiffened. Everyone still wanted to take care of her. "You're not my ..."

"Were you going to say 'boss' or 'father'?" He chuckled.

Ready to protest more, she smiled instead. He was right. She needed to go home for a visit, to rest and see her father. And her mother as well. A week away might help her decide what to do next, and leaving before Willie might be easier than watching him go.

"Derek came in to buy flowers for his mother's birthday. He said he'd come back later to see you. We had an interesting discussion."

"Oh, about what?" Willie began to pull dead blossoms off another plant.

Haleigh rested her hands on a shelf that held potted plants. "How much you've helped him, and that he's going to AA."

Willie nodded. "He told me that."

"He also said attending church with his mother has helped him. He wanted to give his mother the flowers for her birthday because he's given her so much trouble. He's different, Willie. He didn't sneer."

"I've seen the difference too. In fact, he wanted to know when Aubrey would be back in Greenlawn because he had to apologize to her. People do change."

"I know. I have." Haleigh prepared to disclose just how much.

"Do you—" The bell over the door interrupted Willie as a young couple entered. "Oh, I have an appointment to discuss wedding flowers." The telephone rang. "Will you get that, Haleigh?" he said over his shoulder before greeting the couple.

On Saturday morning, Haleigh finished packing her suitcase and backpack and took them out to the car. As the sun peeked over the horizon, she shivered inside her fleece jacket in the cool morning air. She'd seen the Morgans and Katie the night before. Taking one more look around to be sure she had everything, she closed and locked the front door.

Someone stood at the foot of the steps. She jumped and gasped, then held her hand to her chest.

Willie held out a single long-stemmed red rose. "Hello, Halo. I came to say goodbye."

"Not goodbye." Haleigh shook her head, unable to take her eyes from his. "I'll be back." They had taken care of this after work yesterday. Why was he here now? She shivered with anticipation.

He grinned. "That did sound rather final, didn't it? Okay, I came to see you off."

"Thanks, Willie, you're – you're a good friend."

Willie had spent a restless night, anticipating this moment, yet wondering if the timing was right. He'd been patient, he'd prayed, and since her illness, Haleigh's attitude had invited a closer relationship with him. No words had been spoken, but her eyes and body language showed her awareness of him.

His mouth twitched at the corners, and he stepped up next to Haleigh on the porch, handing her the rose. She looked up into his eyes, her breath catching as he gently held her face, warm and soft, between his hands.

"You always say that, Halo. Don't you know I want us to be more than just friends? I've loved you forever, but you never seemed to want more than friendship. I have to know. Will we ever be more than friends?" He held his breath, hoping but uncertain of her response.

"Oh, Willie." Her voice only a whisper, she didn't pull back, but tears filled her eyes. "I don't know. Are you sure that's what you want?"

Exhaling, he dropped his hands and leaned back against the porch railing. "Are you planning to leave again?" Had he read Haleigh wrong?

"Do you want me to stay?"

Of course, he did. "Yes, but only if you want to." *Please want to. For me.*

She brushed tears from her face with her fingers and buried her nose in the rose. She was so beautiful.

"Greenlawn will always be home to me, and you belong with Greenlawn. You're successful, compassionate, and a man of deep faith. You're all a girl could want. I'm not sure I belong in Greenlawn, and I'm not sure I'm right for you."

He turned away from her toward the woods. The trees glowed with color, and goldenrod and purple asters filled the empty lot between the woods and the log home. If she left him, he'd never be the same.

"Willie." Her touch on his arm made his heart skitter. "I'll be here when you get back, I promise. If I decide to stay in Greenlawn, can we at least be friends, like we've always been? Please."

"Friends we will be." He turned with a sigh. "Will you at least think about what I said, and pray about it?" It was hard to look into her eyes.

"I will."

"I'll let you go for now." He grasped her shoulders, so she wouldn't walk away before he said his piece. "But when I get back, we have a lot to talk about." He released her. "I'm not sure what my phone or email access will be, but I'll try to keep in touch."

Haleigh nodded and pushed hair back from her face. He walked her to her car with his arm across her shoulders, as they'd often walked. She slid behind the steering wheel. He closed the door and leaned against it when she opened the window.

"You know, your hands are clean, and you don't have a speck of dirt on your nose." He grinned, despite his heavy heart, then brushed the end of her nose with his finger.

"Same to you, Willie. You're still a good friend."

He wanted to be more.

Haleigh started her car and waved, then she backed out of the driveway. Willie watched her car until it turned out of sight on Main Street, heading away from Greenlawn.

He strode out to the street and on to Floral Creations. The shop and Greenlawn felt empty without her.

The diamond ring sat in its box in his top dresser drawer at home, waiting for his return in four weeks. He had a lot of praying to do.

Haleigh had a lot of alone time in the car thinking about all that had happened since college graduation. She missed her dog, but God had given her so much. Friends, new and old, and another sister-in-law. Soon she'd be an aunt! She enjoyed her work at Floral Creations, and she could pay her bills.

And Willie—their parting had been difficult. She glanced at the rose lying in the passenger seat.

"Mmmm." Haleigh awoke the next morning to the aroma of pancakes. One thing she missed about living at home: her mother's delicious cooking.

She sat up, stretched, and pulled back the curtain to peek out. A clear, sunny day. With a week of vacation ahead of her, she looked forward to helping her mom in the kitchen and taking walks with her dad. Before returning to Greenlawn, she wanted to talk to them about plans and possibilities for the future.

Today she'd attend church with them. She showered, dressed, and got ready for the day.

"Good morning." She entered the kitchen.

"Good morning." Mom sat at the table sipping coffee.

Dad held the pancake turner as he stood in front of the stove. "You'll like these pancakes, Haleigh. Your mom found a new recipe."

"Mom's pancakes have always been good." Haleigh made herself a cup of tea and sat across the table from her mother.

Mom wore her robe and slippers. "Your father and I have had to make some adjustments to our eating habits. Going low fat and low salt are a challenge, but we manage. I've found some good recipes using less fat and alternate seasonings. Pancakes are one of the easier adjustments."

"It's hard to say no to things I always liked to eat. Your mom's willingness to find good-tasting and healthy alternatives has helped." Dad brought the plate of steaming pancakes to the table, and he prayed.

Haleigh took her first bite. "Mmm, these are good. I'll have to get your recipe."

After eating, she cleared the table and washed the dishes while her parents finished getting ready. They sat in the living room for a few minutes before leaving for church.

Her dad leaned back in his chair. "How are you now, Haleigh? You were quite sick."

"I'm okay, except I tire easily. I hope to get some rest this week. I'm sorry I didn't get home sooner, but with everything that happened I couldn't."

"How are the little boy, Timmy, and his dog?" Mom asked.

"They're both doing well. Nancy has a hard time keeping Timmy from overdoing, and King has made almost a full recovery. I'm so grateful. I felt terrible when the accident happened."

"We've been looking forward to having you home. We have a lot of catching up to do. And make sure you take time to rest." Dad got up from his chair. "But right now, we'd better leave, or we'll be late for Sunday school."

Haleigh stood. "Are you teaching Sunday school, Dad?"

"Not yet. I hope to start soon, maybe in another month."

"I'm teaching the fifth and sixth grade girls." Mom held up her teacher's manual. "I took the summer off, but it's good to be back."

The church people welcomed Haleigh, and she enjoyed being with them. The music and the pastor's sermon on faith were uplifting, but she kept thinking about Greenlawn and its people. She'd been a resident of Wellsburg for six years, but Greenlawn was home. And always would be.

That afternoon her cell phone rang, waking her from a nap. Willie.

"I almost called you last night, but I wanted you to have time to get settled in and rested from your trip." The sound of his voice sent a thrill through her. After their parting yesterday, she wasn't sure he'd call but hoped he would.

She yawned. "You were right. I needed a vacation." He probably grinned when she said that.

"Church seemed strange today because I didn't see you. My commissioning service is tonight. I wish you could be here."

"Me too. But someone sent me away." She touched a rose petal. "Mom and Dad will watch it with me on the church's website." She repositioned herself against her pillows. "Are you all packed?"

"Sure am. I leave early tomorrow morning, on the red eye."

"That's the earliest flight out, right? I'll be praying for you."

"I'll miss you, Halo. Four weeks is a long time." His words echoed her thoughts.

Four weeks without Willie stretched endlessly before her. Until now, she didn't know how much she depended on seeing him every day.

"I know. But you and God had this planned before I came back into your life, I know it's the right thing."

"Maybe next time you'll come with me?"

It was a question, an invitation. Friends could go on missions trips together, and it would be fun to go with Willie.

"Maybe."

SHE'D COME HOME for a vacation, at Willie's insistence, so she made no special plans for Monday except an afternoon walk with her father.

"How are you, Dad, truthfully?" He looked healthy to her, but she wanted to hear it from him.

"I'm feeling better every day, Haleigh. My energy level is nearly normal. The doctor says I should be able to go back to work full time in a couple of weeks."

"I'm glad. Everyone said you were doing well, but I had to see for myself."

"I've had excellent medical attention, and your mom takes great care of me. Many, many people have been praying. God has been good."

"I've thought a lot about what you said about trust." She linked her arm with his. "You were right to say I had to learn to trust God. I finally faced my mistakes from the past and discovered that I had been forgiven by God and by my friends. It's like a huge weight has been lifted off me."

"I guess returning to Greenlawn was a good decision."

"I wish I'd gone sooner."

She felt the pressure of Sunshine's leash on her hand and started to speak to her. She had walked this same route with her many times. Tears pooled in her eyes. Sunshine wasn't there.

The grief struck at unexpected times. She turned her head and brushed away her tears, hoping Dad didn't notice.

He did and read her mind. "Do you miss your dog?"

She nodded. "Yes. I still wake up some mornings and reach down to scratch her head. And when I come home from work, I think she'll meet me at the door. It's not as hard now, but I do miss her."

After their walk, Haleigh went to her room and knelt on the floor beside Sunshine's bed. "I'll never forget you, my friend." She placed the dog's bed, dishes, and toys in a black, plastic bag and took them to the attic. One day she'd have another dog.

When she lifted her journal from the bedside stand, the rose caught her eye. She touched its velvety petals. Willie gave her a red rose and said he loved her.

Did she love him? Yes. She'd answered that question when he helped her after Timmy and King's accident. So why couldn't she tell him?

"Father God, I need Your wisdom. What do You want me to do, where do You want me to go, and what should I do about Willie?"

In case Willie called, she made sure her phone was charged and nearby as she wrote in her journal.

On Tuesday, she visited with a couple of friends in Wellsburg in the morning and shopped with Mom in the afternoon. All day, she wondered what Willie was doing.

After supper, she sat on the back patio with her parents. To keep the chill away, Dad started a fire in the patio stove.

"You haven't said much about Willie." Mom pulled her jacket around her. "Have you heard from him yet?"

True, she hadn't said much, but she thought about him a lot. "Yes, he messaged that they arrived safely. He's so excited about this trip, he'd have been disappointed if something had kept him from going."

"And you like working at Floral Creations? Annette says Willie sings your praises about your work." Mom leaned against Dad when he sat beside her on the patio sofa.

"Willie's a great employer, but I probably won't stay there forever." She lowered her eyes to the fire. Mom was digging for information.

"Are you going to remain in Greenlawn?"

"At least until the Sousas come back. Greenlawn is home, and

I might get an apartment and stay." Could she bear to remain in Greenlawn as Willie's friend? What if he fell in love with and married someone else?

"We thought maybe you would." Dad got up to poke the fire. "You haven't said anything about returning home to live."

"I considered coming back after Timmy's accident. Everything fell apart, and I wanted to get away."

Dad sat again and leaned forward. "Have you made any decisions about what you'd like to do next?"

"I've had a lot of time to think lately." Haleigh pushed back her hair. "I enjoy working for Willie. I've learned a lot about the florist business, and I've met a lot of nice people I wouldn't have met on my own." She folded her arms against her middle. "I know I don't want to go back to school full time, at least not right now. If I stay in Greenlawn, I'll continue to work for Willie, if he wants me, and take some on-line courses."

Dad continued to probe. "For what purpose?"

"I've thought about working at the Senior Home as program director, but I've ruled out owning a dog kennel. I'm considering counseling, or maybe combining dog therapy with counseling."

Her mother raised her eyebrows. "And ...?"

The stove cast a circle of light in the middle of the patio. Mom and Dad waited on the other side.

"I knew you'd ask about Willie and me." A cool breath of wind made her shiver. "I don't know yet. I hope to have an answer by the time I return to Greenlawn."

SORTING through her clothing in her old room, Haleigh made a pile of what she'd no longer wear to donate to the Salvation Army. She still had to decide what to take back to Greenlawn.

Willie messaged.

Keeping busy. Packed up and ready to roll out. Maybe out of

contact range for a couple days. Always, Willie. P.S. I miss you, Halo!

She responded.

Getting rested. Enjoying time with Mom and Dad. Returning to Greenlawn Saturday. Haleigh.

P.S. I miss you too.

Touching the fading rose and inhaling its lingering fragrance, she remembered the hope and longing in his eyes when he said he loved her, and the hurt and disappointment when she refused to profess her love for him.

For six years she'd deserted him, but the day she returned to Greenlawn, he welcomed her back. He gave a job and did his best to encourage her and help her overcome fear and guilt from the past. He was with her throughout the trauma of Timmy and King's accident, always an example of faith, love, and service to everyone.

He'd shown her commitment, and he'd taught her love. And she wanted to tell him in person, but he was thousands of miles away.

ON FRIDAY NIGHT, after her parents went to bed, she walked through the house from room to room, turned off lights, and climbed the stairs to her room, in her heart saying goodbye.

On Saturday morning she packed her car mostly by herself, not wanting her father to lift anything that would hurt him. Her winter clothing took up much of the space.

"In the spring, when the Sousas return, I'll find an apartment in Greenlawn." She slid her suitcase into the place she'd left for it in the trunk. "Then I'll come back and get the rest of my things."

"We'll try to fit in a trip to Greenlawn soon, now that my heart is healthy again." Dad closed the trunk.

"Good, I'll look forward to your visit."

"Do you have everything?" Mom peered into the back seat of the car. "You might squeeze in a couple sheets of paper."

Haleigh laughed. "I hope I do. I checked my room and didn't see anything left behind."

After hugging her mother then her father, she got into the car, started it, and rolled down the window. "I'll call you when I get home."

"And if you have any trouble along the way ..."

"I know, Dad, I'll call you."

Crossing off Monday on her wall calendar, she counted the days until Willie's return.

Tia had classes that day, so Mrs. White came in to work in her place. "Have you heard from Willie lately?" she asked.

Haleigh didn't want to discuss her relationship with Willie with his mother, but she talked about him because she couldn't talk *to* him.

"An email yesterday."

"I had a message this morning," his mom said. "He expects to be away from the mission base for a couple of days, and he's not sure what phone or internet service will be."

Haleigh thought Mrs. White might say more, maybe ask her a question. But a couple of customers came in, and they never continued their discussion.

People still had reasons to buy flowers, and Jesse still had calls for planting trees and shrubs, but business at Floral Creations had slowed, as Willie expected.

On Tuesday, she met Katie for lunch at the café.

"I have the church drama for Christmas planned. Will you help sew costumes, girlfriend?"

Haleigh raised her eyebrows at Katie's unexpected request.

"Come on, you can sew. I know better than to ask you to act. You can either sew costumes or sing. Those are your only choices."

"Looks like you've made it for me." Haleigh laughed. "What makes you think I can sew that well?"

"You did a beautiful job on your bridesmaid's dress. Mrs. Hayes is going to be in charge, but she needs an assistant, so I thought of you. How about it?"

How could she refuse Katie? "Well, okay." Mrs. Hayes could help her with any problems she had.

"Great! I'll let Mrs. Hayes know, and she'll be in touch with you. Thanks, Haleigh. That takes a load off my shoulders. And, by the way, you can sing in the choir too."

Smiling, Haleigh shook her head. Katie could keep life interesting.

"Now." Finished with her salad, Katie set down her fork. "It's time to confess. You've made it a point not to talk about Willie this week, so what's going on?"

Haleigh avoided Katie's eyes, concentrating on folding her napkin precisely and laying it on the table. "Why do you think anything's going on? Willie's in Africa, and I'm here." The corners of her mouth twitched.

"Quit stalling, Haleigh. Fess up. I know you, and I know Willie. I could see it on his face every time he looked at you. I can't believe he left for a whole month without some sort of understanding with you. Besides, you look like the proverbial cat who caught the canary."

"Do I look guilty?" She pushed a lock of hair behind her ear. "He wants to be more than friends. When he gets back, we'll talk." She bit her lip. "I love him, Katie. Sometimes I worry that he'll change his mind or meet someone else on this trip."

Katie shook her head. "Never. Not Willie. He has loved you

since high school. Everyone knew it except you. He felt terrible when you moved away. I always thought he was waiting for you to come back. He busied himself with school and starting a business. He didn't take time to date anyone. And Aubrey said he was excited when he heard you were coming back."

"I was stuck on my own problems, too selfish to think much about others."

"You shut all of us out for a while."

"I'm sorry." She played with the edge of her napkin. "I thought our friendship was over."

Katie made a brushing motion with her hand. "That's in the past. God has given us a new beginning. Isn't He good?"

"Yes, I've been forgiven and accepted since returning to Greenlawn. And I'm blessed to have you as my friend."

Katie put up her hand for a high-five.

26

The following week, Willie's third week away, crawled by. On Thursday morning, Haleigh arrived at the shop before Mrs. White. Shortly after she opened for business, the bell on the door jingled and Jesse entered.

"Hey, Jess."

"Hi, Haleigh." He leaned against the counter. "I heard from Uncle Sam yesterday. I have to report for basic training on Monday."

Haleigh stopped arranging flowers. "Already? I thought you had a couple more weeks at home." She supposed she could view Jesse's leaving as though he was going to college. But the military was an alien world to her, very different from anything she knew. It would be hard to see him go.

"That's what I expected as well." He shrugged. "I'll become a government employee just a little sooner than expected."

She stood across the counter from him. Except for his bigger size, he reminded her of Willie, auburn hair, brown eyes. "How is your mother taking the news?"

"She's a bit shaken." Jesse tapped his fingers on the countertop. "She expected me to stay home a little longer. Mom and Dad will drive me to the airport early Monday morning."

"Willie will be disappointed that you're not here when he gets back." Not that it would make any difference to the Air Force.

"So am I." He sorted through the floral gift cards on the counter rack. "But when Uncle Sam calls, you don't have the option to say, 'Wait a few days until my brother gets home.' Maybe it will be easier without so many goodbyes."

"I didn't mean to sound as though I blamed you, Jess. It will be hard for all of us." They both looked up at the sound of a car driving into the parking lot. "My first customer of the day."

"I have to check up on a few things for Willie today." Jesse pushed himself away from the counter. "Mom said to tell you she'll be here, only a few minutes late."

Haleigh reached across the counter to lay her hand on his arm. "Okay, Jess. Have a good day."

On his way out, Jesse greeted the customer who entered.

A few minutes later, Mrs. White arrived. She ran the cash register and answered the phone but didn't say much. Several times Haleigh caught her staring into space and thought she understood. Her youngest child, although now a man, would be leaving home.

WHEN HER ALARM clock rang on Sunday morning, Haleigh turned it off and fell back to sleep. She burned her toast and scalded her tongue with hot tea. The raw, rainy day added to her misery.

She missed Sunday school and decided to drive to church. She slogged into church with soggy shoes, cold feet, and ankles splashed with muddy water from the parking lot. With just enough time to hang up her wet coat, she slid into the back pew and sat huddled in a corner, willing herself to be warm. She didn't take her usual seat with the Whites, not wanting to attract attention to her messy appearance or disturb the worshipers settled in for the service.

Slipping off her shoes, she placed her feet on a dry section of carpet, tempted to tuck them under her to warm them up. She hoped no one would ask, "How are you?" She could lie and say, "Fine," or she could go into an explanation about why she was miserable. Neither seemed like a good option.

Although she checked several times a day, and she made sure her phone was on and charged, Willie hadn't been in touch since Friday. And then it had been a brief call because they were disconnected.

As the congregation rose for the first hymn, she saw Katie a few rows ahead, looking at her over her shoulder. Katie's smile was like a ray of sunshine bursting through gray clouds.

But who was the young man standing beside her friend? Not Nathan, who had dark hair. This person was blond.

Haleigh forced herself to pay attention to the words she sang, that God doesn't make mistakes, He knows all things, and enduring trials purifies the person who trusts Him.

Mr. and Mrs. White sat toward the front with Jesse. He'd be leaving tomorrow. Another change. Another goodbye. If only Willie was home.

How much of the Scripture reading had she missed? She checked the church bulletin and turned to Psalm 130, verses 5 and 6.

I wait for the LORD, my soul waits, And in His word do I hope. My soul waits for the Lord more than those who watch for the morning— Yes, more than those who watch for the morning.

"Have you ever been disappointed?" Pastor Pete asked. "Have you ever expected a person to act a certain way or do a certain thing, and they disappoint you because they don't do it your way? Maybe you have disappointed yourself. Or circumstances have let you down."

Was he talking about her or to her? Haleigh sat up straighter and began to take notes.

"Maybe you're focusing on the wrong person."

Warmth permeated Haleigh's body as her clothes dried. She wiggled her cold toes against the carpet.

"When you focus too much on people, you limit your relationship with God. You look to other people for love, comfort, and guidance. Of course, we need one another. That's the way God made us. But there are times we ignore God and the help He has promised to give us.

"He is holy—perfect, and sinless. He is just—fair in His dealings with people. He is unconditional love. He proved it by giving His Son as a sacrifice for our sins. He is omniscient. He knows more about you than you do."

Haleigh forgot her cold feet and her worry about Willie and Jesse. She wrote furiously.

"Living in dependence on God includes trusting His power and believing He controls everything. And that includes accepting yourself with your limitations and unique abilities. Trust God to be sufficient to fulfill all your expectations as you understand Who He is and what He can do."

That must have been Gram's secret. After the stroke had left her in a wheelchair, unable to do the things she loved, she had accepted her limitations because she trusted God to give her all she needed. She didn't allow her physical limitations to keep her from enjoying life and reaching out to others. The residents of the nursing home had benefitted from her love, and so had Haleigh.

The service ended with prayer. Haleigh searched the floor for her shoes and found them under the pew. They were still damp, but she slid her feet into them anyway.

When she looked up, Jesse sat across the aisle from her, an unusually solemn expression on his face.

"Are you okay? We thought you'd missed church."

His concern touched her. She smiled and stood. "Now I am."

"Will you join us for dinner, Haleigh?" He got up. "Mom fixed my favorite meal."

"Yes, I'm planning to. Your mother invited me yesterday. This morning was not exactly stellar, and if I go home, I may just feel sorry for myself again."

Jesse put out his bent arm, and Haleigh linked hers through it. Only a few people remained in the building. Katie wasn't one of them, so in no time they were out in the parking lot. Jesse rode with Haleigh in her car. Parked in the Whites' driveway, Haleigh switched off the ignition and Jesse turned toward her.

"This will be the last day I see you for a while."

"I know, Jess, and I'm not sure my heart will take it." She laid her hands on her chest. For Jesse's sake she stifled the tears threatening to spill.

"I'll miss you too. You've always been like another big sister to me, though you're not very big."

Haleigh punched his arm lightly. He grinned, a grin so like Willie's it left a lump in her throat.

"Take care of my brother for me, okay? You know how he feels about you, and I think you feel the same about him."

Haleigh nodded.

Clearing his throat, he opened the door. "And I think we'd better go in before Mom's roast burns."

"Yes, we'd better." He'd rescued them both.

HALEIGH FELT the stillness as she unlocked the door and stepped into Floral Creations Monday morning. Tia would be in a couple of days this week, and Mrs. White would be back tomorrow. Haleigh didn't like working alone, but she was accustomed to the routine, and business was slow. She kept her phone handy.

After she quickly checked the plants in the greenhouse and made sure the merchandise was in order, she worked on an arrangement as she waited for the first customer.

The bell over the door jingled, and Haleigh looked up as Tia entered.

"This is a surprise. I thought you'd be in class."

"I do have a class later this morning, but I wanted to stop by and talk to you," Tia said. "It looks like I picked a good time."

"Monday mornings are pretty quiet. The Whites took Jesse to the airport this morning."

"He'll be missed." Tia pointed to Haleigh's arrangement. "That's pretty. You certainly are a big help to Will around here. Do you think you'll be staying?"

Haleigh shrugged. "I've decided to stay in Greenlawn, but I don't know how long I'll work at Floral Creations."

"Even if Will asks you to?"

Haleigh raised her eyebrows.

"Well, it's obvious you like each other." Tia chuckled. "Everybody knows there's chemistry between you two, even if you try to deny it."

Haleigh's face warmed, and she smiled. "I don't imagine you came here to talk to me about my relationship with Will White, did you?"

"No, I had something else to tell you." Tia glanced at the door and around the shop. "I wanted to tell you about Stuart Webber."

Stepping up to the front counter, Haleigh gave Tia her undivided attention. This had to be important, or Tia wouldn't have come.

"Have you had more trouble with him?" Since the day her co-worker came in with bruises, she'd worried about her.

"Did you know he crashed his Mustang last week?"

"No." She hadn't heard anything about Stuart recently, which was fine with her.

"Well, he did." Tia leaned forward. "You were right, Haleigh, he is a jerk! You know the day I came into the shop with the bruise on my cheek?"

"He did that to you?"

"Yes and no." Tia examined her nails. "He got mad at me and pulled open a door. It hit my cheek. I was so embarrassed. I had a black eye too. He said it was my fault." She looked up. "But, Haleigh, it was his fault. He has such an awful temper!"

She'd tried to warn Tia.

Tia rubbed her fingers against the edge of the counter. "That's why he crashed his car, because of his temper. He left, mad because I wouldn't go out with him again. He grabbed my wrists, insisting I didn't mean it. I told him he needed to get help with anger management. He peeled out of the driveway and had an accident just before he got home! It was such a beautiful car." Tia sighed. "It ran like a dream, and he even let me drive it once."

"Did Stuart get hurt?" Tia's concern for the car rather than Stuart might be funny if the situation wasn't serious.

"Maybe some bruises and a damaged ego, but he totaled his car. I think he's getting help now. His parents realized they'd spoiled him, and they're getting counseling for him."

Still concerned, Haleigh asked, "Are you going to date him again?"

Tia shook her head. "No, until I feel safe and comfortable with him, I won't. Probably never."

"I'm sorry it didn't work out, Tia. I am glad he didn't hit you, and you weren't in the car when he had the accident. One of my best friends almost died in a car accident."

"That was the accident when Leanna died. Will's sister was in the car, too, and the driver was drunk. At least Stuart doesn't drink." She adjusted her purse strap on her shoulder. "Well, I better go, or I'll be late for class. But I wanted to tell you thanks for being my friend and trying to help me, even though I wouldn't listen to you. And good luck with Will." Tia whisked out the door, the bell jingling behind her.

"Thank you, Father," Haleigh whispered as she pushed a stem of mums into the foam base. She'd promised the customer she'd have the arrangement ready by ten o'clock. At least she hadn't failed entirely with Tia. Her persistence had won a friend, and maybe the opportunity to tell her about Jesus. She'd pray for Stuart as well.

WHEN MRS. WHITE came into the shop the next morning, she had dark circles under her eyes and tired lines on her face, as though she hadn't slept much. Haleigh put her arms around her, and she clung to Haleigh for a long time.

"Are you all right?" Haleigh rubbed her back. She wished she could do more for this wonderful woman who'd been a second mother to her.

"I will be." Mrs. White took a tissue out of her pocket and wiped her face. "This is one of those times it's hard to be a mother. You always know they'll be leaving one day, but when it finally happens, it's hard to let go."

"You don't have to be here today. I think I can handle the business. It's rather slow."

"No." She sat at the cash register. "It's better for me to be here today. Less time to think. Jim had to go to work, and the house is very empty. The company of a friend is welcome."

"I understand. I'm glad you're here. And Tia will be in this afternoon. Have you heard from Jesse yet?"

"No, he won't be allowed to contact us right away. He has to send his clothes home, and I'm sure he'll be in touch as soon as possible." Mrs. White opened the cash register drawer. "Have you heard from Willie?"

Haleigh straightened a display of cards. "No, not since Friday."

"His father and I are concerned. We haven't heard from him since the middle of last week. I know communications are not great between there and here, but I wonder if we should contact the mission board to see if they know the reason."

Haleigh nodded. "That might be a good idea."

"I know I have to let go of my children, but this isn't like Willie. By the way, what have you heard from Aubrey?"

"Aubrey loves her class of fourth graders, and Jeremy has one more semester after this." Talking about family helped keep her mind off Willie.

"I think, since you're here and there are no customers at the moment, I'll start cleaning." Haleigh pointed toward the greenhouse. "I want to wash down the greenhouse and check the plants left there. The shelves out here need dusting, and maybe you and I can rearrange the shop. I know Willie will be getting his holiday stock in soon, and I'm sure he won't feel like cleaning when he gets back. What do you think?"

Mrs. White laid her palm against Haleigh's cheek. "I think Willie is lucky—no, blessed, to have you for an employee. It's a good idea. It will keep our minds off ... other things."

Willie's lack of communication made Haleigh's stomach jittery, although she tried not to worry. *Trust God.* He was probably in an area that didn't have phone or internet service.

She spent the morning cleaning and organizing the greenhouse, and dusted and vacuumed Willie's office after lunch. Sitting in his chair for a moment's rest, she daydreamed about Willie. She peered out at the front counter. Good! Tia, who replaced Mrs. White for the afternoon, was busy cleaning the cubby holes under the front counter and didn't see her.

That evening, restless and worried, Haleigh waited for an email or phone call, but neither came. She started to walk to the Morgans', then remembered that Nancy had the evening shift at the Senior Home and Timmy had a sitter. Katie, too, had evening shift.

After she'd walked up and down the road a couple of times, she called her parents and asked them to pray for Willie.

Tired from cleaning all day and worry, she went to bed early. When the alarm clock rang, she awoke, surprisingly refreshed. Maybe she'd hear from Willie today.

27

Haleigh had just put away her purse and coat and returned to the front counter when Mrs. White came in the door.

"We're waiting to hear from the mission board. Jim called last night. They hadn't heard of any problems with the project team, but they'll let us know as soon as they can."

"Good. I'm sure it will relieve your mind to know."

"And yours?"

Her question brought heat to Haleigh's face, and her eyes held knowing. Haleigh smiled and nodded.

Working outside, Haleigh discarded old and dead stock, neatly stacking bags of mulch and topsoil in the storage area, raked the lawn, swept the sidewalk, and greeted people as they walked by. She wrote down some ideas for holiday decorating, although Willie might prefer his own.

Back inside while Mrs. White took lunch break, her phone rang.

"We heard from the mission board." Willie's mother sounded calm.

"Is anything wrong?"

"No. Over the weekend his team conducted church services

in an area without reliable internet service. A storm delayed their return to the mission station. Then they lost power there. He'll probably be in touch with us soon."

Her sigh of relief came from deep within. "I'm glad he's all right."

"The person I spoke to said the team is scheduled to return home Monday morning."

"Good." She had so much to say to Willie face to face, things she couldn't write about in a message or email, or even talk about over the phone.

"Are you sure you won't need me this afternoon? I'd be happy to come in after my doctor's appointment."

"No, that's okay. If I need help, I'll call Je ... oops! I forgot he's not here. I'm sorry."

"That's all right. It's hard to remember that Jesse's not here."

"I'll call if it gets busy, but today has been slow like the rest of the week. I'll be closing by five anyway."

When they ended the call, the shop was quiet and empty. Haleigh was sorry she'd told Mrs. White not to come in. Because he'd expected Jesse to still be here, Willie didn't arrange for extra help.

Sitting in Willie's office chair, she picked up the book she'd brought to read. The bell on the door jingled, and she jumped up.

"Katie!" She waved.

Katie's head swiveled until she spotted Haleigh. "Hi. I'm off today and came to visit. Have you heard from Willie yet?"

"Oh, Katie, I'm so glad to see you." Haleigh walked up to her friend and gave her a hug. "You arrived at the right time."

"Is something wrong?"

She checked the parking lot for customers. "No. It's been quiet here this afternoon, but I've been worried about Willie."

"Is he okay?"

"He's fine. His team had been away for the weekend and got

held back by a storm. Then the mission station lost power. I expect I'll get an email from him today."

"When is he coming home?" Katie set her purse on the counter.

"Monday morning." Only five more days.

"I brought you a chocolate bar. That should fix things." Katie pulled two out of her purse.

"Oh, Katie, thank you! Just what I needed. What would I do without you?"

Katie held up her index finger and opened her mouth to start her list.

"Don't answer that!"

With a grin, Katie bit into her chocolate bar.

"By the way, who was sitting next to you in church on Sunday?" Haleigh took a bite of chocolate. *Mmm*, it melted in her mouth.

"Just Chad." Katie shrugged. "We're friends."

"Oh, Chad. He's a nice guy. I talked to him on the hike, and he helped Jesse and me with King. I'm sorry I didn't get to talk to you on Sunday. The day started miserably, and I was running late."

"Jesse left on Monday, right?"

"Yes, and he's missed."

"I'll bet not as much as someone else."

Haleigh smiled and without comment took another bite of her candy bar.

Only two customers came in, but the afternoon passed quickly with Katie to talk to.

"Mrs. Hayes appreciates your help with the costumes for the Christmas play. She showed me the six angel robes you made, and she said you did good work."

Haleigh sat in Willie's chair and Katie across the desk from her.

"I take that as a compliment coming from a dressmaker. I

needed something to do with my time in the evening. The robes were simple to sew."

"And thank you for joining the choir."

Since she'd decided to remain in Greenlawn, Haleigh wanted to become more involved at church. "I enjoy it. The Christmas music you've chosen is beautiful."

"Thank you. I've talked to the choir director about performing the music at the Senior Home. Maybe we should have the kids come in wearing their costumes. I think the residents would enjoy that."

"I agree. Be sure to let me know if there's something more I can do to help you. You've done a fantastic job organizing everybody."

Katie stayed until Haleigh locked up for the day and agreed to meet her for lunch the next day.

That evening she received an email from Willie, describing the weekend events and the storm. She responded right away.

We were worried when we didn't hear from you for so long.
Thank God you're safe. You'll be flying home on Monday, right?
Are you sorry you can't stay longer?

I have much to tell you when we have our talk.

She added news about work, church, and Greenlawn.

Again, she counted the days until his return. One minute her stomach fluttered, the next it clenched with fear.

Would he have changed his mind?

WITH THE HELP of Tia and Mrs. White, she finished cleaning and organizing the shop and greenhouse. Now she had less to do at work and more time to think.

On Friday she closed at five, and because business was slow, planned to open only from ten to noon on Saturday.

She stopped at home before going to the Morgans' for supper. Nancy had the day off and invited her to spend the evening with them.

"You know what, Haleigh?" Timmy bounced on the sofa beside her.

"No, Timmy, but I want to know." She knew he would probably tell her anyway. How she loved this little boy!

"Daddy's coming home in one month! That's thirty days. Mommy is letting me mark it on the calendar." Timmy ran to get the calendar to show her. "I put an *X* over each day, and this is the day we'll see him." He had circled the date in red.

"Oh, Timmy, that's wonderful! I'm sure your mommy is happy about that too."

"I sure am!" Nancy smiled and patted her rounded belly. "He expects to be here when the baby is born, and for Christmas too. I'm so grateful."

"Jason and Carmella's baby is due in November, just before my birthday."

"And when is Will coming home?" Nancy got up from her chair.

"Monday. He's finishing his last project helping a family."

"Lots of good things are happening!" Timmy spread his arms wide.

King walked over to Haleigh and laid his head in her lap. He looked up at her, wagging his tail. She scratched between his ears. "Lots of good things."

28

*M*rs. White called Haleigh at the shop on Monday morning. "Willie's flight has been delayed. He'll let us know when to pick him up."

"That means he may not make it today." Haleigh's heart sank. Why hadn't he called her? Probably because his parents planned to pick him up, and he knew they would relay the message to her.

Haleigh now had more sympathy for the missionaries the church supported in remote parts of the world. Never before had she realized the difficulty of not being able to make a phone call or send an email.

"We're not sure what time he'll be in, but maybe you'd like to go with us. I'm sure Willie won't mind if you close the shop a few hours early."

"That sounds wonderful! Thank you." Haleigh's spirits lifted.

"Do you need my help today?"

"If you'd like to come in for a while, that's fine." She didn't want to refuse the company this time. "I have a couple of arrangements to make, and I need to water the plants left in the greenhouse."

"I'll be there in half an hour."

Haleigh sighed and put down the phone. Only a few more hours. She felt like a child waiting to open presents on Christmas morning.

While she waited, she planned what to wear to the airport. Willie said she looked nice in blue, so she'd wear the new light blue knit top with her navy slacks.

Mrs. White ran the cash register, and Haleigh answered questions on the phone about bulbs and rose bushes. One customer came in for some cut flowers and two for their arrangements. A college student stopped in to ask about employment. Haleigh gave her an application and told her to bring it back next week.

All morning they waited.

When she returned from buying a sub and a can of diet soda for lunch, Mrs. White left, promising to call her when they heard from Willie. Haleigh waited until four-thirty, then decided to call the Whites.

Pulling her phone from her pocket, she heard the door open and turned.

"I'll be right ..." She stopped, speechless.

"Hello, Halo." Willie grinned.

Tears filled her eyes. "I expected to meet you at the airport. I thought your flight was delayed. But you're here." She swiped her tears with the back of her hands and smiled.

Closing the door behind him, he set down his duffle bag. "My flight was delayed."

Mesmerized by his approach, she waited. He looked a little tired and pale, but the smile was pure Willie, and it was for her.

"But when I discovered that another team member would pass this way, I asked him to drop me off, so my parents wouldn't have to drive to the airport. So, I got home sooner."

"Are you all right?" She reached up and brushed a lock of hair off his forehead.

He caught her hand, his touch electric. "I am now." He put his other arm around her waist and pulled her closer.

"I'm glad you're home." Encircling him with her arms, she laid her head against his chest. "I love you."

Gently he held her face between his hands and looked into her eyes. "I love you too." When he kissed her, she responded to the softness of his lips, and a thrill passed through her down to her toes.

Haleigh pulled back from the kiss. "Willie?"

"Hm?" His gaze melted her, and he kissed her again.

Breathless and wobbly, she almost forgot what she wanted to say. "What if a customer comes in?"

"Well, I'm the boss." He chuckled. "I locked the door when I came in."

"Oh." She relaxed against him again, listening to his heartbeat, breathing in his scent, feeling the warmth and security of his arms.

"Just a minute alone to say hello." He stroked her hair.

"Do your parents know you're here?"

"They knew I was on my way, but I came here first. You said you had something to tell me."

She tipped her face up. "I'm staying in Greenlawn."

Willie stepped back, placing his hands on her waist. "How long?"

"Greenlawn is home. When the Sousas return, I'll rent an apartment in town."

"Is there something else? You said you had much to tell me." He ran his fingers down the side of her face, and she leaned into his touch.

"I'd like to keep working for you."

"You and I make a great team. I'd be foolish to turn down that offer. Is there more?"

This was the hardest. "You've always been my good friend." She caught his hand as he drew it away and chose her words carefully. "I love you, Willie White. Can we be more than friends?"

A smile spread across his face. "Is that what you want?"

When she nodded, he pulled her into another embrace. "God answered my prayers. He said, 'Yes.'"

This kiss was warm and welcome and wonderful but didn't last long.

"We'd better go." Willie stepped back. "Have you taken care of the money yet? We can stop at the bank and deposit it on the way home."

"Not yet, but we didn't have much business today, so there's not a lot."

Each look or touch as they worked side by side counting the money made her shiver.

Willie threw his bag into the back seat of her car and slid into the front passenger seat as Haleigh started the engine.

"Jesse was disappointed not to see you again before he left."

He rested his head against the back of the seat. "So was I, but it was out of our control." He lifted his head and cleared his throat. "I was a little jealous of my brother."

"You were? Why?" Haleigh eyes widened.

"You always seemed so comfortable around him. He could put his arm around you, and you didn't shrug him off. You and he joked around a lot."

"Is that what caused the tension between you two? I'm really sorry." It took a lot to irritate Willie, but Jesse was one of the few people who could push him over the edge.

"Why did you do that?"

"Well." Haleigh bit her lip. "I think it's because I was falling in love with you and tried to deny it. Jesse is such a tease anyway. I assure you, he's like a younger brother to me."

"That's good to know. Sometimes Jesse did things just to irritate me because he knew how I felt about you. He knows how to raise my ire." Willie brushed her cheek with the back of his hand.

His presence proved a distraction to her driving. "Do you want me to drop you off? Maybe your parents would prefer to greet you alone."

"No, Halo. They won't mind, and I want you there. Do you know how hard it was to be on the other side of the world from you for a whole month?"

"I think I do." She checked her rearview and side mirrors. "Especially when you didn't contact us for so long."

"I guess you and Mom worried, huh?"

"Your poor mother! I think she experienced empty nest. After Jesse left, she looked lost, and she'll be glad to have you home."

"Can we go out later for dinner? I need to get unpacked and cleaned up ... say about six thirty?"

Haleigh pulled into the Whites' driveway. "Are you sure? Maybe you should rest tonight."

"The most restful thing I can do is be with you. Please?"

Haleigh smiled. "Okay. I'll say hi to your parents, but I'll have to go home to get ready for tonight. Do you want me to drive?"

"That's probably a good idea. Jet lag hasn't struck yet, but it may at any time. It'll be safer if you drive. Is the Hillside Diner all right? I don't think I'm up to going too far tonight."

"I love that place, and the food is good."

He leaned over to brush her lips with a kiss that held a promise for her.

AFTER DRESSING in a dark purple blouse, a coordinating floral print skirt, and black pumps, she applied a light layer of makeup and a dab of floral fragrance. She examined herself carefully in the mirror, then took a deep breath, put on her coat, grabbed her purse, and headed out the door to her car.

When she pulled into the driveway, Willie was outside waiting for her. Her breath caught. He looked wonderful, dressed in khaki dress slacks and a brown shirt, with a matching tweed sports jacket.

He slid into the passenger seat. "You look beautiful." He leaned over and kissed her.

Her lips tingled. "Thank you. You look nice too." Butterflies danced in her stomach.

In the few minutes it took to drive to the diner, Haleigh had so much she wanted to tell Willie, but he appeared to be deep in thought. Or maybe he was just tired.

The atmosphere of the Hillside Diner held an unusual sparkle. The touch of his hand made her feel alive, and her insides quivered each time he looked at her.

As they waited for their food, he listened quietly as she talked about her week in Wellsburg and some of the happenings in Greenlawn in the past month.

He laid his hand over hers on the table. "Somehow you're different. More at peace, more confident. Did something happen?"

"God happened." Haleigh leaned forward. "I'm learning to trust Him. I'm looking forward, rather than backward. A friend told me, many years ago, to get a new life, and I am, finally."

"Have you let go of your guilt for Aubrey's accident, and Timmy's?"

Pulling her hand back, she folded both hands in her lap. "Though I wish I could have stopped it, what happened to Timmy was an accident. As to Aubrey's accident, you didn't know why that was so hard, and I was afraid to tell you." She licked her lips.

His eyes invited her to trust and confide in him.

"It seems childish now. Just before Aubrey's accident, I prayed Leanna would go away. When she died, I felt responsible, even though Derek drove the car. I also blamed myself for Aubrey's injury. If I'd been a better friend, I might have convinced her to not get in that car. It sounds dramatic, but I wanted to die."

"I wish you'd talked to me, Halo." He held out his hands, and she placed hers in them. "I wanted to help you. But you moved away and shut me out. I was hurt."

"I'm sorry." She cupped his cheek in her palm. "I was too ashamed to tell you. You always cared about people, wanted to help them. I thought you'd reject me."

He squeezed her hands.

"I enjoyed my pity party and allowed the anger and guilt to take control of my life. Timmy's accident brought it all back. But I've been forgiven by God and my friends, and I'm ready to go on."

The waitress brought their food, and Willie prayed.

Covering his mouth with one hand, he yawned. "Honestly, I'm not bored with your company. I think the long day is catching up with me."

"I understand. Let's eat, and I'll take you home."

She had more to tell him, and she wanted to ask about his trip, but it was enough for now to be with him.

"Are you trying to get rid of me?" His eyes held a teasing glint.

"No, but I don't think I can carry you into your house if you fall asleep."

"That would be interesting." He smiled and brushed his fingers across her cheek.

His electric touch paused her breathing, and her face warmed under his gaze. As they left the diner, he grasped her hand and intertwined their fingers.

"That was nice, Willie. Thank you."

"You're welcome, Halo." He kissed her hand. "For me, the company was the best part. Before you take me home, may I show you something?" He escorted her to the driver's side and stopped before opening the door for her.

"Of course. Where do you want to go?"

"You drive, and I'll tell you where to turn."

"Hmm. This should be interesting." She slid behind the wheel. What was he up to now?

WILLIE DIRECTED Haleigh to stop along a road about a mile from the log home. Getting out, he removed a flashlight from one jacket pocket and turned it on. He checked his other pocket for the small, black box he'd placed there before leaving home that evening. It was still there. He walked around the car and opened her door.

Her hand fit well into his, her skin soft and warm against his work-roughened fingers.

"The ground is a little rough here, so be careful." The beam of the flashlight revealed a stony and uneven path.

Pulling her arm through his, he led her up a knoll, the cold air waking him fully. The moon spread its light across the landscape, and stars twinkled overhead.

She looked up. "Sometimes I think of the stars as fireflies in heaven."

Clicking off the flashlight, he returned it to his pocket and turned her to face him. His heart thudded and his mouth felt dry.

With a trembling hand, he brushed her hair back from her forehead. "You always did notice stars and fireflies."

"I haven't been up here for years, but I always liked this spot" She shivered. "It would be a beautiful place for a house."

Gazing at her in the moonlight, he waited for her to look into his eyes, then kissed her, holding her close. She responded, wrapping her arms around his neck, her lips warm and soft. The contact ignited sparks that made his heart beat crazily and his entire body quiver.

He finally broke the kiss, not because he didn't enjoy it, but he had something to say.

Stepping back, he withdrew the box from his pocket and held it out to her.

She looked at the box, then at his face. "Willie." She whispered his name.

"Halo, I love you. I've loved you forever. I'm having a house built here. Will you share my home with me? Will you marry me?"

"You're poetic, Mr. White." Her eyes reflected the moonlight. "I love you. Yes, I'll marry you."

Willie turned on the light, and she opened the box. "Oh, Willie, it's beautiful!" Even in the dim light, the diamond sparkled. Willie removed the ring carefully from the box and slipped it on her finger.

"Perfect!" she said, looking at the ring, then at him. She laid her hand against his cheek. "I love you, Willie White. God is so good to me."

"To both of us." He kissed the back of her left hand. "I've had a lot of time to think about this, all the way home from Africa. Will you be willing to have an early March wedding? That way we can be married before the spring gardening rush. By then the house should be ready, at least enough for us to move in. The foundation is already laid." Willie pointed the flashlight toward the cement structure. "If the weather holds, they can start framing right away."

She giggled. "You've been planning. I'm not sure that's fair."

She laid her head against his chest, he rested his cheek against her hair, and they stood for a moment with their arms around each other. He breathed in the fragrance of her hair and his heart raced.

"I'd live in the greenhouse with you if I had to, Willie. March will be fine for the wedding."

"The greenhouse ... an interesting proposal. But I don't think that will be necessary." He kissed her again, the kiss broken by another yawn.

Haleigh pulled away. "I'd better get you home. It's too cold for you to sleep out here." She shivered and hunched her shoulders. "We'll plan the wedding another time. Shall we tell your parents tonight?"

"It makes sense, since you're taking me home. Is that all right with you?"

"Certainly. Afterward, I'll go home and call my parents. I don't think this will be a surprise to either your parents or mine."

"I think you're right." He took her hand and turned on his flashlight.

"Our mothers get to plan another wedding together. Maybe they should start a business."

Laughing, Willie pulled Haleigh close to his side, treasuring the moment. Six months ago, he'd wondered if this day would ever come. But she said yes!

In the light of the moon and his flashlight, they followed the path back to the car. As he held the door open for her, she turned to him.

Her hand cradled his cheek. "I can hear Gram saying, 'See, I told you God has a plan for you.' That includes you, my best friend and the love of my life."

Bless Gram.

He kissed Haleigh again, then she got in and he closed the door.

Tired as he was, he wasn't sure if Haleigh's yes would keep him awake or help him sleep tonight.

ABOUT THE AUTHOR

Beth began her writing career when a poem about her lamb she wrote in second grade was published in the school newspaper. She wrote puppet plays that she performed with her brother for elementary school talent shows, and later wrote ventriloquist routines for her husband to perform with his dummies.

Beth grew up in a rural New York, the youngest of seven children. After graduating from Hartwick College in Oneonta, New York, she married Frank. They have three adult children and five grandchildren, plus one in heaven. She enjoys reading, sewing, music, and time spent with her family.

For 38 years, Beth worked alongside Frank in Christian ministry with Child Evangelism Fellowship and in pastoral ministry in several churches. She taught Bible classes to children, teens, and women and directed holiday programs. She remains active in church music ministry.

A 4-H member for nine years, she became a 4-H leader when

her children belonged to 4-H. She homeschooled her children for 12 years.

A life-long lover of books and reading, *A Heart's Journey* is Beth's third contemporary Christian romance novel. *Meadow Song* and *Heart's Desire* are her other two. Lillenas Drama accepted some of her church holiday manuscripts for publication in their Christmas, Easter, and Thanksgiving *Program Builders*. Several devotions appeared in *Penned from the Heart* and *The Secret Place*. Her short story for preteens, "Sadie and the Princess," is included in *Heartwarming Horse Stories,* available from Amazon.

Meadow Song

Artist Kate Greenway escapes her home town after the death of her finance. She finds a meadow to paint in, a young girl, and the girl's handsome uncle Jack Chambers and begins to move forward in her life. When Kate's mother develops cancer, Kate has to return home to care for her. Jack cannot make a commitment. She tells Jack the Master Potter can create something new out of the broken pieces of their lives.

Destination: Romance by Amy Anguish

It's not every day you bring a boyfriend back as a souvenir.

Katie Wilhite is ready to settle into her new job as a librarian now that college is through, but friends Bree and Skye want one more girls' trip, and when Bree insists this is her bachelorette fling, Katie agrees. What she didn't agree to was allowing fun and flighty Skye to dictate the itinerary or for her anxiety to kick in harder than ever ... right in front of a cute guy.

Camden Malone had no idea when he agreed to be the voice of reason on his cousin Ryan's vacation that the trip wouldn't stay in New Orleans as planned. But when Ryan plots with Skye so that the guys can tag along with the girls all week, he isn't nearly as upset as he should be.

Not with Katie's fiery temper and flashing eyes intriguing him more by the minute.

Can Katie relax enough to trust Camden and a possible future, or will she continue to push him away as only a vacation fling? And can Camden move past a rocky history of his own to be able to jump into a better future? For a trip that was supposed to be all about fun, there's a lot of romance going around.

Perfectly Placed by Liana George

Nicki's tasked with making New Hope the perfect place for orphaned children.

So why has everything gone wrong?

Six weeks after leaving China, Nicki Mayfield returns to complete two critical tasks: restore order at New Hope Orphanage and re-connect with the little girl who stole her heart. However, between a stubbornly stone walling supervisor, missing documents, and personal tragedy, Nicki faces challenges at every turn. Is she the best person to bring order – and longevity – to the place these children call home?

Then, with the help of an unexpected ally, Nicki makes a life-altering decision that upends her well-planned life and the lives of those around her. Will she lose it all, or has she found the way to save what matters most?

Stay up-to-date on your favorite books and authors with our free e-newsletters.

ScriveningsPress.com